"You'll Be Flying Back to Tokyo?"

"Yes, to meet my uncle." The words clearly brought home the fleeting nature of their relationship. "By then his business should be finished and we'll fly back to the States."

"And if he doesn't get the contract?"

She studied him from across the table and turned the question around. "If he gets it, what will *you* do?"

"Are you always so touchy about your uncle?"

"I'm not touchy. It's just that business is business and . . ."

"And you never mix business with pleasure. Well, I propose that we dispense with business and get right on with the pleasure."

ERIN ROSS

saw most of the world as a flight attendant and now puts her unique experiences to good use in her writing. Among those experiences: water skiing off Wake Island, motorcycle riding on Guam, surfing and scuba diving in Hawaii, and getting lost on the subway in Japan without being able to speak a word of the language.

Dear Reader,

Silhouette Special Editions are an exciting new line of contemporary romances from Silhouette Books. Special Editions are written specifically for our readers who want a story with heightened romantic tension.

Special Editions have all the elements you've enjoyed in Silhouette Romances and *more*. These stories concentrate on romance in a longer, more realistic and sophisticated way, and they feature greater sensual detail.

I hope you enjoy this book and all the wonderful romances from Silhouette. We welcome any suggestions or comments and invite you to write to us at the address below.

Karen Solem
Editor-in-Chief
Silhouette Books
P.O. Box 769
New York, N. Y. 10019

ERIN ROSS
Flower of the Orient

Silhouette Special Edition

Published by Silhouette Books New York

America's Publisher of Contemporary Romance

Other Silhouette Books by Erin Ross

Second Harvest

SILHOUETTE BOOKS, a Division of Simon & Schuster, Inc.
1230 Avenue of the Americas, New York, N.Y. 10020

Copyright © 1983 by Erin Ross

Distributed by Pocket Books

ISBN: 0-671-53607-9

First Silhouette Books printing July, 1983

10 9 8 7 6 5 4 3 2 1

All of the characters in this book are fictitious. Any resemblance to actual persons, living or dead, is purely coincidental.

Map by Ray Lundgren

SILHOUETTE, SILHOUETTE SPECIAL EDITION and
colophon are registered trademarks of Simon & Schuster, Inc.

America's Publisher of Contemporary Romance

Printed in the U.S.A.

To Gerry, who shared—
To Lisa, who encouraged—
And to Hiromi Cross, who
corrected my abominable Japanese.

Flower of
the Orient

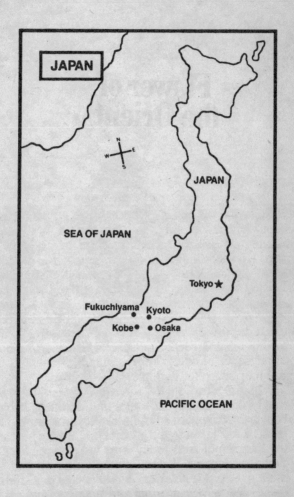

Chapter One

Lisa Howard carefully maneuvered the small rented Blue Bird out of the hotel parking lot and then sat waiting for a break in traffic which would allow her onto crowded Showa-Dori. It was only one o'clock in the afternoon, and already downtown Tokyo was a tangled mass of traffic. As she watched the endless stream of cars, she realized that Uncle Leonard's admonition to take a taxi to Yokohama had been motivated by more than his usual protective attitude toward his only niece. But Lisa, so accustomed to the convenience of having her own car back in the States, had merely scoffed at her uncle's warning.

"If I take a taxi, there's no telling where I'll end up," she'd said. Her soft blue eyes had sparkled, knowing how much they both enjoyed the playful teasing. "Yesterday I was taken to the Nihombashi Bridge instead of the Museum of Art. Today is my last chance to see the Bunraku Puppets. I don't want to end up watching sumo wrestlers instead." She'd planted a quick kiss on his forehead. "I'm a big girl now, Uncle Leonard. I'll be just fine."

But now, facing the bumper to bumper traffic, Lisa wasn't so sure. Perhaps it would be wiser to turn around after all. Even the infamous Tokyo subway couldn't be worse than this. Gingerly, she tried to manipulate the car back into the garage, gesturing broadly to the queue of drivers already lined up behind her. But the angry blaring of horns informed her that the effort was futile. Like it or not, she was committed to Showa-Dori and the congested ride south to Yokohama.

Uncomfortably aware now of the other cars lined up behind her, Lisa watched intently for an opening. The oncoming cars refused to let her in, their frustrated drivers intent only on their own destinations. Just as it seemed that there would never be a break, a blue Datsun in the extreme left lane signaled an intended turn into the garage. Immediately Lisa reached for the gear stick, so awkwardly placed near her left hand in this Japanese-made car, and rapidly shifted into first. The car barely moved. Irritated, Lisa realized that she must have put it into high gear by mistake. Hurrying now, she manipulated the unfamiliar shift, finally settling it into the proper gear and letting out the clutch. Then, as she pressed her foot down hard on the pedal, it happened. The Blue Bird spurted forward just as an impatient car behind her darted around to the left forcing Lisa to slam on the brakes in front of the Datsun. The Datsun swerved and screeched to a stop, crashing noisily into the right front bumper of the Blue Bird.

For a moment Lisa was too stunned to move, and it was in a kind of dream that she watched the car on her left continue on toward the street. Amid a blare of horns it forced its way onto Showa-Dori, seemingly oblivious to the chaos it had left in its wake. Before she could get out of her car, a very tall, very angry man, wearing a dark, three-piece business suit, jerked open the driver's door of the Blue Bird.

"Where in the name of heaven did you learn to drive?" he roared. "Or did you? Either stay in the garage or move onto the road. But for god's sake don't bound out in front of a person and then stop dead."

Lisa took a deep breath, fighting to suppress the angry retort which sprang to her lips. The first thing she had to do was assess the damage, not get into a sparring match, she told herself. Still, her legs felt surprisingly unsteady as she tried to make her way past the tall, broad-shouldered body blocking her path to the front of the car.

"Excuse me," she said, looking at him pointedly. He shifted his stance, but hardly enough to allow her to pass. Their eyes locked in a battle of wills, and Lisa was infuriated with herself when hers dropped first. Turning her shoulders parallel to the car, she again tried to move past him.

"I said, excuse me," she repeated angrily. When he still wouldn't move, Lisa gave a sigh of exasperation and boldly stepped forward. It was only when her breasts came into contact with his chest that she realized how badly she had misjudged her clearance. Her sharp intake of breath was more like a gasp as she became aware of the uncompromising, muscled feel of him, and the scent of spicy, very masculine aftershave. She knew her face was flushed as she looked up to find him eyeing her speculatively.

"I—I said excuse me." She wondered if anger were the reason for her racing pulse.

Without a word, he finally moved back, and Lisa hurried around him to see what damage had been done. To her relief the Datsun was hardly scratched, and the

Blue Bird had suffered only a cracked headlight. The bumpers were locked, however, and once again Lisa was uncomfortably aware that the Datsun's driver was standing much too close to her.

"It—it doesn't seem too serious," she stammered. "I'm really sorry, but when that other car pulled out. . . ."

"I know, you lost your head," the man finished for her. He turned his back before she could answer, removed his jacket, then climbed on top of the bumpers and started to rock the cars free.

Lisa found herself at an unaccustomed loss for words, and she stood by mutely and watched him work. The man appeared to be American, in his mid-thirties, perhaps, very tan, with thick, dark chestnut hair, which was flying helter-skelter over his eyes now from his efforts with the fenders. His eyes, which she had good reason to know were a rich, dark brown, were framed by thick eyebrows and long, heavy lashes. He had an appealing, almost magnetic vitality. He was a leader— Lisa felt it very strongly. As he grappled with the bumpers she could see the rippling muscles which had had such a peculiar effect on her only moments before. Now that he was at a safe distance and she could examine him more objectively, she realized that his remarkable physique seemed somehow out of place in his conservative and very expensive suit. For that matter, so did his tan. Surely here was a man who would be more comfortable out of doors than behind a desk. Despite herself, Lisa was intrigued. She had to admit that he was very good-looking. In fact, if he hadn't been so rude, she might have felt attracted to him. As it was, she was just anxious to get as far away from him and these other demented Tokyo drivers as possible.

When he had finally bounced the cars free, the man impatiently brushed the dirt off his hands. His eyes traveled over her coolly. "You're staying here at the hotel, I assume," he said. "And from the way you handle the Blue Bird I'd guess you haven't been in Japan long."

Lisa bridled under his gaze and the annoying accuracy of his assessment. "I've been here long enough to see that you all drive like madmen," she replied hotly. "Doesn't anyone show any courtesy in Tokyo?"

"Not on the roads," he replied levelly. "And until you can cope with that, I suggest that for your own sake, if not for the safety of the rest of the city, you stick to taxis or public transportation and leave the driving to those who know what they're doing."

"I know perfectly well what I'm doing," Lisa snapped. "It's just that this traffic is impossibly heavy, and the Blue Bird's not what I'm used to. And of course I didn't expect that other car to dart out from behind me so suddenly."

"Well, that's just what you *can* expect around here. You might at least take the time to familiarize yourself with a strange car before launching out in it as if you owned the road."

"I never even made it to the road," Lisa protested, then realized this hardly improved her position. "And I do understand the Blue Bird's gears. But in all the confusion . . ."

"Which you will find on a Tokyo road most of the time," he broke in caustically. "I suggest you get your act together before you get behind that wheel again." He nodded his head toward the crowded Showa-Dori. "Better drivers than you have been eaten alive out there."

Half a dozen colorful retorts sprang into Lisa's head,

but before she could get even one of them out he was back in the Datsun, skillfully weaving his way into the subterranean garage beyond.

"Of all the nerve!" she sputtered in frustration. A persistent blast of horns interrupted her angry thoughts. Her car was still obstructing the exit, and from the withering looks directed at her by the drivers forced to make their way around the Blue Bird, it was clear she had better move at once. But where? A quick look to the rear told Lisa it was still impossible to make her way back into the garage. There seemed no choice but to come to grips with the little compact. Resolutely she climbed back into the car, carefully put the gear lever into neutral before starting the engine, then gently glided the stick into first, double-checking its placement before depressing the accelerator. This time, thankfully, the tiny car slid smoothly into motion, and Lisa guided its nose just to the edge of the crowded street. Remembering the way the other car had brazened its way onto Showa-Dori, Lisa boldly moved the Blue Bird into a tiny space between two passing vehicles and grimly refused to back off. A clamor of horns greeted her efforts, but she was in. With a sigh of relief she settled back in the seat and concentrated on directing the little car through the dense stream of traffic toward Yokohama.

Eventually she had found the Bunraku Puppets, but not before a frustrating string of misunderstood directions sent her several miles out of her way. In desperation, she had invested in a small tourist's guide to the Japanese language which promised to answer all her travel questions instantly. Unfortunately, the guide could not demonstrate the intonations necessary to make words intelligible, and Lisa still spent most of the afternoon struggling to be understood. Back at the hotel she was relieved to discover that there was little need for the book in the underground shopping arcade. Just as the clerk at the main desk had promised, most of the shopkeepers spoke excellent English, enabling her to pick up several souvenirs, including a brightly painted parasol, some delicate rice-paper prints and a heavy, intricately hand-carved Buddha.

Now it seemed her luck had run out. For ten minutes she had been trying futilely to communicate with the smiling young woman in the lovely blue-flowered kimono behind the counter of one of the hotel's novelty shops. Lisa shifted the colorful parasol and her other parcels under her left arm, then thumbed once again through the Japanese phrase book searching for the right combination of words.

"Chisai ningyo sagashite i-masu," she said, trying a slightly different intonation this time. She repeated the words in English as if this would clarify the statement. "I'm looking for a smaller doll."

The girl's expression didn't change, although Lisa thought she could detect anxious bewilderment behind her smile. Not for the first time, Lisa was tempted to give up. Then her eyes strayed back to the row of exquisite Japanese dolls displayed in a mirrored cabinet behind the register and she knew she had to give it one more try.

"Chisai ningyo wa arimasen ka? Don't you have any smaller dolls?"

The young woman's face beamed with sudden comprehension. *"Hai, arigato gozaimasu."* She bowed, smiling broadly. In halting English she repeated proudly, "Yes, thank you."

Lisa sighed. At last they were getting somewhere.

"Chisai ningyo o kai-tai no desu ga," she told the girl. "I want to buy a smaller doll."

Immediately the girl's smile vanished, and she held out her hands in a clearly recognizable gesture of confusion.

Now what had she done wrong? Lisa wondered. In desperation, she reverted to the one phrase which had elicited a positive response. *"Chisai ningyo wa arimasen ka?* Don't you have any smaller dolls?"

As if by magic the girl's smile reappeared. *"Hai,"* she said with a relieved bow. "Yes."

"You could go around like that all day and never buy a thing," a low voice said from behind Lisa's shoulder.

Startled, Lisa whirled around, forgetting for the moment the long parasol she still held under her left arm.

"You!" she cried, alarmed to see the man from the garage standing directly behind her.

There was an appalling crash of glass as the umbrella swept an oversized jar of candy off the counter. As Lisa made an instinctive grab for the container, the pointed tip of the parasol jabbed hard into the man's side, causing him to double over in silent pain.

"You really are a walking disaster area, aren't you?" he said through clenched teeth. "If I'd known you were going to attack me, I would have left you to muddle along on your own. You have a strange way of showing your appreciation."

"Appreciation for what?" Lisa asked angrily. "For startling me half out of my wits and causing me to break the candy jar?" Then, as she saw him still holding his side, she was instantly repentant. "I *have* hurt you, haven't I? I really didn't mean to. But I was so surprised to see you again that I . . ."

The man held up a hand and cast his dark eyes—

really remarkable eyes, Lisa thought through her distraction—toward the heavens. "I know, don't tell me, you were confused again. I'm beginning to see that in your case that must be a more or less normal condition." He stood stiffly, one hand still massaging his side. "I was just trying to point out that as long as you ask this poor woman negative questions she's going to keep answering you in the affirmative."

"I suppose you realize I haven't the foggiest notion what you're talking about," Lisa told him, his seeming double-talk only adding to her consternation.

"I mean that if you ask a Japanese a question in the negative, such as, 'Don't you have any smaller dolls?' the answer will always be a polite yes, meaning, 'yes, we don't have any.'"

"That's ridiculous."

"It may be ridiculous, but it's very Japanese."

"Well, it makes it very difficult to communicate, doesn't it? Besides," she went on, embarrassed now that she knew that the error had been hers, "I was told that all the shop clerks in the hotel arcade spoke English."

To her surprise, he turned to the girl behind the counter and, in rapid Japanese, spoke intently to her for several minutes. At length he turned back to Lisa, bowing slightly to her in mock courtesy as the clerk had done several times during their talk. "The young lady's name is Ariko, and she is merely standing in today for the regular proprietor, who is ill. She apologizes for her miserable English and also for the store's deplorable lack of stock. She says she's very sorry, but they are out of smaller dolls. However, if you try the shop across the mall, she's confident you'll find a wide selection there." His face was lit by a sudden grin, and Lisa was astounded by the way it transformed his rather somber features. A large dimple appeared in his left cheek, lightening the rest of his face, and the dark eyes sparkled with golden brown highlights as he went on. "And, in the interest of good Japanese-American relations, I'm happy to tell you they speak English over there."

Lisa was at a loss for words. It was obviously her turn to apologize, but she hardly knew how to go about it. Despite her reluctance, she had little choice but to continue to use the stranger as an interpreter.

"Please tell Ariko I'm sorry, too, for misunderstanding her, and also for breaking the jar." As an embarrassed afterthought, Lisa looked down at what was left of the large container and the jumble of tiny cellophane-wrapped squares of candy spread out over the floor. Stooping, she tried to pick up some of the shattered pieces of glass.

"You'd better leave those for the girl," he said, getting down beside her. "With your luck, you won't have a finger left using your hands like that." She jerked away as he moved forward to remove a large piece of glass from her grasp, her patience with his patronizing attitude very nearly at an end. As she did, the fragment tore across his hand leaving a ragged cut along the outer palm. Lisa heard him curse under his breath, then watched as he quickly pulled out a handkerchief to stem the flow of blood.

"I—I'm really sorry," Lisa stammered, reaching out to help.

"Good God!" he cried, pulling away. "There's no need to come at me again. Haven't you done enough damage already?"

Lisa followed his gaze to her right hand and saw she was still clutching the jagged section of glass, holding it, in fact, almost like a weapon. Startled, she sat back on her heels, horrified at her unaccustomed ineptness. Then Ariko was around the counter, squatting beside them, protesting loudly in Japanese. Lisa did not need a knowledge of the language to understand the girl's distress.

"We're being asked to leave," he said, getting to his feet. "Very politely, of course, but very emphatically. She takes full responsibility for the candy jar and asks us not to concern ourselves any further."

Lisa stood, her attention divided between the young woman who was now sweeping up the remains of the glass with a small brush and dustpan, and the man's hand, bound tightly with the handkerchief. Why was it that every time he was around she acted like a complete idiot? Normally, she was a controlled, responsible woman, but around this man she became all thumbs. Well aware that her face was embarrassingly flushed, she tried again to make amends, consciously avoiding the stranger's eyes as she spoke.

"Please tell Ariko that I'm very sorry for disrupting the shop and that of course I insist on paying for the damage." She reached into her purse, pulled out several Japanese bills and placed them on the counter. "I believe this should cover the cost of the candy and the jar and any inconvenience I've caused."

Lisa was acutely aware of the piercing dark eyes which had not left her face. "I'm very sorry about your hand," she went on, looking up at him quickly. "You really should get it properly bandaged as soon as possible."

In her hurry to arrange the awkward parasol under her arm, the heavy statue of Buddha slipped from her grasp and fell crashing onto his foot. Blushing furiously, Lisa quickly stooped to retrieve it. As she did, the sole of her shoe slipped on some loose pieces of candy, causing her to drop the other parcels, as well as herself, onto the man in the process. Two strong hands reached out to break her fall, and the man held her for a long moment cradled in his arms, her cheek pressed so tightly to his chest that she could count the quick, steady beats of his heart. It was only when he bent his head and spoke soothingly into her ear that she became aware of her own racing pulse.

"It's all right," he murmured. "I've got you now. I won't let you fall."

Lisa raised her head to find his dark eyes mere inches from her face. The intimate proximity only served to heighten her confusion, making her breathlessly aware of the hard body which was pinned against her own. Although she'd not had a drop of liquor all day, she felt intoxicated by the nearness of him. The feeling was exhilarating, and even though Lisa resented having to be rescued by him, she was strangely loath to break away.

"I'm—I'm all right now." Gently, she pressed her hands against his chest in an effort to be free. "Really," she repeated, "I'm all right."

"I don't know," he said doubtfully. "In the best interests of the hotel I think you should stay right here."

She looked up to find him laughing down at her. His condescending tone was infuriating. "I said I'm all right now," she told him sharply. She strained against him, struggling to be out of his arms.

And then she was free, released so suddenly that she was thrown by the force of her exertions onto the glass counter behind her back, rocking the knickknacks which were displayed on the top. Instinctively she reached out to steady them, but her rescuer was quicker. To hide her embarrassment, she stooped to retrieve her packages from the floor.

"No, no," he said quickly. "Allow me. There's no telling what other tortures you've got in store for us. Here, let me help you restock your arsenal." With exaggerated care he placed the bundles back in her arms. "Now, do you think you can handle all this? Or is that asking too much of someone as disaster-prone as you?"

The insult immediately retriggered Lisa's anger, while at the same time increasing her annoyance that she could have felt such a surprising reaction in his arms. "I'll manage quite nicely, thank you," she told him with infinite courtesy. "As I would have managed in the first place without your unsolicited and definitely unnecessary interference."

Her blond hair tossed defiantly as she walked proudly to the door. Once there she turned back with a frosty smile. "Not that it hasn't been nice," she told him politely, "but in the future I'd like to ask you most humbly"—here a mock bow—"to keep yourself *and* your uninvited help well out of my way!"

Lisa was still smarting from her experiences when she joined her uncle and his friends for dinner that evening in the hotel dining room. A quick shower and change of clothes had left her refreshed but had done little to erase the unpleasant, and admittedly confusing, memories of this afternoon's fiascos. Although she reassured herself that the episode outside the garage, while embarrassing, could easily have happened to anyone, the scene at the novelty shop could not be dismissed so easily. It was simply not like Lisa Howard to act like such a klutz, or, for that matter, like some swooning idiot. Never in her life had she trembled like that in a man's arms, not even Jeff's. The knowledge that she could be so easily affected by another man left her dazed and frightened.

As she sat down at the table she realized that her only consolation was that she would never see the man again. Tomorrow she would be in Kyoto and two weeks after that she'd be back at her office in Evergreen, California, where it would be business as usual. What happened today would become regrettable incidents in an otherwise memorable trip.

"You know Marion and Clyde Gilbert, don't you, Lisa," her uncle was saying, indicating the middle-aged couple who completed their foursome.

"Of course," Lisa said pleasantly, determined not to let this afternoon's difficulties spoil dinner. "They've been your friendliest rivals for years. It's nice to see you again, Mr. and Mrs. Gilbert."

The woman, plump, graying and in her fifties, smiled warmly at Lisa. "Please, there's no need to be so formal. After all, we've been doing business, or perhaps I should say trying to take business away from your uncle, for too many years to be anything but Clyde and Marion." She hesitated, a pained expression crossing her full face, and Lisa knew with a sinking heart where the conversation was headed. "I want you to know how very sorry we were to hear of the accident, my dear. It must have been a very great loss."

Clyde Gilbert cleared his throat, and the look he gave his wife was a clear command to be quiet. "It's been over two years, Marion," he reminded her pointedly. "I'm sure it's a subject the poor girl would rather forget."

Lisa's thin smile silently acknowledged her agreement, although not for the reason Clyde Gilbert had in mind. It was her husband everyone mourned, of course: Jeff Howard, reckless, talented head test pilot for Mason Aircraft, the company that Uncle Leonard had founded after World War II. But Lisa's grief had not been for her lost husband, or even for a marriage which had been doomed almost from its beginning. For all their closeness, even Leonard Mason had not suspected the real reason for her sorrow.

"How was your afternoon, honey?" her uncle was asking gently, and Lisa knew that he was deliberately bringing her out of her thoughts. "I assume you found Yokohama and the Bunraku Puppets all right?" He turned to the Gilberts, skillfully launching them into safer waters. "You know this girl is really something. Three days in Tokyo and she's off on her own all over the countryside as if she'd lived here all her life."

Lisa almost choked on her glass of water. Uncomfortably she returned her uncle's grin, hoping he would never find out just how far off the mark he was this time.

"I understand you arrange all the cultural exchanges for the city of Evergreen," Marion Gilbert commented.

"I'm only the assistant director, Mrs. Gil—er, Marion," Lisa answered. "Normally the director, Mr. Allen, would have taken this assignment. But since Uncle Leonard's trip to Japan coincided with our plans to go to Kyoto, it was simply more practical for me to accompany him than to fly the director over at the city's expense."

"She's being too modest, of course," Leonard Mason said, laughing. "But I guess it doesn't hurt when your uncle owns his own aircraft corporation."

"What's so important in Kyoto?" Clyde Gilbert asked.

"We're inviting a well-known Kabuki theater group

to come to Evergreen," Lisa answered, "in exchange for our ballet troop. I'll be going to Kyoto tomorrow to make the final arrangements."

"And the Bunraku Puppets, dear?" Mrs. Gilbert asked. "Will you be having them over, too?"

"We haven't decided yet who will follow the Kabuki troop. Several possibilities have been discussed; the Bunraku Puppets, for instance, the Noh theater, or any number of private art exhibits. I've been looking into as many possibilities as I can while I'm here."

"What fascinating work," Marion Gilbert exclaimed. "And you're so young to hold such a responsible position."

"I'll be twenty-six next month," Lisa explained patiently, a little annoyed that she still looked so much younger. Later on she might appreciate wide blue eyes and a saucy, slightly upturned nose, but for now, as she tried to appear efficient and businesslike, they seemed more like liabilities.

Lisa was relieved when a waiter appeared to take their dinner orders. And she was pleased when, over soup, salad and a disappointingly American steak dinner, the conversation turned away from her and onto speculation about this morning's tests at the airfield.

"Franklin did a good job, I thought," Clyde Gilbert said, referring to the pilot who had put the Mason plane through its paces. "But then he's one of the best in the business."

"He always puts on a good show," Leonard Mason agreed. His eyes narrowed slightly as they caught the other man's gaze from across the table. "Of course nothing like Brannon."

Lisa noticed a subtle change among the three at the

mention of Keith Brannon's name. Brannon, president and founder of Brannon Aeronautics, was the third rival in contention for the much-coveted contract which had brought Mason and the Gilberts to Japan. Fugi International, one of Japan's leading industrial firms, would soon be awarding to one of the three competitors, a multimillion dollar contract to produce fifteen business jets over the next three years with an option for five additional planes in the following year. The smart money was on Mason Aircraft to win the prize, if only because of their experience and their high degree of technical ability. But more and more frequently, Keith Brannon's name was being mentioned as a real possibility.

"He always makes the most difficult maneuvers look like child's play," Marion Gilbert was saying.

Her husband laughed good-naturedly. "Maybe he just doesn't realize that what he's doing up there is damn dangerous. I was talking to him after the test this morning, and you'd think he'd just come in from a Sunday stroll."

"Oh, I don't know about that," Uncle Leonard disagreed. "Keith Brannon is one of the best pilots in the business. He just has the knack of coaxing a little bit more out of his machines than the rest of us."

"*And* out of the ladies, I hear," Gilbert added with a sly wink. "If you can believe all the stories they tell about him in the papers, he's quite the predator with the ladies. The love 'em and leave 'em type. I saw a spread on him not too long ago in a national news magazine. I'll say one thing. He sure can pick them."

Marion Gilbert poked at her husband playfully with her elbow. "Really, Clyde, you know you can't believe a thing those magazines print."

Her husband laughed again. "I may not be able to vouch for the story, but they sure didn't fake those pictures. The ladies looked much too pleased with themselves to be pretending. But then, who can blame them? Let's face it, for all the headaches he's giving the rest of us in the business, Keith Brannon is one hell of a good-looking guy."

Lisa felt a sudden chill run down her spine. A simple change of name and this conversation could have been about Jeff. Good lord, she thought. Was this how their friends had discussed her husband's extracurricular affairs? How many men had leered, as Clyde Gilbert was doing at this very moment, when someone mentioned Jeff's latest paramour? Lisa pushed away her plate. Suddenly she had lost all taste for dinner.

"When will Fugi announce their decision?" Marion Gilbert was asking the men.

Her husband shrugged. "Who knows? We've submitted our initial bids, and now that they've seen the planes in operation it's just a matter of waiting until their board comes to an agreement. My guess is that we'll probably hear within three to four weeks."

Lisa felt her uncle's gaze upon her and knew he had noticed her sudden tenseness. A reassuring pat on her hand said that he had correctly guessed the reason as well. Although she had been too proud to confide the more humiliating details of her marriage, Lisa sensed that Uncle Leonard had not been deceived by the outward pretense of normality.

"I propose a toast," he announced in what Lisa recognized as a firm move to close the subject. "To the best plane, to the most qualified company, and"—here he paused and smiled at his companions—"to a fine dinner with very dear friends."

Their glasses clinked and each silently sipped the

cool amber liquid. In the companionable silence which followed, Leonard Mason turned to his niece.

"What time do you want to leave tomorrow, honey?" he asked. "The flight takes about forty-five minutes, so you can judge accordingly."

"Mid-morning will be just fine," Lisa replied. "My appointment's not until after lunch." At the inquiring looks from the Gilberts Lisa explained, "Uncle Leonard is flying me to Kyoto tomorrow morning. I'll be there for a couple of weeks and then return to Tokyo in time to fly back to the States with him."

"With your Kabuki troop?" Mrs. Gilbert asked.

"No, they won't be coming for several months yet. These things are arranged well in advance."

"I can see that," Mr. Gilbert laughed. "Say, you be sure to tell us when and where this troop of yours will be performing. Marion and I don't want to miss that, do we . . ."

"So sorry to interrupt, Mr. Mason," their Japanese waiter said, bowing apologetically, "but there is a telephone call for you at the desk."

Leonard Mason's eyebrows rose. "I wonder what that's all about." He placed his napkin on the table and rose. "You'll excuse me, won't you? I shouldn't be long. It's probably not important."

But Lisa could see by the look on her uncle's face when he returned to the table that it was very important. Her heart sank at the thought that he'd been given an additional responsibility just now.

"It was from my office," he told her. "More headaches with the Baldwin contract." He frowned. "I don't see any way around it, honey. I've got to fly back to the office and straighten the mess out myself. I'm afraid it means I won't be able to fly you to Kyoto tomorrow after all."

Lisa's concern was obvious, but not for herself. Ever since Leonard Mason's heart attack the previous year she'd been after her uncle to lighten his heavy workload. Life was too short, she'd argued, to run around doing the work of two men. At his age he should be able to relax and delegate responsibility. The advice had fallen on deaf ears, and for weeks Lisa had worried that he looked too tired.

"Can't someone else handle it?" she protested. "Surely you've got enough on your mind right here with the Fugi account."

Leonard Mason patted her hand, and she knew from the look in his eye that her arguments were useless. "Sorry, honey," he told her with a sheepish smile. "Don't worry, I ought to be back in a day or two. It seems to me the real problem is getting you to Kyoto. Do you think you can get there okay on your own?"

"Of course I can." She sighed, accepting his decision. "Didn't I find Yokohama today without any problems?" Lisa felt only a slight tinge of guilt at the lie. Right now it was more important that Uncle Leonard not have to worry about her as well as his business. "I'll just ride the 'Bullet' train," she said, forcing a smile. "I hear it actually reaches speeds of 130 miles per hour. Going that fast you might say I'll still be flying to Kyoto."

The next morning, however, Lisa received a better offer than Japan's high-powered "Bullet" train to take her to Kyoto. At six-thirty, Marion Gilbert called to tell her they had found another pilot. If they could get her to the airport by eight o'clock, she would be in Kyoto before nine.

Hurriedly, Lisa dressed and threw a few last-minute articles in her suitcases. By seven-thirty the Gilberts had picked her up at the hotel and they were on their way to the airport.

"You didn't have to drive me yourselves," Lisa protested.

Marion Gilbert immediately shushed her. "Nonsense, dear. As you're the niece of our favorite competitor, we feel it our duty to see you safely on your way. Besides, we'd arranged a little sightseeing trip this morning and we were planning an early start anyway."

Promptly at eight o'clock, the Gilberts' car pulled up in front of a small, sleek jet aircraft anchored just north of the airport tower. Several men in khaki coveralls were swarming over the plane, some loading fuel, others making last-minute checks on the aircraft before takeoff.

Lisa gave an involuntary gasp at the sight of the plane. "You can't mean . . . don't tell me *that's* the plane I'll be on!"

The jet's smooth bullet-shaped fuselage and slightly swept-back wings were unmistakable. Just yesterday morning she had watched it soar like a giant predator over the skies of Narita Airport.

Clyde Gilbert cleared his throat. "That's the plane all right," he said awkwardly. "And by the look on your face I can see you've guessed who the pilot is."

"Keith Brannon!" Lisa spoke the name in a kind of daze. "But I don't understand. Why on earth did you ask *him* to take me?"

Marion Gilbert was looking at Lisa in confusion, obviously surprised by the younger woman's reaction to their plans. "We didn't think you'd mind, dear. When we found out Mr. Brannon was flying to his main office in Kyoto this morning, it seemed a shame not to take you along at the same time." When Lisa continued to

stare at the plane as if it were an object from outer
space, the older woman stumbled on apologetically.
"It's such a short flight, dear, less than an hour. You
don't even have to speak to him if you don't want to.
You'll be there before you know it."

A more objective part of Lisa's brain recognized the
wisdom of this logic. Still, her body seemed made of
lead, incapable of moving from the car. The years
melted away to a time when she had sat much like this
and watched her uncle's mechanics ready the latest
Mason aircraft for Jeff's final testing. Only then there
had been real fear, not the vague apprehension she felt
now.

Lisa started when the door next to her swung open.
"It's after eight," Clyde Gilbert told her, glancing
nervously at his watch. "They'll be boarding soon."

For one wild moment, Lisa had the impulse to ask
the Gilberts to take her to the "Bullet" station instead.
The train would get her to Kyoto in plenty of time for
her appointment this afternoon. Then, as Marion shifted uncomfortably on the seat next to her, she realized
that she couldn't impose any further on the Gilberts'
friendship. She was behaving irrationally. The ride in
the Comet was simply a matter of convenience. No
matter how much she disliked the idea of flying with
Keith Brannon, the flight would be over in less than an
hour.

Feeling a little foolish, Lisa tried to cover her momentary panic by stepping quickly from the car. She
saw that Clyde Gilbert had already unloaded her two
suitcases and overnight case from the trunk. Picking up
one of the bags, she walked briskly with him toward the
Comet.

"One last thing," Gilbert said as they neared the

plane. "Keith Brannon doesn't know you're Leonard Mason's niece. We thought you'd be more comfortable if we simply introduced you as a friend. Since you still go by your married name, there's no problem. Of course, if you want to tell him who you are . . ."

"No, no," Lisa put in quickly. "There's no need to go into unnecessary explanations."

The two stood just to the right of the Comet's nose and watched as the crew completed their final inspection and fueling of the craft. Lisa felt a grudging thrill of admiration as her eyes ran over the smooth contours of the plane. Every line was a masterpiece of economy, every curve, pure condensed strength. Even stationary, the craft exuded tremendous power. For one brief moment Lisa forgot the shadows of the past and was lost in the sheer beauty of the machine before her. What would it be like to take it up, she wondered; to let it soar beyond the cluster of clouds fringing the eastern horizon?

Lisa felt Gilbert's hand on her arm and she turned. "There he is," he said. "See? The tall man with his back to us speaking to one of the ground crew. That's Keith Brannon."

Lisa studied the back of the man who was rapidly establishing himself as the single greatest threat to her uncle's corporation. Tall, at least six-foot-two, the man was wearing tan cords and a brown leather flight jacket. His dark hair was longish and tousled by the sharp morning breeze whipping across the airfield. Lisa felt reassured. He looked harmless enough, at least from the rear. There was no reason why she couldn't survive his company, at least for the short flight to Kyoto.

Then the man turned around, issuing short, clipped orders to the members of the ground crew, and Lisa's heart jumped. It couldn't be! It wasn't possible! But as he walked closer to where they stood, she saw very clearly that it was.

For some reason the fates had cruelly entangled her with the one man in Japan she had hoped never to meet again. Her impertinent stranger from the hotel yesterday, the man she had told emphatically to stay out of her life forever, was none other than the infamous Keith Brannon!

Chapter Two

I've had the pleasure," Keith Brannon was saying, the look on his face just slightly less surprised than her own. "Although I certainly didn't expect to see the young lady again so soon. She was rather explicit on that point the last time we met."

"I had no idea you two knew each other," Clyde Gilbert said, looking at them in amazement. "Lisa didn't mention it." He smiled tentatively, seeming to sense the undercurrent between the two. "Well, then, that makes it easier, doesn't it? I appreciate the favor, Brannon. Since it's not out of your way. . . ."

Keith Brannon's eyes were fastened on Lisa's, but she couldn't read his look. As for herself, she realized that she had been standing stock still, almost afraid to breathe during the exchange between the two men. He was obviously as shocked as she to find himself in this situation. Why didn't he simply end the charade by refusing to take her on board? Why didn't *she* refuse to go?

"I'm glad to help out, Gilbert," he was saying. "I'm sure the young lady will be no problem." Then, under his breath he added, "As long as my insurance premiums are paid up."

The cut startled Lisa out of her daze. "That was totally uncalled for," she snapped, for Gilbert's sake trying to keep her voice lowered.

"I beg your pardon?" Gilbert was confused.

"It's nothing, don't worry about it," Keith Brannon said. "Just some personal business between the young lady and me."

Clyde Gilbert looked at them both sharply. "Yes, well, I'll leave you to it, then." He turned Lisa's luggage over to one of the ground crew. "Have a good flight now. See you in a couple of weeks, Lisa. Good luck with your Kabuki people."

With a last wave, Gilbert moved back to the car where Lisa could see his wife peering eagerly out the window. Lisa knew Marion Gilbert was consumed with curiosity about the notorious Keith Brannon. Well, given a choice, she would gladly trade places with her. The short fifty minutes to Kyoto was looking longer every minute!

Keith Brannon motioned for Lisa to board the plane, indicating that she could sit either in the cabin or in the cockpit. Then, without another word he went back to his preflight preparations.

That's cool enough, Lisa thought, unsure whether to be relieved or insulted by his abrupt dismissal. But as she mounted the steps to enter the roomy cabin, she decided that it was much better this way. Keep it on an impersonal basis, she told herself. She'd sit back here behind the cockpit like any other passenger. There was no need to even see him after takeoff.

Midway through the cabin Lisa stopped, unconsciously comparing the interior of the Comet to that of her uncle's latest plane, the Silver-Star. The Comet's was by far the more luxurious. Its compartment was sumptuously done in soft tans and browns with a highlight of rich burnt sienna woven through the velvety fabric covering the dozen or so seats. The carpet, deep brown and thickly piled, felt wickedly soft and resilient beneath her feet. Everything was expensive, and Lisa was alternately turned off and attracted by such extravagance.

Choosing a window seat, one of two plush swivel chairs which shared a small cocktail table, Lisa put down her handbag. Just ahead was the cockpit, its door open, its interior tantalizingly close. Lisa wondered if it, too, differed from its counterpart on the Silver-Star. She had been on board the Star only half a dozen times before Jeff's death, but even those infrequent visits had been enough to convince her that the craft was a marvel in up-to-the-minute technology. Could Keith Brannon possibly have improved on the Mason Aircraft design?

She looked out one of the port windows. The few crewmen in her line of vision were still busy completing their preparations. Just to the right, she could see Brannon standing with a mechanic watching the last of the fueling. Her eyes were drawn once more to the cockpit. Perhaps there was time for one quick peek before the pilot came on board. If she hurried, she could be back in her seat well before takeoff.

Lisa wasted no more time. She made her way quickly to the door of the cockpit and looked inside. At first glance, it was not unlike the Silver-Star, with dual panels set in the standard configuration, pilot on the left, copilot to the right. But there was something different about the controls. Although many of the dials and gauges were similar to those in her uncle's plane, a number were located in slightly different positions on the panel, and several more were unfamiliar. Fascinated, she moved over to the right to get a better view, running her hand over the half-moon-shaped stick as she slid into the copilot's seat.

It had been almost three years since Lisa had been in the cockpit of a plane; a far cry from the days when she had spent nearly every free moment strapped into a seat next to her Uncle Leonard preparing for her first solo flight. She smiled at the memories, especially those of her uncle's quiet patience. During all those years she must have given him more than his share of bad moments. Yet, as far as she could remember, he had never once raised his voice to her. Lisa shook her head. But then Leonard Mason could hardly be labeled a typical uncle.

Nearly sixteen years ago, when she was only ten, Lisa's parents, Lloyd and Sharon Mason, had been killed when their single-engine plane went down during a sudden spring blizzard over the Sierras. Despite serious reservations, and a lifetime of confirmed bachelorhood, Lloyd's partner and older brother, Leonard Mason, had taken in the orphaned child. To their mutual surprise the experiment proved to be an unqualified success. As the years passed, Leonard had become both mother and father to her, a loving bond forming between them which was closer than many father-daughter relationships.

Those had been wonderful, exciting years, full of the joy of discovery. Leonard Mason had shared with his young niece not only his life but his one overwhelming passion, flying. With infinite patience, he had passed on to her all the skills he had accumulated as one of the country's finest pilots. And slowly, as her trust grew, he had helped her to conquer the fear of flying which had burdened her since her parent's fiery death. By the time she was sixteen, Lisa was a confident, proficient pilot in her own right. That year she soloed and received her license. More important, with Uncle Leonard's help she had faced and won the first major battle of her young life.

Lisa failed to hear the thump of the cabin door being closed. It was only when a hard, lean arm brushed against hers and Keith Brannon eased himself into the pilot's chair that she realized that she had overshot her mark; they were ready to take off.

"You'd better fasten your seat belt," he told her matter-of-factly, his eyes fixed on the control panel. As he flipped the "battery on" switch, which Lisa knew turned on the plane's electrical system, she could see that a neat square of bandage had been placed over his cut, a grim reminder of their previous encounter.

Quickly, Lisa stood, intending to move back into the cabin, but a long brown arm reached out and pushed her firmly back into the copilot's seat.

"I said, fasten your seat belt," he repeated in a tone which did not brook disobedience. Not waiting for a response, he looked out at the member of the ground crew who was plugging in the auxiliary power unit which would allow the engines to start. At a signal, Brannon reached out and started the port engine.

"But, I'm not sitting here, I . . ." Lisa's voice was lost as the drone of the starboard engine joined that of its counterpart.

Keith Brannon shoved a small black manual into her hands. "Here, make yourself useful," he told her, his voice carrying clearly over the noise of the engines. "In a few minutes we're going to start our taxi to the runway. It would help if you read off this check list for me." He indicated the long line of checkoff procedures every pilot must go through before taking off. Lisa was familiar with most of them, having used them for years each time she'd flown. "And for the last time," he clipped, "fasten that belt!"

Lisa hesitated, then decided that leaving the cockpit now would only make an already bad situation worse. Obediently she locked the belt tightly across her lap. She watched Keith signal to the crewman to pull the chocks, the blocks that prevent the plane's wheels from moving, then saw him switch on the microphone to talk to the tower.

"Narita Tower," he said crisply into the mike, "this is Comet 053 in the transient parking area. Request taxi clearance to runway 25 left."

There was a crackle of static as the tower okayed the request, ordering the jet to hold short of the runway before taking off. Brannon pushed forward on the throttle and the sleek plane began to glide smoothly over to the runway area.

"Okay," he told her, "now start reading off that checklist. You won't understand most of it, but that doesn't matter, just read off each item in turn." He looked at her pointedly. "Or is that more than you can handle?"

She nodded to him, clenching her teeth, infuriated, as before, by his condescending attitude. More than anything she wanted to wipe that smug, self-satisfied look off his face by telling him that as a qualified pilot she knew as much about the checkoff list as he did. But the admission would only raise embarrassing questions, questions she was not prepared to answer. Right now all that Lisa wanted was to be off this plane and out of Keith Brannon's life. With great effort she held her tongue, reading through the checklist with exaggerated care, making sure he heard each item clearly. Once or twice she thought that he looked at her surprisedly when she correctly pronounced an unusual or difficult word, but for the most part, he simply listened, going through the designated motions in order.

When they reached the runway, Keith turned the plane into the waiting area and began his final instrument check. Methodically, he moved the controls back and forth, then turned the wheel to the right then to the left to make sure that the ailerons and rudders were free and operational. When he was certain everything was in perfect working order, he once again picked up the microphone and requested and received final clearance for takeoff.

"We're going to start our run now," he told Lisa, speaking in the sort of tone one might use to reassure a small child. "It's not much different from the run a commercial airliner makes, but sometimes people get nervous in a private plane, especially sitting up here in front. We'll be going pretty fast, about 120 knots, before we actually lift off, so don't go getting squeamish."

"Don't worry, Mr. Brannon," she said icily. "I'll do my best not to faint on you."

The sunlight pouring through the windshield accentuated the lean, straight lines of his face as his dark eyes probed hers.

"After yesterday I don't know what to expect from you. There's been a near disaster each time I've seen you. I must be out of my head to take someone as accident-prone as you up with me." Cutting off her angry retort, he said, "So let's make the best of a bad situation, shall we? Are you ready?"

Lisa nodded, furious. He gave her one more quick look, then lined the jet up with runway 25 left, pushing each of the engines separately to one hundred percent power as a final check. Satisfied, he released the brakes and sent the plane hurtling down the runway.

Within minutes they were airborne, soaring above the layers of smog blanketing industrial Tokyo, then banking smoothly to the left for their flight south to Kyoto. Lisa held her breath as she felt the tingle of excitement never present when she flew simply as a passenger on a commercial flight. The sensation was not entirely welcome. For more than two years she had managed to put the world of airplanes, pilots and, most of all, sleepless nights behind her. Distance had made it easier. Now it was coming back too clearly, the thrill of darting down the runway and the exhilaration which came at the precise moment of takeoff, when the earth, with all its petty affairs, was left behind.

Lisa closed her eyes and savored the moment, trying to block out the fact that she was not up here alone. Again she was amazed by the quiet of these little jets. The Comet's engines, as well as the Silver-Star's, were in the tail of the plane, not in front as they were in propeller-powered aircraft, and so engine noise was greatly reduced. It was an eerie, almost ethereal feeling, sailing silently through the heavens, and Lisa knew that she could never be indifferent to the sensation.

"Look, over there," Keith Brannon said, breaking the quiet. He was pointing to an enormous cone-shaped mountain to their right. "That's Fujiyama, Mount Fuji. It's the tallest mountain in Japan, over twelve thousand feet. To the Japanese it has deep spiritual significance."

Lisa eagerly looked down on the famous landmark. The dome of the volcano was capped with snow and slightly lower down she could see a layer of clouds encircling it like a ring, hiding the tip of the mountain from viewers below. As they flew over she saw that one side of the mountain was more furrowed and ragged than the other, and when she looked directly down upon the peak flames of snow seemed to be shooting out from its depths.

"It's beautiful," she said, more to herself than to her companion.

"Japan is beautiful," Keith replied, "although parts of it are being ruined by industrialization."

"Aren't you partly responsible for that?" Lisa accused, remembering the Gilberts' comment about Brannon's company in Kyoto. "Doesn't your corporation do its fair share of polluting?"

"My company is under strict, self-imposed guidelines regarding waste disposal," he answered crisply. "And we recycle whenever possible. Preservation of this land of the gods is everyone's obligation, though too many have forgotten that recently."

"Land of the gods?"

"The ancient Japanese believed that theirs was the only country specially protected by the gods. For centuries they worshipped their emperor as a direct descendant of the gods. In fact, it was only thirty-seven years ago that the current emperor publicly renounced his divine status."

Lisa watched Keith make a slight adjustment in their altitude, noting that the altimeter was holding steady now at 35,000 feet. Then he pushed a small black button on the side of the wheel, and Lisa knew they were on automatic pilot.

Keith got up and stretched. "How's about some coffee? I plugged in the pot when I came on board. It should be just about ready."

"Sounds good," Lisa answered, remembering that she had had no time for breakfast this morning. "Black, please."

He turned to leave the cockpit, then stopped at the

door. "Oh, incidentally, I've put the plane on autopilot. It's flying itself, you might say. Even so, someone has to stay alert up here. Although the Comet's equipped with a radar warning system to signal the approach of other aircraft, I'm counting on you to keep a close watch while I'm back in the cabin. If you see anything, *anything at all,* call for me immediately. I'll only be gone for a few minutes." He looked at her warily. "Oh, and be sure you don't touch anything while I'm back there. Understand?"

"Yes," she clipped, his distrustful tone shattering their temporary truce. "Don't worry, I won't disturb any of your little gadgets."

"Good. I'd hate for us to make an unexpected landing before we reached Kyoto."

Lisa stared at the instrument panel for several minutes after he left the cockpit, trying to collect herself. When she moved to loosen her seat belt she was astounded to find the hands in her lap fumbling and unsteady. Annoyed, she grasped the buckle firmly, releasing the belt in one smooth movement to a more comfortable position across her waist. Damn it all, anyway! What was it about Keith Brannon that made her feel like an awkward, bumbling schoolgirl?

Lisa stared out the window but was too distracted to appreciate the occasional glimpse of checkered land which peeked through the clouds. Not since her years with Jeff had she experienced such a frustrating lack of self-confidence. Her elopement with the handsome test pilot, barely a month after graduating from Berkeley, had been a surprise to everyone. To Leonard Mason it had been a shock. At first Lisa had attributed her uncle's misgivings about her marriage to normal paternal protectiveness. Then her own disillusionment had set in. It was soon obvious that her rash new husband possessed an almost neurotic drive for attention and recognition. No plane was too experimental, no stunt too difficult for Jeff Howard to tackle, or, she thought ruefully, to brag about later. The press ate it up, and Jeff's continual brushes with death soon became legendary. Unfortunately, Lisa's bouts with insomnia became correspondingly frequent. Her self-esteem plummeted until, after two years, little remained of the carefree, secure young woman so carefully cultivated by Leonard Mason. Where he had fostered self-confidence, Jeff had demeaned; where Uncle Leonard encouraged independence, Jeff had demanded submission; and where her uncle showered love, her husband taught her the bitter hurt of rejection.

With a painful wrench of her neck, Lisa was suddenly jarred out of her chair, and her thoughts, and sent flying upward to the full extension of her seat belt. Even before she had recovered from the jolt the autopilot had started to correct the heading, compensating for the violent downdraft which had hit the plane. But Lisa knew the autopilot would adjust in direct proportion to the severity of the dive, an over-correction which could severely stress the plane and cause structural damage. Something had to be done at once or there was a real danger to the aircraft, and to them.

Quickly, Lisa disengaged the autopilot by depressing the small button which was also on the copilot's wheel, then took the controls, gradually leveling out the plane.

The jet responded beautifully as Lisa smoothly eased it back into the proper heading, and soon she relaxed, reveling in the sheer thrill of flying this marvelous machine. How easily it handled. How effortlessly it reacted to her slightest touch. Lisa's mind went back to that other sunny morning almost ten years before when she'd taken her first solo flight. Now, as then, she was struck by the sheer joy of flying. Only now did she fully realize what Jeff had taken from her.

Lisa's fingers clutched the wheel possessively. Up here it was as if the past had never existed. Her cares seemed to melt away as she maneuvered the trim Comet through the intermittent blankets of clouds. Gone were all thoughts of yesterday, and with them her antagonism toward the man who had made this glorious experience possible. How could she stay angry when he had brought such an important part of her back to life? For a wonderful, brief space in time, all was well.

The moment was rudely shattered as the door to the cabin flew open. Without turning, Lisa could feel Keith Brannon's presence behind her.

"What the hell do you think you're doing?" His voice boomed through the cabin, jarring her almost as violently as the turbulence had.

She spun around. He stood in the doorway, hands pressed against the frames of the door. A dark brown stain was still spreading across his shirt and pants, giving her a clear vision of what must have occurred in the cabin when they hit the disturbance.

"I might have known I couldn't leave you alone for five minutes without something going wrong. What the hell do you think you're doing with those controls? You damn near scalded me back there!"

"Yes, but there was a down . . ." Lisa was about to say "down draft," but realized in time that she could hardly be expected to know that term unless she was a pilot. "There was a gust of air all of a sudden," she amended hastily. "I was afraid the autopilot couldn't handle it."

He looked at her in disbelief. "You know you really are something else," he said in wonder. "Who the hell are you to decide what the autopilot can and cannot handle?" Quickly, he slipped back behind the pilot's wheel and scanned the instrument panel. "We're lucky," he said finally. "No thanks to you there doesn't seem to be any harm done, aside, of course, from almost boiling me alive. Fortunately, the autopilot must have had time to make the proper correction before you grabbed the controls." For the first time the full impact of what she had done seemed to hit him. He looked at her suspiciously. "How did you know how to bring it back under manual control, anyway?"

"I . . . I saw you push the same button on your wheel before you went back to the cabin," she improvised quickly. "I just assumed it must be the autopilot."

Keith shook his head and a shock of chestnut hair fell over his forehead, lending an almost boyish look to his tan face. Brushing it aside, he turned in his seat until he was facing her. "So you thought you'd go ahead and push yours and take us for a little joyride. Without even considering the consequences, of course. No wonder you're always getting yourself into trouble."

Lisa felt her face flame. "Why, you . . . you . . . overweening, self-centered egotist! How dare you presume to tell me what I was thinking. I was genuinely worried about the plane. We might have crashed. You weren't here and I did the best I could under the circumstances. You ought to be thanking me instead of shouting insults."

"Oh, I do beg your pardon," Keith said with infinite sarcasm. "You should have told me I had an aeronautic expert on board." He moved closer, turning in his seat until his face was uncomfortably close to her own. His eyes were deadly serious as they probed hers uncompromisingly, and Lisa was aware of a disturbing increase in her pulse rate. "Listen, my dear Miss

Howard," he told her deliberately, "this is a very complex, highly sophisticated machine. It is not a toy for little girls who want something to play with, especially those who have a penchant for breaking everything that comes into their hands." He leaned back in his seat, but his eyes still held hers contemptuously. "Now, no more fun and games, okay? For the rest of the flight I want you to at least try to stay out of trouble. I know that won't be easy, but for both our sakes, make an attempt. Understand?"

She nodded, still too angry to trust herself to speak. For the next half-hour they flew in silence, Keith Brannon making an occasional adjustment to the controls, Lisa lost in her own stormy thoughts. It was almost over, she kept telling herself. Soon she would be off the Comet and on her way to the hotel, and after that she'd be too busy to remember the past two days. At one o'clock this afternoon she would meet with Hiruka Yakamoto, director of the Kabuki Theater Troop of Kyoto, to begin final negotiations for the group's trip to Evergreen. Then there was the Noh Theater, Japan's ancient stylized drama, which she hoped to see sometime this week, and several art exhibits her employer had urged her to view. Yes, there would be little time to worry about the insufferable Keith Brannon.

They were commencing their slow descent for landing at Itami International Airport when Lisa sensed a change in Keith's handling of the plane. His relaxed, almost careless posture became suddenly alert, his body tense and vigilant. Even as Lisa was absorbing this at a subconscious level, her trained eyes were already scanning the instrument panel, trying to pinpoint the difficulty. An ominous red light, glowing in the center of the control panel, gave her the terrifying answer. It was the "fire" light, indicating that they had a fire in the port engine. As Keith coolly checked the tailpipe temperature gauge, her own eyes went to the duplicate instrument on the copilot's panel in front of her. The arrow was well into the red zone. A stab of fear went through her as she realized their danger.

Lisa watched Keith spring into action, his strained face intent, his movements swift but strictly controlled. She said nothing, trusting his ability to handle the situation. She knew instinctively that if anyone could bring them out of this in one piece it was Keith Brannon. Quickly, he pulled the throttle on the left engine to the off position then hit the engine fire-extinguisher button. She watched with relief as the temperature gauge dropped slowly back into the safe zone. With a sigh, Lisa relaxed, letting out the breath she had been unconsciously holding throughout the emergency. Only now was she conscious of the queasiness in the pit of her stomach and the irregular flutter of her heart.

Within minutes the red light was off, signaling that the immediate danger was over. Only time would tell how much damage had been done before the fire had been brought under control—time which could now be measured in minutes. The test would come when they attempted to land. And they were rapidly approaching the airfield.

"Itami Airport, this is Comet 053," Keith was saying evenly into the microphone. Calmly, as if he were talking about yesterday's stock report, he went on to explain their emergency situation, requesting a "straight-in" approach at the field. As soon as the clearance was approved, Keith turned to Lisa.

"I suppose you heard," he said, watching her apprehensively as if he were afraid that she might fall apart on him. "There's no use denying we've got a problem. We've lost our port engine, although that in itself is no cause for panic. This plane can easily fly *and* land with only one engine. Just to be safe, though, I've radioed the tower and they're giving us a straight-in emergency approach. That means we have priority over any other aircraft, either taking off or landing." He reached over and patted her on the lap, his hand remaining there lightly to send erratic signals up her spine which had nothing at all to do with the emergency. "I want you to tighten your belt now and stay calm." He smiled, and his dark eyes were reassuring. Again his tone was placating, as if he were addressing a frightened child. "Think you can hang in there?"

Lisa struggled with a conflicting set of emotions. Alternately, her hand wanted to slap the condescending expression off his face, then longed to rub lightly over the strong fingers which still rested on her thigh. The very capriciousness of her feelings finally brought her mind under control as fifteen years of training came to the fore.

Lisa looked at him coolly, her face composed, almost casual. "Now that the engine fire light is out and the tailpipe temperature is down I can hang in there quite nicely, thank you," she told him calmly. "You just concentrate on bringing us down in one piece. I'll take care of little Lisa all by myself." Pointedly, she removed his hand from her knee.

Keith looked momentarily startled, but a crackle from the radio sent his attention quickly back to his landing procedure. He maneuvered the jet over the let-down point, then started to drop altitude, setting up for their "straight-in" to the field. Reducing air speed, he released the landing gear, then smoothly lowered the flaps and expertly greased the plane onto the runway. Looking out the window, Lisa could see several firetrucks running alongside them, their presence simultaneously frightening and reassuring. But she knew there would be no need for their services now. They were in Kyoto and they were safe.

Keith was out of his seat almost as soon as he had brought the plane to a complete stop in the taxi area. Motioning for her to follow, he made his way quickly through the cabin, unfastened the door and let down the ramp.

"Because of the danger of fire or explosion we can't take the plane into the terminal area until it's been completely checked over," he told her as he helped her down the ramp and onto the field.

Nodding, Lisa allowed him to lead her a safe distance from the jet. There they turned and watched as the crash crew, well covered in their protective uniforms, made their way swiftly but cautiously over the plane, paying special attention to the port engine. The men had been at work only minutes when Lisa saw a small green Toyota race across the field toward them. With a protesting screech of rubber it twisted to a stop just short of the plane. Both doors of the car flew open and two men bounded out. The first man, a tall, slender young Japanese, conservatively dressed in a dark business suit, hurried toward them, his face a mask of worry. Close behind him was the second Japanese, older, heavier and wearing coveralls.

"What happened?" the younger man asked anxiously as soon as the two reached the pilot. "Why did you come in on emergency clearance?"

"The port engine fire light went on," Keith told him, then went on to explain briefly what happened after the red light flashed. Almost as an afterthought, he seemed to remember Lisa, who had been standing by patiently throughout the exchange. "Lisa, this is Etsu Okura, my general manager here at our airport office."

Etsu bowed formally to Lisa, then reached inside an inner pocket to hand her a small white *meishi,* or name card. Remembering that this was a serious custom in Japan, Lisa pulled a similar card from her purse and just as solemnly, presented it to him. Bowing politely, she smiled at the young man. *"O-hayo gozai-masu, Etsu-san, Hajimemashite. Dozo yoroshiku,"* she said, happy that she had memorized the useful phrase from the tourist's grammar guide. "Good morning, Etsu, I am pleased to meet you."

The man's face broke into a broad grin, and he bowed again, obviously delighted with her attempt at his difficult language. Keith was also smiling, but he looked slightly surprised as he slapped a hand on the older man's shoulder. "And this is Hiroshu Hamada, my chief mechanic."

Again they bowed, and Lisa repeated her greeting to everyone's amused satisfaction.

"You're doing very well," Keith told her beneath his breath as the four walked toward the Toyota. "We haven't had a single disaster since we landed. What's gotten into you? Are you losing your touch?"

Before Lisa could retort he was engaged in earnest conversation with the two men, addressing them rapidly now in Japanese. By his hand movements and several anglicized words, Lisa gathered that he was telling the mechanic what he wanted done with the plane after the crash crew finished their work. Evidently it was to be towed into the hangar and gone over thoroughly by his own crew. From the anxious expressions on both the Japanese men's faces, she knew that the matter would be taken seriously. When he was satisfied that his instructions were understood, Keith bowed to the men and placed Lisa in the car.

"I'll be taking Miss Howard to her hotel, Etsu," he said in English, obviously more for Lisa's benefit than Etsu's, "so I'll pick up my own car at the hangar. After that I'll be going on to the office. I want a complete report on the plane as soon as Hiroshu locates the problem. With the Fugi account just around the corner, we can't afford episodes like this. So get on it quick, *hai?*"

Chapter Three

$\mathcal{T}$his is a far cry from the Datsun," Lisa said, sinking comfortably into the elegant silver-gray Maserati. Despite her protests that taking a taxi would do just as well, she found herself enjoying the ride, grateful for the opportunity to pull herself together before reaching the hotel. She leaned back against the posh seat and felt her nerves unwind, releasing the tension that had built up during the emergency. The sensation left her pleasurably lethargic. She watched languorously as they passed out of the airport complex and made their way slowly through the city toward the center of Kyoto.

"The Datsun's just a rental I use when I'm in Tokyo on business," Keith Brannon explained. He turned to her questioningly. "Speaking of business, you haven't told me why you're in Kyoto. Or for how long."

Briefly, Lisa explained her job and the cultural exchange which had brought her to Japan.

"Have you actually seen our Kabuki troop?"

Lisa shook her head, causing a cascade of blond hair to spill about her shoulders. "No, but of course we screened movies and any number of slides before we settled on the Kyoto group. I'm meeting with their director this afternoon to begin final negotiations. Later on I'll have a chance to see them perform live."

Brannon was quiet for a moment as he manipulated the late model Maserati through heavy morning traffic. "None of which explains how you knew about the fire light and the tailpipe gauge," he said unexpectedly, shattering Lisa's hopes that her momentary lapse had gone unnoticed in the confusion of landing. His dark eyes explored hers as they waited at a crowded intersection. "I thought you might have something to do with aeronautics after all."

"No, no," Lisa said quickly—too quickly, she realized as his gaze intensified. She forced herself to slow down, to appear casual. "It's just that a very good friend of mine is a pilot," she went on cautiously. "Occasionally he points things out to me when I go up with him." All of which was true enough, Lisa rationalized. Uncle Leonard had taken her up since she was a child.

"A boyfriend?" Keith asked, refusing to let the matter rest.

Lisa was annoyed by his persistence. "I don't see why that should concern you."

"Well, well, touchy, aren't we?" Keith's voice, though still low, held an edge of sarcasm. "You're right, though. Your personal life . . ."—here he gave her a peculiar sidelong look—"no matter how interesting it may be, is none of my business. I was just going to comment on your astonishing cool up there. I'm surprised you handled it so well."

"You mean you're amazed that I didn't go to pieces on you, Mr. Brannon? Believe it or not, I do sometimes act like a responsible adult."

"Keith," he told her, his mouth twitching in a

suppressed grin. "Since we've faced death together, I think we should be on a first-name basis, don't you?"

When she didn't answer he went on more seriously. "And of course responsibility has nothing to do with it."

"To do with what?"

"Our little emergency. Most people would panic under similar circumstances. In fact, it would be more or less normal behavior for a novice. Fires of any kind generally bring out the worst in us, much less one at 35,000 feet." Again, his eyes brushed over her with interest. "You handled yourself like a pro up there."

"Yes, well, having flown before helped." Lisa shifted uncomfortably in the custom seat. "I've been meaning to ask you about that conversation you had with the girl in the novelty shop yesterday," she said, anxious to change the subject. "You speak Japanese like a native."

"Not quite." He laughed. "But I admit I've become fairly proficient."

"Then you've lived here awhile?"

"About ten years. I was a Marine pilot during the Vietnam War. My buddies and I spent as many of our R and R's in Japan as possible, and, well, I fell in love with the country. In my spare time I began learning the language, practicing it whenever possible during my leaves. When I got out of the service I decided to spend some time here before going back to the States. Finally I admitted I didn't really want to go home, so I started my business here. All in all it's worked out well. My company is headquartered in Kyoto."

"And you don't miss the States?"

"Oh, every once in a while I get an itch to fly home. I still have some family in the Midwest, and they seem to enjoy seeing the prodigal son periodically."

"And vice versa?"

He grinned. "Okay, I admit there's still a streak of the provincial in me. My family have been farmers for generations. Despite my space-age surroundings I guess I'm still a country boy at heart."

Lisa spent several minutes digesting this surprising insight into Keith Brannon. She wondered what her uncle and the Gilberts would think of their infamous playboy's rural background. Of course even an ex-farmboy could grow into a rake, she supposed. Sneaking a sidelong look at him as he effortlessly guided the high-powered sportscar along crowded Kyoto streets, she could well understand why women found him attractive. He certainly possessed the kind of dark good looks which appealed to many women.

Her eyes strayed to the strong brown hands resting confidently on the wheel. Yesterday those same hands had molded her tightly to his body. If she closed her eyes, she could still remember the hard, muscular feel of his chest and smell the heady aroma of his aftershave. Good lord, she groaned silently. Did his appeal extend even to her? Resolutely, she put the thought out of her mind. She had learned her lesson. There would be no more pilots in her life.

"You're awfully quiet," Keith said, breaking the silence.

"Sorry, I guess I was daydreaming. Is it far to the hotel?"

"Just a few blocks now. It's pretty centrally located, as a matter of fact." His dark eyes were lightly mocking her now. "Why, are you in a hurry to be rid of me?"

"No, of course not," she said quickly. "I appreciate the flight to Kyoto. And of course the ride into town. You've saved me a lot of hassle."

Still it was a relief when they reached the hotel and

he handed her over to the doorman. With a final thank-you she hurried into the lobby, not bothering to look back as Keith drove off into the heavy downtown traffic. Within minutes she was ensconced in a comfortable, if unpretentious room, chosen by her for its reasonable price and convenient location. Now that she was on a city expense account she could no longer indulge in the luxurious accommodations that Uncle Leonard had insisted upon in Tokyo. But it would hardly matter, she told herself practically. She would be too busy to notice her surroundings, *or,* she added firmly, brood about overbearing playboys who were best forgotten.

Even after she had unpacked, more than two hours remained before Lisa's one o'clock appointment with Hiruka Yakamoto, the Kabuki director. She showered, then sent down for a light lunch. After lunch, she laid out her clothes, choosing carefully, discarding several outfits as too flashy or too revealing, until she settled at last on a simple but expensive beige linen suit and soft cream-colored blouse.

These preparations completed, Lisa sat down on the edge of the bed and went over the papers in her briefcase. Although she had thoroughly familiarized herself with the plans before leaving the States, she was determined that her first major assignment out of the country would go as smoothly as possible.

After Jeff's death Lisa had been delighted to land the job of Assistant Director of Arts and Culture for the city of Evergreen. With a major in speech and drama and a minor in fine arts, she had been ideally suited for the position. But she had to admit that the big attraction had been the job's almost total removal from the world of aeronautics. Here, she felt, she could forget. Here she could rebuild her life.

Lisa sorted through the preliminary arrangements for the Kabuki troop's stay in California, then checked the final contract papers, even though it was unlikely that they would get that far during their initial visit. She had been well coached not to expect to wrap up her business in one or even two visits. "Yakamoto will want to move at a relaxed pace," her employer had told her. "It would be considered poor manners for you to rush him in any way. Take things slowly and let him take the lead."

So Lisa had allowed two full weeks in Kyoto. She would meet with Yakamoto, see the Kabuki players perform live for the first time, then take in the other attractions that might subsequently follow the troop to Evergreen. When her business was concluded, she hoped that she would still have time to sightsee on her own, to explore one of the oldest and most beautiful cities in Japan.

When Lisa could find no flaw in her preparations, she dressed carefully, then brushed her long, glossy blond hair back from her face. Fashioning it into a tight chignon at the nape of her neck, she secured the mass of thick hair firmly with tiny, invisible combs. She opened the door to the closet and pivoted before the floor-length mirror, critically examining the effect. Just as she hoped, the tailored suit deemphasized her slim yet sensuously curved figure. Unfortunately, the severe hairstyle hadn't been quite as successful. Although it did make her appear older than her nearly twenty-six years, it also accented her large, clear blue eyes and porcelain complexion. Still, the overall image that peered back at her from the mirror seemed more mature, she decided, and Lisa was satisfied that she had done the best she could.

Just after noon she grabbed her handbag and briefcase and took the elevator to the lobby. Stopping at the main desk, Lisa asked for detailed written instructions both for the cab driver taking her to Minami-za where the Kabuki troop performed and for the return ride to the hotel. Today she was taking no chances. She wanted no repetition of yesterday's fiascos. Lisa was determined that this afternoon everything would go exactly as planned.

And it did. At least until she returned to the hotel later that afternoon. Yakamoto had been a charming host, enthusiastic about the exchange and agreeable to the arrangements. After a tour of the theater proper they had concluded their meeting amicably, agreeing that Lisa should attend the troop's next live performance the day after tomorrow.

Back at the hotel, Lisa was glowing with pleasure over the success of her meeting as she waited for the elevator that would take her to her fifth floor room. She was just stepping into the lift when a low voice spoke almost directly into her ear, "You look like the cat that swallowed the canary."

Lisa was so startled that the high, thin heel of one of her pumps caught on the slight uprise leading into the enclosure, causing her to fall forward, briefcase and purse flying, before two strong arms grabbed her from behind.

"I see you're up to your old tricks," Keith Brannon exclaimed, steadying her against the back of the cage. "Do you always fall into strange men's arms like this?"

Regaining her equilibrium, Lisa pulled out of his grasp, her pulse beating rapidly. Chagrined, she reached for her scattered belongings, only to realize that the heel of her right pump was dangling almost off the shoe.

"Oh, darn," she said in annoyance, and raised her

foot for a closer inspection. Immediately she teetered, lost her balance and fell back against the pilot, causing him, in turn, to career into the elevator operator.

"Sumi masen," he said to the slight Japanese man who was nearly thrown off his stool. "I beg your pardon." Once again Keith pulled Lisa to her feet. "You really are unbelievable, you know that? It's a wonder our plane landed in one piece this morning with you aboard." He handed over her briefcase and handbag, making sure they were securely in her possession before letting go. "I'm surprised there's anything left of Kyoto after an afternoon with you on the loose."

The angry retort that sprang automatically to Lisa's lips wilted to a rueful shake of her head. "You always seem to catch me at my worst. For your information my meeting this afternoon went perfectly."

Keith's mouth twisted into a crooked smile. "Somehow, I find that very difficult to believe." The elevator jerked to a stop, and he took her firmly under the arm. "This is your floor. You'd better lean on me getting out. We can't afford any more casualties."

Flushed with embarrassment, Lisa permitted him to escort her off the lift, then stopped as soon as they were in the hallway and removed both shoes so that she could walk evenly. "I can manage quite nicely now," she told him with a fair show of dignity considering the circumstances. "My room is just down the hall. There's no need for you to . . ."

"Then it's moved. You know as well as I do that room 575 is all the way to the end of the corridor and around the bend. I feel I owe it to the hotel to see that you get there without any more accidents. Come on now, don't argue." Without waiting for her approval, he grabbed her arm and started to lead her briskly down the hall.

Lisa's eyebrows flew up in astonishment, and digging in her heels as determinedly as possible without benefit of her shoes, she refused to move. "Just how would you know which room I'm in?" she demanded angrily. "And where do you get off ordering me around like this? You have no right. . . ."

"For your own good I'm giving myself that right," he replied calmly. His grip on her arm intensified. "Now come on, I'm through arguing with you. We're going to be late as it is."

Lisa was so startled that she allowed herself to be led off toward the end of the corridor. "Late for what? What in the world are you talking about?"

"We're going to dinner, didn't I tell you? I thought it was time you got out of these Westernized hotels and saw something besides the tourists'-eye-view of Japan. You're never going to know what the countryside is like if you stick around here."

With a pang of guilt, Lisa realized that that was exactly what she had planned to do, enjoy a relaxing bath followed by a nice safe dinner in the hotel dining room.

"But where—?"

"My general manager Etsu Okura has asked us to his home for dinner. He lives with his parents just outside the city. Evidently you made quite an impression on him this morning at the airport. He insisted that I bring you over for an authentic Japanese meal. On behalf of us both I graciously accepted."

"Without even asking me? You have a lot of nerve, Keith Brannon. For all you knew I might have had previous plans." She looked at him suspiciously. "I'm surprised you're not at the airfield supervising work on your precious Comet."

Keith smiled and took the room key she was holding

from her hand. Inserting it into the lock, he pushed open the door and stood aside, allowing her to enter first. "Perhaps I prefer to supervise you." There was a hint of wry amusement on his lean face. "Your lines beat the Comet's any day."

Lisa walked past him to toss her purse and briefcase on the room's only chair, glad for an excuse to hide the unwelcome flush that was invading her cheeks. By the time she turned back to him she had decided it was safer to ignore his last remark. "Have you had a report on the extent of the fire damage yet?" she asked, keeping her voice impersonal.

To her surprise he laughed out loud, a hearty, resonant laugh, masculine and full, and Lisa knew with a flash of irritation that he had seen through her act. At her look of consternation, Keith forced a semiserious expression onto his face. "I appreciate your concern," he said with mock politeness. "But it's nothing serious. My mechanics found the problem less than an hour after we landed. Hamada is ordering a new part from Tokyo."

"A new part? That's all?" Lisa couldn't hide her surprise. "Surely after the fire . . ."

"Ah, but there was no fire. It turned out to be just a faulty transducer in the fire warning system." He looked amused. "So you see? This morning's crisis was much ado about nothing."

Lisa was still trying to digest this surprising diagnosis when he went on, "Now that you've had your aeronautical update, how's about it? Dinner, I mean. The Okuras will be very disappointed if you refuse their invitation."

"But I . . ."

"Have you ever had a real Japanese meal or been in a native Japanese home?" he pressed.

"No," she answered honestly. "But really, Mr. Brannon, I don't think that tonight would . . ."

"Keith, remember? Now, let me have a look at you." He turned her around in front of him, his eyes taking in every detail of her tailored outfit. "No, that's out. Put on something softer, something with more pizzazz. And your hair, for God's sake let it down again." She watched him openmouthed as he walked to the door.

"Oh, and hurry, will you? I said we'd be there by six."

The Okura house was located high on a hill overlooking varicolored strips of city below. Lisa was amazed at the difference between Kyoto's glamorous central district and the serene countryside. Even the air smelled fresher, and she inhaled deeply. Now that she was out of the city, Lisa was glad Keith had persuaded her to accompany him. Throughout the half-hour drive he had been at his charming best, settling her solicitously in the Maserati, pointing out places of interest along the way and narrating interesting pieces of Japanese history to which she listened intently. He had the gift of making the stories come to life, and Lisa could almost visualize the colorful samurais and shoguns of the past as they waged their bloody battles for power.

"The city was established in 794," Keith told her as they sat in the car for a few moments before going up to the house. "An ancient emperor selected this spot because it was entirely surrounded by mountains. He named it the City of Peace or Heian-jo. But by popular acclaim it soon became Kyoto, or 'capital,' and it remained the capital of Japan for eleven centuries until its place was usurped by Tokyo."

"It's all so—so different up here, so serene."

Keith smiled and turned to her softly. "That's why I

wanted you to come, Lisa, to experience firsthand the real soul of Japan." He moved his hand to the back of her seat, allowing it to rest lightly on her shoulder. Lisa trembled as she felt the warmth of his flesh through the sheer fabric of her dress. Her body stiffened imperceptibly as his fingers traced lazy patterns on her bare neck, all too aware of his nearness and the searing sensation his hands made.

With a slight shifting movement, he inched closer, and his free hand closed over the fingers that lay on her thigh. She was sure he hadn't missed her sharp intake of breath, or the chill which tingled through her body as his hand touched hers. Still, she made no effort to move away.

Kyoto stretched below them, its streets forming the classical Chinese grid. Lisa's eyes stared at the pattern even as her mind whirled in confusion. Keith's thumb gently massaged her wrist, then moved to the sensitive area of her palm. The scene below blurred. It was as if nothing existed in the universe except the handsome, virile man next to her.

"I could look at this sight all day," he murmured. The fingers of his left hand traced the underside of her chin, then ran lightly down to the hollow of her neck. Lisa's breath caught, and she would have been powerless to speak even if it had been necessary. But Keith required no answer. He went on softly, "It's so very, very beautiful." She looked at him quickly, but his eyes were not on the view. They were resting on her face.

Lisa swallowed hard but could not relax the constriction of her throat as his fingers moved to explore lower on her neck. When she tried to speak, her voice was noticeably thick. "It . . . it is remarkable."

She couldn't tear her eyes from his face; the strong, lean lines, classic yet playfully boyish. Never before had she been so affected by a man. Surely he must be aware of the mad thumping of her heart and the thrust of her breasts as they reacted to his touch. She trembled as the hand on her shoulder moved even lower, seeking the warm, deep cleavage above the scoop-neck of her dress. Lightly, his fingers traced over the swelling peaks and into the valley between.

"God, Lisa. I've wanted to touch you like this since I first saw you in the parking lot yesterday. When you brushed against me it was all I could do to keep my hands off you. I thought if I stayed angry about the accident, I'd come to my senses. But it's no use. Today I want you even more."

His lips found hers, teasing them with the merest hint of a kiss.

"You're making me dizzy," she groaned when she could no longer stand the taunting, feather-light touch.

"I know how to fix that," he whispered into her mouth, and his lips came down hard on the pink, yielding softness of hers, claiming them with a passion that had lost all forbearance. The muffled gasp that came from deep in her throat left no doubt that he had answered her need. She made no resistance when his tongue parted her lips and started a thorough, delicious search of her mouth.

"Lord, you taste as good as you look," he said huskily when they finally broke apart. "We didn't have to come here for dinner. We could have stayed at the hotel, and I could have feasted on you."

Lisa's mind hazily recognized danger. Having him this close made it impossible to think rationally. Things were moving much too fast. The last thing in the world she wanted was to be emotionally involved with Keith Brannon!

Lisa shivered and moved closer to the door. "I . . . I

think we'd better go in now," she said, realizing that her voice sounded strained.

She turned to find Keith looking at her searchingly, the desire in his eyes all too obvious. Then, with a long, regretful sigh, he reached for the door handle.

"You're right. It would involve great loss of face if we were late for dinner." His eyes searched hers one last time. "But, later . . . There's always dessert. . . ." His voice trailed off meaningfully.

Lisa quickly straightened her dress as he came around the Maserati to open her door. Reaching out a hand, Keith helped her to her feet, then allowed his other arm to circle her slender waist. When he pulled her to his chest she felt her blood racing like hot lava through her veins. His hands massaged her back, then lowered to cup her hips, molding her so intimately to his body that Lisa was left in little doubt about his very male need for her. She moaned, and involuntarily her hips swayed ever so slightly against his, causing him to draw her even more tightly to his aching body. She felt his breath hot and eager against her neck.

"I can't get you close enough," he groaned. "It's all I can think of." With a wrenching effort he pushed her away, but his hands remained firmly positioned on her upper arms. His eyes held hers, and he bent his head and let his lips brush gently over her mouth.

Then he was leading her up a slight incline and through a gate which led into a spacious, carefully tended garden. Behind it stood a charming Japanese house of the old style, weathered to a rich cinnamon color and constructed along simple, straight lines. The roof was peaked and made from heavy, curved ceramic tiles, some of them quite ornate on the hips and ridges. In the center of the garden was a large pond inhabited by dozens of beautiful and colorful carp, which were swimming around a small island connected to the rest of the garden by a graceful wooden bridge. To one side of the pond was a hill and a gently flowing waterfall, its faint trickling sound breaking the otherwise perfect silence of the sanctuary. The serenity was just what she needed to calm nerves still frayed from the encounter in the car. When she looked at him she could still feel his body pressed against hers . . . his lips resting ever so lightly on her mouth . . . his . . . Good lord! Enough! What was this man doing to her?

Lisa forced herself to concentrate on the beauty of the setting, not on the man who, even now, was creating unwelcome tingles where his hand rested on her arm. Fortunately the scene was truly lovely. Scattered about the garden were evergreens, dwarf pines and Japanese maples, some of which were sculptured in simple but elegant designs. Concentric circles of raked sand were placed at pleasing intervals, and Keith explained that they represented the waves of the ocean, a recurring theme in Japanese landscaping. Here and there throughout the garden Lisa saw beautifully carved stone lanterns and artistically placed rocks of all sizes and shapes. The only thing that she couldn't find were flowers. Curious, she mentioned this to Keith.

"The Japanese garden is a place of order and serenity," he told her as they crossed over the narrow bridge toward the house. "It expresses the Buddhist philosophy of ruling out the inessential and seeking harmony with nature. Etsu has no blooming flowers because he wants to express the unchanging essence of nature. Flowers bloom and die, but rocks and evergreens remain for a lifetime."

"Well, he's certainly captured the peace, hasn't he? This is one of the loveliest gardens I've ever seen."

"Which makes it the perfect setting for you," he breathed in her ear as they came up to the house.

Lisa was spared a reply when she saw that the sliding door to the house was already open. Composing herself, she walked with Keith up the steps to the *genka,* or entrance hall, to find Etsu standing inside the doorway, his handsome face beaming as they approached. For a moment Lisa hardly recognized him, so drastically had his appearance changed from the staid, conservative businessman she'd met at the airport earlier in the day. Instead of the tailored suit, Etsu was wearing a tan kimono covered by a short dark-brown coat with several crests woven into it. On his feet were a pair of two-toed socks which Lisa knew were called *tabi.*

Behind Etsu stood two women, the older of the pair wearing a gray kimono with very little decoration. By contrast, the younger woman, whom Lisa judged to be about nineteen, was dressed in a colorfully embroidered kimono that made her stand out dramatically from the rest of the family. To Etsu's right was a middle-aged man of great dignity, who stood smiling at them benignly. This was undoubtedly the patriarch of the Okura family, Lisa decided, Etsu's father.

"Welcome to our humble house, Mr. Brannon-san, Miss Howard," Etsu said politely as the whole family bowed to them in unison. With infinite respect, he motioned to his family. "Please allow me to introduce my mother and father. And this is my sister Toshiko."

Once again everyone bowed, and Lisa and Keith removed their shoes, which were arranged neatly before the door, and put on fresh *tabi* provided by their host. Promptly another sliding panel, or *shoji,* was opened, and they entered an interior room where they were graciously seated on large square cushions. Lisa

saw that the floor of the room was covered in traditional Japanese style with thick rice-straw mats called
tatami. At one end of the room was a little raised
platform in an alcove which, Keith whispered, was a
tokonoma. Inside the alcove hung a long handpainted
scroll, the only picture in the room, and beneath it a
lovely vase holding just three flowers. The room was
simplicity itself, Lisa thought, amazed by the straight
geometric patterns and sparsity of furniture. Still, she
had to admit that it had an air of purity and serenity
unmatched in Western homes. The only piece of real
furniture, at least by American standards, was a low,
oblong black lacquered table set in the middle of the
room and surrounded by six more of the large cushions.
Lisa assumed it was there that they would eat dinner.

"Miss Howard, you grace our humble home with the
light of your presence," Etsu said formally. And then
with a grin, "I'm so glad you could come."

"I'm very happy to be here, Etsu," she said, smiling
warmly. "But really, I wish you'd call me Lisa."

There was a titter of embarrassment as Etsu translated for his parents. This was followed by a respectful
silence when Etsu's father bowed his head slightly and
addressed Lisa formally in Japanese.

"My father apologizes, Miss Howard," Etsu told her,
"but begs me to explain that it is very difficult for us to
pronounce your name in Japanese, since there is no 'L'
in our language. Therefore, with your permission, he
asks if we may call you 'Hana-san' instead. It means
'flower,' and he chose it because your lovely pale
yellow hair and blue eyes remind him of the fairest of
spring flowers which bloom each year on the hillside.
He says it is an honor to behold such beauty in his
humble house."

Lisa blushed as Keith broke into peals of laughter. "You *have* made an impression, Little Flower of the Orient," he told her teasingly. "You may be the best thing that ever happened to Japanese-American relations. That is, if there's anything left of the country after you leave."

"*Domo arigato gozaimasu.* Thank you very much," Lisa said, trying to ignore Keith's sarcasm as she bowed politely to Etsu's father. "I would be honored to be called Hana-san."

As they sat down at the highly polished table for dinner, Keith winked and squeezed her hand, leaving Lisa feeling unaccountably euphoric, as if she had passed an unspoken test. She knew that she had pleased him and that the warmth in her cheeks could not be totally explained by the potent rice wine so generously served before the meal. Even without the benefit of a mirror, Lisa knew that she had never looked better, and the knowledge added immeasurably to her enjoyment of the evening.

Keith had been placed facing the *tokonoma,* the seat of honor, Etsu explained, while Lisa, as second guest, had been seated with her back to the alcove. The food appeared on the table so quickly and silently that Lisa decided that the Okura servants could rival any magician. As soon as the steaming dishes were in place, a red lacquered tray was put in front of each diner. On the tray were chopsticks neatly wrapped in paper, a small bowl for rice, and a larger bowl for the main course. Lisa hardly knew where to begin. Artistically arranged before her were pickled turnips, radishes and peppered string beans, two soups—one a delicate fish soup and the other clear—and bamboo sprouts that had been cut into very thin pieces and cooked in brown

sauce. In addition to these was a dish of *sashimi,* raw
fish daintily sliced and rolled in a sheet of seaweed,
and, of course, the inevitable *gohan,* or rice.

Using Keith as her guide, Lisa made her way through
all the courses, delighted to find the dishes not only
pleasing to the eye, but also delicious. Even the
sashimi, which she sampled with some trepidation, was
surprisingly tasty, and her efforts with the raw fish
earned her another reassuring wink from the far end of
the table.

After the food was cleared away Lisa rearranged
herself on the cushion, feeling relaxed, almost lazy
now. Vaguely she realized that she had probably consumed far too much *sake,* but the warm glow of the
wine was pleasant, and she settled back comfortably to
enjoy the easy flow of conversation. The outside *shoji*
had been parted to reveal a misty, enchanting view of
the garden, the graceful bridge and waterfall taking on
an ethereal quality in the moonlight. It was exquisite,
Lisa thought languidly, and soon the soothing drone of
Japanese receded as she became lost in the beauty and
serenity of the evening.

It was some time before she realized that the tempo
of the conversation had changed and become strained.
Rousing herself from her meditations, Lisa saw that
Toshiko was addressing Keith with some animation,
darting mischievous looks at her brother as if she were
telling an amusing story at his expense. The expression
on Etsu's face, however, was ominous, and Lisa saw
that both parents wore ill-concealed frowns. Finally,
Mr. Okura shifted abruptly on his cushion.

"Shizuka ne shina-sai!" he told his daughter sharply,
and Lisa needed no translator to know that the girl had
been told to be quiet.

There was an awkward silence as Toshiko placed a

small, delicate hand over her mouth and looked around at the others in acute embarrassment.

"Domo shitsurei shimashita," she said in a soft, choked voice. Very formally Toshiko bowed low to her father, then to her brother, and finally to her mother and their guests. To Lisa she said in halting but understandable English, "So sorry, Hana-san. I have been indiscreet. I must leave now, for I have many duties to perform." Lisa could see tears glistening in Toshiko's eyes as the girl bowed a final time, then hurried from the room as quickly as the hobble skirt on her gaily flowered kimono would allow.

There was a noticeable lull in the conversation after the girl's departure, and Lisa was relieved when, a short time later, they were able to make polite thank-yous and take their own leave.

Chapter Four

What was that all about?" she asked as soon as they were settled in the car. "That poor girl was all but expelled from the room. What did she do that was so terrible?"

"She was teasing her brother," Keith answered, guiding the car down the winding hillside road. "And in doing so she revealed some rather embarrassing facts about his love life. I gather Toshiko isn't always as prudent as she might be."

"My goodness, that sounds intriguing. What's so confidential about Etsu's love life that it has to be kept top secret?"

Keith smiled. "I think it's more the *lack* of a love life that he'd like to keep under wraps," he replied dryly. "Etsu is very much in love with a girl he'll probably never be able to have, a lovely young *geisha* called Miyume, or 'Beautiful Dream.'"

"A *geisha!*" Lisa exclaimed. "I didn't think they had those anymore."

"They do. But not nearly as many as they used to. It's almost prohibitively expensive to train them properly anymore, although Kyoto still has two of the finest *geisha* houses in the Orient. That's where Miyume took her training. And now that it's completed Etsu rarely sees her anymore."

"How did he meet her?" Lisa asked, affected by the story.

"They grew up together. Miyume was almost ten years younger than Etsu, but I think he's always loved her. Miyume's mother was a very famous *geisha* in her day and began to train her daughter when she was only six years old. By the time she was twelve, Miyume was sent to serve as a *maiko,* or an apprentice, here in Kyoto. That meant she attended to the bath and dress of an older *geisha* and very quietly poured *sake* at parties. Now she's a full *geisha* herself. And a very beautiful one, I might add."

"But isn't there anything Etsu can do? Surely they can't stop Miyume from marrying for love, can they? I mean, she's not in prison."

"No, but she might as well be. It's cost a great deal of time and money to train Miyume in the arts of the true *geisha.* Both her mother and others have a lot invested in her. Miyume understands this and honors her obligation to her benefactors. It's her duty to serve as a *geisha* until such time as a man comes along with enough money to buy her contract, thereby satisfying everyone involved."

Lisa was incensed. "But that's terrible! You make it sound like she's a commodity."

"A very expensive commodity," Keith said wryly. "Much too expensive for Etsu, I'm afraid."

"You mean that's the only way they can get married? Etsu has to buy her contract?"

"The only *honorable* way, yes. You have to remember, Lisa, that things are done differently in Japan.

Honor and 'face' are still all important here. It would be unthinkable for Etsu and Miyume to break with tradition.''

Lisa thought about this as they drove, fuming at the unfairness of Miyume's existence and the futility of the romance. She hardly noticed Keith slowing the car until he had pulled the Maserati off the road, coming to stop on a wide ridge overlooking Kyoto. Her heart skipped a beat as she remembered his earlier promise about having "dessert" later. Was this gorgeous setting to be the table where he planned to enjoy his late-night snack? Her body tingled at the thought. But was it from fear or anticipation?

Keith turned off the ignition and leaned back in the driver's seat, seemingly lost in the spectacular view below them. When he made no move toward her, Lisa gradually relaxed, leaning back in her own seat to look out over the mountain. If her thoughts were tinged with regret, she studiously ignored them, focusing instead on the easy companionship they were sharing. Better to enjoy a brief friendship than a fleeting, hopeless love affair, she told herself sensibly. No strings, no expended emotions, no awkward goodbyes. Lisa sighed softly. Why was the thought so damn depressing!

For several moments they sat quietly, each admiring the host of twinkling lights that made up the city below. Would she ever be able to think of Japan and not remember Keith Brannon? Lisa wondered. Would his memory always conjure up visions of peaceful gardens and whispering waterfalls, or glittering lights at midnight on a Kyoto mountainside?

Keith's low voice broke through her thoughts and the hush which had settled over the hill. "Well, what do you think of my city now?" he asked, not bothering to hide a note of pride.

"I love it," she answered softly. "It's almost as beautiful by night, isn't it?"

"More so. Darkness has a nice way of hiding the imperfections."

Lisa smiled. "I'm surprised to hear you admit there's anything about Japan that isn't perfect."

"Ah, but imperfections make us appreciate true beauty," he answered, shifting toward her in the seat.

"Very philosophical," she replied, uncomfortable with the move. Suddenly he was too close. She felt suffocated by his nearness, his scent, his strong male body nearly touching her own.

"But very true." He reached out and took her hands, and she felt a shock as his skin came into contact with her own. His hands were warm and dry and surprisingly gentle as they massaged hers, tracing little patterns around each finger. "Take you, for example," he said. "If you hadn't stopped so suddenly in the parking lot yesterday, I might never have met you. Just think what we would have missed." One of his hands went to her face and softly traced her cheek line and the perfectly arched contour of her lips.

Lisa was alarmed at the dangerous promise in those dark eyes and the sudden wild acceleration of her heartbeat. She had to stop him now, while she still had the strength to resist. "Keith . . . please, I don't . . ."

His fingers brushed aside her objections as they glided across her mouth. Strong fingers ran through the silken gold of her hair, then moved to her back where they continued their maddening movements along her spine. With tantalizing slowness his face drew closer to hers, his eyes holding her spellbound.

"No," she cried, and realized vaguely that even now the protest was weaker than before. As his face came to hers she felt the last vestige of resistance evaporate into

the cool night air. Every fiber of her body, every
nerve-ending tingled with desire for him. Even as a
small voice inside her screamed caution, she longed for
him to move closer. She wanted to absorb him completely, totally. "Keith . . ."

His lips silenced further argument. But had that one
word been an argument or a plea for fulfillment? she
wondered. She felt as if she were on a wild, wonderful
roller coaster ride, heedless of the dangers or the
ultimate destination.

He drew her closer, and she felt the power in the
arms that gripped her as if afraid she might fade into
the night. For one, brief, lucid moment, Lisa knew that
even had the word been a protest, she would still be
here in his arms, awaiting his caress, his kiss.

Keith's lips grazed her mouth, causing her breath to
catch. His lips traveled a path of fiery pleasure across
her cheek to the tender lobe of her ear, exploring every
crevice, every curve of sensitivity. Lisa felt giddy, but
whether it was from the unaccustomed *sake* or the
sensations he was arousing, she couldn't tell.

"I've never tasted a sweeter dessert," he whispered
against her lips. "But it's only whetting my appetite. I
have a hunger to consume it all."

Then his tongue was describing deliciously moist
circles on her neck, his breath sweet and warm as his
mouth moved to the low-scooped neckline of her dress.
His tongue found the deep hollow between her breasts,
and she moaned softly.

"You really are beautiful, Little Flower," he whispered. "You're like a lovely rosebud that needs to be
tended and coaxed until its petals open into full
bloom." His lips slid further into the deep valley, and
she felt an electric charge course through her body.
"Bloom for me, Lisa," he groaned.

With practiced skill his tongue and teeth gently nibbled one of the nipples outlined sharply now beneath the thin cotton fabric of her dress. With infinite patience he teased it until Lisa ached with longing.

"Oh, my God," she moaned. "What are you doing to me?"

"I'm just listening to your body, Little Flower," he whispered. "It's telling me how good it is between us. How incredibly good. Don't you feel it?"

"Yes," she murmured, and twisted beneath his touch. "I . . . I've never felt like this before."

"Then you've been deprived for too long. Let me take care of you, Lisa. Listen to your body."

His hands stroked her back, coming to rest on the gentle curve of her spine. When they dipped even lower to caress her hips and thighs, and the sensitive, feminine area between, Lisa held her breath, mesmerized by the waves of pleasure he was evoking. When his hands pressed against her even more intimately, she gasped, not realizing that her own fingers were raking his back until she heard him moan softly into her neck.

Through a haze of desire Lisa tried to remember the reasons why she must resist. One part of her wanted him to take her, to give her the love and fulfillment that she had never found with Jeff. Another, more rational side, argued only that she was in danger. Lisa forced her bewildered mind to focus on Jeff. She fought to remember the pain, the confusion, the humiliation. She had to remember. She had to keep the memory alive so that it wouldn't happen again!

"No, Keith, please. . . ." Terrified of her own weakness, Lisa tried to pull away, tried to break the spell of the *sake* and the moonlight and the dark, handsome man so close to her. But her plea fell as harmlessly as feathers onto a stone. His lips would not be deterred.

They claimed hers fully now, firm and demanding, taking what she was powerless to withhold. For one wild moment Lisa surrendered totally to him. Against her will, against all reason, Lisa's hips arched toward his, pressing, writhing. Mindlessly her hands tangled in his hair, then pulled his tensely corded body closer, molding it to her own.

At her totally uninhibited response, Keith seemed to explode. With a little groan, he parted her lips with his tongue, probing her mouth until she was drowning in a sea of sensations. With sudden dismay she realized how much she wanted him, how desperately she longed for the union of their bodies.

She was hardly aware when his hands moved to undo the buttons on her dress, and the touch of his roughened hands on her sensitive breasts startled her. Reason returned and with it the clear knowledge of what was happening.

Lisa struggled to free herself from Keith's arms. "No, please. . . ." Her voice caught and the words escaped as a bare whisper of fright. His lips only came down harder, robbing her of breath. Still pinioned beneath his iron grip, she felt her fear grow until it was nearly suffocating. With strength born of desperation, she pummeled him wildly with her fists. "Let me go! Please! Jeff . . . let me go!"

Lisa was released so suddenly that she fell back against the car seat. It seemed an eternity before the dark, angry face came into focus, mere inches from her own. For a long moment he didn't move, and Lisa lay completely still, too dazed to stir, mesmerized by the hated name that echoed again and again in her ears. Had she actually called it out? Was his hold still so powerful, even from the grave?

Only when he had himself firmly under control did Keith shift to the other side of the car. "Who's Jeff?" he asked hoarsely.

With fumbling fingers, Lisa hastened to refasten the buttons of her dress. She was embarrassingly conscious that her own breathing had still not returned to normal. Unable to look into his accusing eyes, she kept her face diverted as she worked.

"I asked, who's Jeff?" he repeated.

Still, she kept her eyes away from his. When she finally spoke her voice was uneven, barely audible. "No one . . . no one, really," Lisa stumbled. "An old friend, that's all."

Keith reached a long arm across the seat and grabbed her chin, tilting it upward until she was forced to look into his face. "Just an old friend?" he challenged. His eyes studied her skeptically. With a little grunt of disgust, he abruptly removed his hand. "With that kind of friend you really don't need any enemies, do you? You sounded as if you were scared to death of the guy. What did he do to you?"

"Nothing," she whispered.

"Come on, Lisa," he told her abruptly. "Give me more credit than that. It's obvious he meant a great deal to you . . . one way or the other. You don't call out another man's name at a time like that without his having touched your life pretty dramatically."

"Perhaps he did," she managed hoarsely. "But it was a long time ago." She knew that the story was feeble, that Keith must realize there was more to it than that. If he only knew how much! Jeff had touched her life, all right. He had affected her so profoundly that even after two years his name was still on her lips. She looked at Keith. Only a short distance separated them in the small car, but now they seemed miles apart. She knew that she had hurt him deeply. He deserved some kind of explanation. She cleared her throat and tried.

"Jeff was a man I knew from another time, Keith," she said softly. "Another time, another place . . . when I was a much different person. But it's all over now. I haven't . . . I haven't seen him in a long time."

Keith's eyes probed hers through the moonlight. Lisa felt as if he were picking apart her mind, sifting through her fabrication in search of the truth.

"That's it?" he probed. "You don't want to tell me anything else?"

She shook her head. "No, I . . . I really can't. It's all over, Keith. There's no sense dredging up the past."

"I'm not so sure," he disagreed. "Sometimes you have to confront the past in order to put it in its place. Whoever this guy is he's still in your life whether you know it or not. Anyone who can cause you to do a hundred and eighty degree turnaround like that wields too damn much power, Lisa. One minute you were as eager as I was and the next you were fighting me off as if I were a rapist. Do you always run hot and then cold like that?"

"No, I . . . I must have had too much *sake,* that's all. I'm not in the habit of doing this sort of thing. You took me by surprise."

Keith's face was strained. "You wouldn't play games with me, would you, Lisa?" he said tightly. "You're a beautiful, desirable woman. And I'm a normal male with all the natural impulses. Did you really think I wouldn't respond when you came on to me like that?"

Lisa trembled, hating herself for the way her body had reacted to his touch. "I don't know what you mean. Of course I'm . . . I'm not playing games. I told you, I just had too much *sake*. Now please," she went on miserably, "I'd like to go back to the hotel."

He glared at her for a moment, then turned and with a fury of roaring gears started the Maserati.

"I'll be very happy to do just that," he told her shortly. "You know I've been wondering about you, Miss Howard," he went on caustically. "You're really quite an enigma. For someone who's such a bull in a china shop you can be remarkably agile when you want to."

His eyes glinted at her through the moonlight. "Is that something else you turn on and off at will?"

Lisa spent a miserable night. For hours she tossed fitfully on the hard hotel mattress, struggling to sort out her hopelessly tangled feelings. The very human response he had aroused in her tonight was all the more frightening because she should have known better. Two years of punishment should have taught her *that* much. At least with Jeff there'd been some excuse; she'd been so much younger then, much less in control of her emotions. For all his good intentions, Leonard Mason had hardly prepared Lisa for the real world. Even her years at Berkeley had been spent under his close supervision. At twenty-one she'd been no match for Jeff Howard.

The first time they'd met, or more accurately, the first time that Jeff really noticed his employer's niece, was at Lisa's college graduation party. In his enthusiasm, Leonard Mason had invited a number of his employees as well as Lisa's friends to the celebration. Lisa was flattered to be singled out by the handsome test pilot and frankly enjoyed the envious stares directed at her by every other female in the room. When Jeff asked her out for dinner the following evening, she readily accepted. Two weeks later when he asked her into his bed she was equally powerless to resist. One month later they were married.

In her eagerness to please him, to prove herself worthy of the great Jeff Howard, Lisa ignored any number of danger signals. Naively she confused her husband's passion and possessiveness with affection and his bouts of criticism with a desire to help her grow up. If she were slow to respond to his abrupt, frenetic lovemaking, it was her fault for being so inexperienced. Even his late-night drinking sprees left Lisa with a niggling guilt that somehow she had failed him at home.

Two months before his death, a time when Lisa's self-esteem had reached an all-time low, she stumbled onto what must have been humiliatingly obvious to the rest of their friends. From the earliest months of their marriage Jeff had been unfaithful to her; he had enjoyed other women as freely as if they'd been just another fringe benefit of his job. In typical Howard fashion he'd shown surprise, then indignation when she'd finally confronted him. Even Lisa had to agree that Jeff put up a convincing argument—a man well cared for at home had no need to fool around; somehow she was to blame for his infidelities. But there'd been little time to question this warped logic. She'd barely had time to collect the tattered shreds of her dignity when she made an even more momentous discovery: She was pregnant!

Lisa still found it amazing that she'd been so over-joyed by the news. How easily her happiness blotted out the awful memory of how the miracle had come to be. Quickly her body forgot the degradation and pain which more and more often accompanied Jeff's love-making. All that mattered was the seed which had been planted, the new life growing inside her. Lisa's unborn baby became the focus of her life, persuading her to clutch blindly at Jeff's promises to reform. A child needed a father as well as a mother, she reasoned. She even deluded herself into thinking that fatherhood might have a settling influence on Jeff. She made a face in the darkness. And someday she might walk on Mars! How could she have been such a fool?

Lisa's pillow was damp as she shifted positions on the bed. Frustrated, she pounded her fist into the hard, unyielding mattress and pulled the now totally disheveled blankets up until they nearly covered her head. Why was she dredging all this up now? For months after Jeff's death she'd struggled to forget, reasoning that only by burying her old life could she begin a new one. Now she wasn't sure. Maybe Keith was right when he said forgetting wasn't the answer. Perhaps the only way to build a sound, solid future was to construct it upon the hard-learned lessons of the past.

As the faint light of dawn swept lazy fingers through the Kyoto clouds, Lisa admitted that Keith Brannon had come along at a very bad time in her life. Next month she would be twenty-six. For over two years she had striven to rebuild her self-esteem. She had changed her job, her apartment, her friends. For the first time in her life she could say that she had accomplished something on her own; she was self-sufficient and content, beholden to no man. Now, after knowing Keith Brannon for only two days, she felt as if she were back to square one. The realization was scary. The handsome pilot was Jeff Howard all over again. Some level of her consciousness must have recognized the truth, and she had reacted with all her old insecurities.

The similarities were blatantly obvious, starting with Keith Brannon's prowess with the ladies. The love 'em and leave 'em type. Wasn't that the way Clyde Gilbert put it? Lisa cringed when she realized how very close she had come to succumbing to him. Just as she had with Jeff, she thought disparagingly. Would she never learn? It was as if two years of hard-earned progress had been wiped out in less than forty-eight hours!

Lisa turned over again, heedless of the tangled mess of blankets that caught at her waist. No, she told herself firmly, Keith Brannon could cause her grief only if she let him. She was just beginning to discover the real Lisa Howard, and the small taste she'd had of independence left her hungry for more. Her confidence and self-respect were still too fragile to be risked because of a fleeting physical attraction to a man she had every reason to distrust. The choice was hers. This time there would be no excuse if she let someone else make a mess of her life. She would have only herself to blame if she made the same disastrous mistake twice. For the remainder of her stay in Kyoto she had to avoid Keith Brannon at all costs!

The decision made, Lisa felt a sense of welcome relief and with it overpowering weariness. She yawned and closed her eyes against the ever-increasing invasion of light into the room. Still, she thought as she drifted peacefully on the brink of sleep, the touch of his hands on her skin had been exciting—intoxicating, unlike anything she'd ever experienced. What would it be like to make love to such a man? she wondered drowsily. To give herself to him completely . . . unconditionally . . . blissfully . . .

Chapter Five

The knocking was insistent, an abrasive intrusion which she fought to reject.

"Go away," she mumbled, and rolled over to pull the lumpy pillow firmly over her head.

But the noise went on, pausing only a moment as if to recharge, then continuing even louder. Reluctantly, Lisa opened heavy lids and tried to focus on the small travel clock she had placed on the nightstand. It was barely eight-thirty. A quick, if bleary, calculation revealed that she had been asleep less than three hours. Not enough, she thought wearily, and once again sought refuge beneath the covers. "Come back later," she called out in muffled tones.

A disturbingly familiar voice rose above the pounding. "Hey, sleepy head, open up in there."

Lisa sat bolt upright, her pulse racing. There was no mistaking that voice. Keith Brannon! What in the world was he doing here?

Lisa threw a light robe over her sheer blue nightgown and padded barefoot across the room, acutely conscious of her sleep-tousled appearance. She opened the door a crack and peered out.

"What do you think you're doing here at . . ."

She stopped short. Before her, looming tall and unbelievably handsome in the dingy hallway, stood Keith, smiling boyishly. In one hand he held a single exquisitely formed yellow rose. Last night he had said he wanted her to open for him like a rose. Was the flower an indication that he had come back to try again?

"The desk clerk said you were still in your room," he said, "so I decided to surprise you." With a disarming grin, he extended the rose.

For a long moment Lisa didn't move. The man was persistent, she'd give him that. Was he dangerous, too? She looked into the dark eyes, but last night's fire had been replaced by playful golden highlights that told her nothing.

"Don't you want it?" he said with a wounded look.

Lisa hesitated, looking at him suspiciously. "No strings attached?"

"Of course not," he answered, indignant that she would have to ask such a question. "Do I look like the kind of man to give stringy presents?"

"Keith, be serious!" she said in exasperation. "You know what I mean."

He grinned and spread his hands wide in a gesture of surrender. "Of course I do. And I meant what I said. No strings." Again he extended the bud, his face boyishly pleading. "Come on, Lisa, have a heart."

She looked at the innocent face grinning at her from the hallway and was barely able to suppress a smile. He certainly could be charming, she thought ruefully. But how far could she trust him; how much of this was real and how much a clever act?

"Please . . ." The deep brown eyes spoke eloquently.

Unable—or was she *unwilling?* she asked herself honestly—to resist either the flower or his appeal, Lisa finally opened the door just wide enough to accept the rose.

"It's very nice," she said stiffly.

"Well, at least one of us seems to be welcome," Keith said.

"That's the risk you run when you come by uninvited," she countered. Her quavering nerves left her no choice but to go on the offensive. Last night proved that she couldn't trust herself to react rationally when he was this close. "Don't you believe in calling before you drop over?"

Keith chuckled low in his throat, and he leaned his tall body against the frame of the door. "Sometimes," he drawled. His brown eyes swept her face in amusement. "But not this morning. Sometimes it's more fun to act on the spur of the moment, don't you think?" Without waiting to be asked, he walked past her into the room.

Lisa watched dumbfounded as he sank easily into the overstuffed chair by the window and draped one long leg over the arm. "Aren't you going to close the door? Or do you want the whole floor to share our little visit?"

Lisa's pulse was racing. "Just what do you think you're doing barging in here unannounced?" she flared aggressively. "After last night you've got a lot of nerve to . . ."

The sound of voices in the hallway broke through her harangue, and she teetered for a moment between her desire to have him out of her room and her desire for privacy. The latter won. She marched across the room and slammed the door.

"Tsk, tsk," he clicked, as she whirled around and faced him from the closed door. "Such a temper." His brown eyes twinkled. "You'll have me thinking I'm not welcome."

"Then you'll be thinking right," she shot back. Even as she fumed, she could hardly keep her eyes off his powerful frame. It seemed to fill the small room. She noticed that his clothes were casual: a plaid flannel shirt and a pair of well-worn blue jeans that hugged powerful thighs, making Lisa uncomfortably aware of the hard muscles that rippled beneath the thin material. Over his shirt he had on the same brown leather flight jacket he'd worn the day before, and on his feet were a pair of heavy hiking boots that had obviously seen much use.

Her eyes traveled back to his face, and she noticed, to her annoyance, that he looked remarkably refreshed, as if he, at least, had had no difficulty sleeping the night before. In fact, he looked all too alert as he lazily took in her soft blue robe and the transparently thin gown scarcely hidden beneath. Lisa fought to keep her eyes steady and her face stern as she met his stare, but she couldn't shake the uncomfortable feeling that he could see right through the subterfuge.

The painful prick of a thorn on her thumb broke her concentration, and she looked down at the rose in her right hand. "I'd better put this in water," she mumbled without looking up.

Lisa hurried into the bathroom, feeling as drained as if she'd been engaged in hard physical labor. It was too early in the morning to be sparring with Keith Brannon, she thought wearily. Although in all honesty she wasn't sure that any time of day would be to her advantage. For the first time since Jeff's death she felt out of her league. Damn the man! Why must he persist in upsetting her life?

Lisa continued to chafe as she filled a glass with cold water and dropped in the rose. Automatically, her eyes went to the the mirror and she studied herself critically. Thankfully, the face that looked back at her was not nearly as ghastly as she'd feared. Her blue eyes were wider than usual, but they looked bright enough. Lisa gave vent to some of her frustration by running a brush through her tousled hair. Not that looking better would help get rid of her uninvited guest, she thought dryly. But at least it would give her sagging ego a boost.

"What are you doing here, anyway?" she asked, grabbing the initiative as soon as she returned to the room.

Instead of answering, Keith's eyes moved in wry amusement to the water glass in her hand. "Is that some new trick for preserving flowers?" he asked.

Following his gaze, Lisa looked down to see that the water surrounding the rose was a pale pink. While she watched, a small drop of blood fell from her injured thumb and was absorbed into the liquid.

"I pricked my thumb on a thorn, that's all," she said, putting down the flower and reaching for a tissue. "It's no big deal."

To her consternation, Keith laughed out loud. "I should have known better than to bring you anything as dangerous as a rose. Although I guess I should be grateful you didn't attack me with it." He held up his right hand and she saw that the square of gauze had been replaced by an ordinary bandage. "I'm still recuperating from your last assault."

The grim reminder of their disastrous meeting in the

hotel shop in Tokyo only served to irritate Lisa. "And I should know enough to be wary of Keith Brannon bearing gifts," she snapped. "I'm sure you've got ulterior motives."

"Of course I do," Keith admitted good-naturedly. "I've come to take you for your next flying lesson. After yesterday, I don't want you to be afraid to fly again."

"I'm sure a big business executive like you has more important things to do with his time," she said.

He shrugged easily. "My company's bidding on a new account, and I've been working night and day on it for weeks. I think I owe myself a day off for good behavior." He shifted his long legs on the arm of the chair. "I've decided to spend the time making amends for scaring you half to death yesterday."

"Don't be ridiculous. That wasn't the first . . ." Lisa stopped just short of blurting out the truth. "That's nice of you," she went on coolly, "but I've already planned some sightseeing today."

"By yourself?"

His blatant skepticism immediately rekindled her anger. "Of course, by myself. I'm a grown, responsible woman. I hardly need a nursemaid."

"Don't you? Tokyo may never be the same after your visit the other day. You may not need a nursemaid, but you could sure use a keeper."

Lisa's voice was cutting. "And I suppose you're applying for the job?"

Keith gave a mock bow. "At your service, Miss Howard. I will be delighted to escort you to the far corners of Kyoto. Just name your pagoda."

"No, thank you, Mr. Brannon," she said, mimicking his mock formality. Memories of her Tokyo fiascos were still too fresh to be humorous. "I'll get along quite nicely by myself. I wouldn't think of saddling you with someone as accident-prone as me."

Keith moved from the chair like a lynx, reaching her in two powerful strides. His smile was apologetic as he bent his head down to hers. "Hey, I didn't come here to fight, remember? All I want to do is make amends."

He took both her hands in his and lightly rubbed her injured thumb with his fingers. At his touch, she felt her skin burn as it had the night before. Unnerved by this involuntary response, she tried to pull away. Instead, she found he was holding her even closer as his broad hands moved to her upper arms. Lisa held her breath, fearful he might feel the quiver which ran the length of her body.

"Come on, Lisa," he cajoled, his face so near she could almost count the tiny golden flecks in those dangerous eyes. "You're not giving me much of a chance." As if the words didn't come easy, he bent his head closer until she could feel his breath stir on her face. "Don't you understand? I'm trying to tell you I'm sorry. At least give me an opportunity to make up for yesterday."

"No . . . there's no need . . . really . . ."

His lips brushed hers so lightly that had it not been for her racing pulse, the kiss might have been imagined. "There is *every* need," he said softly, cutting off her protests. "Let me make it up to you."

"But—"

He kissed her lightly on the forehead, then held her at arm's length. "No 'buts' about it. I'll compromise with one tourist attraction, then it's off to the airport." Before she could object he went on, seeming to take her acquiescence for granted. "Now, what's it to be?

Nijo Castle? The Shinkyogoku Arcade? I know, the Gold Pavilion; that's every tourist's first stop. It's sure to be jammed today, but let's have a go at it anyway."

"No," Lisa broke in, Keith's high-handed manner breaking the spell of his touch. Pulling out of his grasp, she walked to the window, anxious to put as much distance between them as possible. Her mind was racing, as out of control as her pulse, when she turned back to face him. "That's not what I had in mind." She purposely made her voice curt. "As a matter of fact, I don't think you'd like my choice at all. It's not on your 'list of tourist attractions.'"

Keith's brows went up. "Oh? What *is* your choice?"

Lisa hesitated. Ever since she could remember, Uncle Leonard had told her stories of the place where, many years before, he had first dreamed of starting his own aircraft company. It had been shortly after the end of World War II, and a very young Leonard Mason was just completing a perilous three years as a crack fighter pilot with "Pappy" Boyington's famous Black Sheep Marine Squadron. The day before he left for home, he made one last trip to the place that had become his haven from the often frantic Allied Occupation. There, in the peaceful seclusion of Shokin-tei, he had quietly decided what he wanted to do with his life, and ever since then, the simple garden teahouse had held a warm place in his memories.

"It's not at all exciting," she told him haltingly. "Certainly nothing as spectacular as the Gold Pavilion. But it's special to someone I care about very much, and I've always wanted to see it."

"Oh? Now you've really got me curious."

Still, Lisa was reluctant to tell him. Revealing Uncle Leonard's private sanctuary seemed almost a betrayal.

On the other hand, she was sure Keith Brannon would find her choice boring, and it might be just the out she needed. A safer, if much less exciting, course of action, she told herself abjectly.

"It's the Shokin-tei," she confessed, "the tea hut in the garden of the Katsura Villa. An old friend visited it once and said it was very beautiful." At his puzzled expression she blinked back her disappointment to ramble on, "I told you it wasn't very exciting."

"Oh, I wouldn't say that. In fact, it's probably one of the most *exciting* places in Japan. Although I'll grant you, not for the usual reasons." He eyed her speculatively. "But you're right when you say it's not the run-of-the-mill tourist spot."

Lisa frowned. This was not working out as she planned. She made one more feeble try. "But you can't really want to spend your morning visiting a lonely garden?"

"Why not?" He grinned. "I told you I was at your disposal. There's one problem, though. The Shokin-tei is one of the few monuments in Kyoto that requires advance permission. It usually takes about twenty-four hours to get a permit."

Lisa grimaced. Despite herself she had been almost pleased that he had backed her into a corner. Now, because of some government red tape, she would have to visit the Shokin-tei by herself, a suddenly lonely prospect.

"Don't look so glum. Remember, Kyoto's my home. I have a friend in the Imperial Household Agency. Maybe she can expedite matters."

Using the phone in Lisa's room, Keith placed a call to the appropriate agency and spoke to his friend in rapid and persuasive Japanese. While he talked, Lisa grabbed some clothes and retreated into the bathroom to change. She had decided to follow Keith's advice to dress casually, choosing a pale pink cheesecloth shirt to go with her blue denim pants and a pair of comfortable low-heeled shoes. After seeing the Shokin-tei, he had explained, they would still be taking that promised flight. Then, he'd added mysteriously, he had planned a surprise that required sensible clothing.

As she applied a touch of mascara to her long lashes and lightly glossed her lips she wondered what Keith would think of his plans today if he knew she was Leonard Mason's niece? Would he still believe that their meeting in the hotel parking lot the day before yesterday, at the height of the competition for the Fugi contract, was an accident? Or that her ride with him yesterday in the Comet had been merely a matter of convenience? The aeronautics business was too competitive, too merciless nowadays to accept that kind of coincidence. She knew what she would think if the tables were reversed; she would accept the more logical explanation that she was an industrial spy charged by her uncle to keep an eye on the opposition.

Lisa nearly laughed aloud at the humor in the situation. From the very beginning she had gone out of her way to avoid Keith Brannon, and with him, the entire world of aviation. Yet if he discovered her identity he would undoubtedly assume just the opposite, that she had deliberately set out to entrap him. Lisa was brought up short. Actually that wasn't such a bad idea. If that didn't get him out of her life, nothing would. Why not go out there right now and admit that she was Leonard Mason's niece?

Lisa continued to brush her hair, but the movement was purely perfunctory. Instead of being relieved by the plan, she found herself quickly manufacturing reasons why she shouldn't take such a drastic step. Why make waves when she probably wouldn't see him again after today? she reasoned. Because of the Fugi contract, wasn't it in Uncle Leonard's best interests if she retained her anonymity, if she went through the motions of a pleasant, impersonal day with him and then said goodbye? Surely she could do that much for Mason Aircraft.

She pulled a face at the image in the mirror. Lisa Howard, the great martyr! Who was she trying to kid with all this rationalization? The truth was she *wanted* to go with him today. Despite everything, she wanted to share these last few hours with Keith. Good lord, she sighed. Why was her intellect having such a hard time winning the war over her emotions?

Lisa took one last look at her reflection, and it seemed that her blue eyes had never looked so huge, so intense. Although the effect was not unbecoming, it nonetheless pointed out her underlying tension, and Lisa irritably closed her overnight case with a bang.

If you're going to play with fire, Lisa Howard, she told herself sharply, *you'd better be damn sure you can take the heat!* Then she stepped back into the bedroom.

"Very nice," he told her with obvious approval. With a devilish glint in his eyes, he added, "It'll take at least an hour until our permit is ready, plenty of time for a bite of breakfast downstairs before we go. I want to make sure you get a good start. You're going to need all your energy today."

Refusing to elaborate further, Keith led her down to the hotel's coffee shop where he ordered a hearty Western-style breakfast for them both.

"Not very Oriental," he told her, "but I can't seem

to lose a craving for sausage and eggs in the morning."
He winked disarmingly. "Must be the farmboy in me, I
guess." And Lisa was left to wonder again about this
inexplicable man who could be rude and overbearing
one minute and totally charming the next.

They had the Katsura Villa almost to themselves.
There were a few other tourists, but essentially the
peace and utter serenity of the monument were undis-
turbed. Lisa chose to explore the villa itself first,
wanting to save the Shokin-tei tea hut and garden,
which had so captivated her uncle, until last.

"I think General Hideyoshi got his money's worth,"
Keith said as they walked through the three sections
that comprised the villa.

"It's almost overpowering in its simplicity, isn't it?"
Lisa was awed by the villa's austere but perfectly
balanced architecture. She wished that she had the
power to transport the entire building and its garden
back to California for the city of Evergreen to enjoy as
well.

"How much do you know about Katsura's history?"
Keith asked as they entered the second part of the villa.
Each section of Katsura was divided into several
rooms, and all were beautifully decorated with priceless
paintings by members of the Kano school. Even the
rooms' fittings were exquisite; all finely detailed and
superbly crafted. Yet, the overall effect was of great
simplicity and restraint.

As they paused for a moment before going on to the
third section of the building, Lisa considered Keith's
question, pleased that she had taken the time to do
some cursory research on the monument before her
trip. "I know that Katsura is the masterpiece of Kobori

Enshu, and that it was commissioned by the military dictator, Hideyoshi, in the late sixteenth century. Other than that I'm afraid I know very little about its past."

"Actually there isn't too much more to know," he said, his expression showing that he found her knowledge impressive. "Enshu agreed to design the gardens only after imposing three conditions on Hideyoshi: he wanted no limit on the cost, no limit on the time and no interference until the project was completed."

"Kobori Enshu must have had quite a reputation." The story, even more than the dreamlike atmosphere, captured her fancy. "How long did it take to finish?"

"Five years. As I said, I don't think anyone would dispute that General Hideyoshi got his money's worth." He nodded toward the last section of the villa. "Shall we see the rest of the building, or would you like to move on to the Shokin-tei?"

"Let's finish the villa first," Lisa said quickly.

Keith smiled but said nothing as they browsed through the third, and last, section of the structure. Even when they had seen the villa, Lisa insisted on taking a circuitous route to the Shokin-tei, a path that allowed them to view the other teahouses first.

The garden was organized around a gracefully designed pond, and Lisa knew without being told that each stone, bush, tree and pebble had been carefully put into place with concern for the whole. Artifice and nature were indistinguishable, and the result was a timeless creation by a man who was one with his environment.

"The teahouses were designed for each of the four seasons," Keith told her, and Lisa noted that he had unconsciously lowered his voice as if he, too, found the setting awesome. "Enshu planned it so carefully that wherever you stand seems to be the best place for viewing the entire garden or even the villa."

"It's absolutely lovely," Lisa marveled. As their footsteps brought them closer to the retreat that had meant so much to her uncle, she sucked in her breath. It was not unlike the other tea huts, yet to Lisa it seemed more profoundly peaceful than its companions. For a long moment she didn't speak.

"Well?" Keith said at last, his low voice stirring the almost palpable silence. "Are you disappointed?"

"No," she whispered. "It's everything I expected."

With almost reverent care, Lisa picked her way over the stones that led across the pond to the tea hut beyond. As she walked she had the eerie feeling that she was threading her way into the past, into the more ordered, simpler world of sixteenth-century Japan. At the front of the hut, she stopped.

"It's so peaceful," she murmured, sensing without turning that Keith had followed her to the teahouse.

"It's hard to believe Katsura ever lived here, isn't it? Not a single pebble or pine needle is out of place. That's what makes it so timeless, so uniquely Japanese."

She felt his arm on her waist, and this time she didn't flinch from the sudden warmth that crept through her body as he bent to kiss her. Somehow here, in this garden of tranquility, his embrace seemed as natural as the sculpted trees that framed them with graceful limbs. Her lips parted willingly as his kiss became more insistent, and soon she was clinging passionately to him, pressing eagerly against his hard and hungry body. It was only the sound of footsteps approaching the pond which reluctantly drove them apart. Still he did not move away, and his arm remained loosely around her waist, his body blocking the path to the teahouse.

"Can we go inside?" Lisa was conscious of the breathless quality of her voice. How could she think clearly when her pulse was pounding like a sledgehammer? Now that the spell was broken, she knew that she had to escape the lips that could so easily make her forget the harsh realities of their relationship. "I'd like to see the tea hut," she repeated, more insistently this time.

Keith made no effort to move. "There's not much to see," he told her softly. His eyes had not left her face, and it was clear that he had little inclination to explore the teahouse. Lisa was afraid that he was about to take her in his arms again when another group of tourists walked toward them from the main building. With a sigh, he finally stepped aside, removing his hand from her waist as she moved past him onto the path. As if sensing her need to be alone in the little hut, Keith allowed her to go on by herself, making no effort to follow her inside.

Lisa entered the Shokin-tei solemnly, very nearly in awe. It was everything her uncle had promised, and much, much more, for of course he had not been able to convey in words the spirit of the little teahouse, the utter serenity one experienced on stepping inside. She felt as if she were entering a room of angles; all squares and rectangles, some solid, some transparent, a jewel of symmetries. No wonder Uncle Leonard had found inspiration in this simplest of dwellings. Its sweeping, uncluttered lines led her eyes smoothly from that which had been created by man to the living universe beyond.

As Keith had warned, the tea hut was unfurnished; nothing drew the viewer's attention away from the straw, paper and wood from which it was constructed. The rustic tea pavilion led her back almost forty years to a young man with a dream. For a moment, as she stood quietly within its austere walls, she felt herself become part of the past, an experience she would always treasure.

And Lisa knew as they left the serene walls of the villa that Keith Brannon would always be part of that memory.

They arrived at Itami Airport just before noon. With the Comet temporarily out of commission, Lisa wasn't sure what to expect, but she was totally unprepared when he stopped the sportscar beside a single-engine Cessna 150, a plane Lisa had flown many times. Before she had been allowed to check out in a jet, Uncle Leonard insisted that she log hundreds of hours in several propeller-driven crafts, one of them an almost exact replica of the small plane moored here. It was a versatile craft, well-known for its easy maneuverability, and Lisa had fond memories of the many hours that she and the Cessna had spent cruising California skies.

Keith smiled as he got out of the car, misreading her startled expression. "Don't look so surprised, Lisa," he told her. "Prop planes have been around for a long time. You'll be perfectly safe." As he began the preflight check of the little craft his eyes once again danced with mischief. "In fact, I hope you'll find this flight a very memorable experience."

Lisa was impressed by Keith's meticulous care as he went over the plane, mentally ticking off each procedure in her own mind as he worked. First he noted the oil and gas levels before draining some of the gas to check for contamination and octane. Then he moved to the propeller and, working clockwise, inspected every inch of the fuselage, wings, tail assembly and tires. Finally, he climbed into the plane and carefully scanned the controls. Only then did he remove the blocks and move the plane out from its protected moorings.

"All set," he said, helping her climb into the right-hand side of the plane. Lisa noted with a pleasant sense of familiarity that the instrument panel in Keith's Cessna was almost identical to the one in the aircraft she'd flown in the States. As she settled into the coffee brown Naugahyde seat she longed to touch the controls, to be in command of the plane herself. Instead, she sat quietly, holding herself in strict control while Keith made one final check of the instruments.

Finally satisfied, he turned to her with a grin. "Ready?" At her nod, he looked around in all directions, then poked his head out the window and shouted, "Clear." With a loud screech and a blurring swirl of propeller, he started the engine and they began the long taxi ride to the runway.

Their takeoff was smooth and faultless, but by now Lisa expected nothing less from the famous Keith Brannon. Whatever else she might say about him, she could not criticize his flying ability. At 2000 feet, they leveled out, and Keith spoke to her in a raised voice in order to be heard over the roar of the engine.

"See, that wasn't so bad, was it?" He nodded toward the control wheel in front of her seat. "Would you like to take the wheel for a while?"

Lisa was tempted. Surely she wouldn't give herself away by simply handling the controls now that they were airborne. Even complete novices were able to do that much. Then she read something in Keith's expression, a sort of challenge that touched off a silent alarm warning her to decline. She shook her head.

"No, thank you. I'd just as soon you did the driving."

For a long moment his dark eyes stayed on hers, and she had to stop herself from squirming beneath the candid scrutiny. Had she guessed wrong? Should she have agreed to take over the wheel? Then it was too late to change her mind, he had turned his face away and was looking out the side window.

"See that road down there?" he shouted. When Lisa nodded, he went on, "Keep your eyes on it."

Without warning Keith lowered the nose, accelerating the Cessna's air speed, then pulled the wheel back with gradually increasing pressure. As the plane began its almost vertical climb, Lisa felt a noticeable, but not uncomfortable, pull that pressed her back into the seat. Out of the corner of her eye she saw Keith glance at her, but she was too busy enjoying the free sensation of the loop to care. In seconds they were upside-down, and as the craft moved through the fully inverted position to complete the second half of the circle, Keith adjusted the back stick pressure to keep the nose moving at a constant rate for the downward arc. Smoothly, they pulled out of the 360-degree loop, and the nose was once again at a level flight attitude. Lisa looked down and was amazed to see that the maneuver had been executed flawlessly; they were once again directly over thè road!

"I think we left my stomach somewhere up there," Lisa said, belatedly remembering her amateur status. "Do you always fly like that?"

"In this plane, yes," he answered. "The 150 is made to order for free maneuvering." Once again he eyed her speculatively. "You seem to have taken it in your stride. If I didn't know better, I'd say you've done this sort of thing before."

Lisa mentally kicked herself. A stunt like that would take any novice's breath away. Yet he was right, she'd hardly batted an eye. "As a matter of fact, I have," she said, searching for a plausible explanation. "My pilot friend has taken me up in a plane very similar to this."

"Ah, yes, your friend." His voice was so low she had to strain to hear. "I take it this is the same person who taught you about the fire light and tailpipe gauge?"

"Yes," Lisa said, averting her eyes. "As a matter of fact, it is."

"Has he also shown you this?"

Again he increased the cruising speed, putting the Cessna into a shallow-dive attitude, then he gently coaxed it into a barrel roll, a maneuver Lisa particularly enjoyed. And she had never seen it performed better. They described a wide, lateral circle, inverting gently as they curved around like some giant-winged bird. Smoothly they swung back to the point where the plane had first crossed through the horizon.

This time Lisa was not caught off guard. Even as she relished the beautiful precision of the movement, she remembered to grimace and clutch the sides of the seat with white knuckles until they were once again level.

"You didn't care as much for that one, huh?" he said, noting her reaction. Not waiting for an answer, he banked the plane sharply to the left. "Let's see what you think of this one."

Their speed once again increased, and Keith moved into another stunt which Lisa immediately recognized as the Cuban Eight. She knew this maneuver combined the loop and a diving aileron roll to describe an aerial figure eight. Keith started the stunt just like the loop, but when the nose was about forty-five degrees, he relaxed all back stick pressure and they went over the top in an inverted position. As they came down he executed a rapid aileron roll, and for a split second they hung suspended with the nose of the little plane pointing directly toward the ground. But instead of pulling back on the controls to describe the upward curve of the second circle as Lisa expected, he suddenly let go of the wheel. Whirling out of control, the Cessna continued to plunge downward, and Lisa could see the ground racing toward them at dizzying speed. An icy fear clutched her heart. They were going to crash!

"Lisa!" The command reverberated in her ears, slicing through her panic.

She reacted instantly. Without thinking, without consciously willing it, her hands fastened onto the wheel. Long years of training caused her to act instinctively, and as if they possessed a will of their own, her hands exerted firm but gradual pressure, easing them up out of the disastrous dive. The little Cessna gave one rebellious shudder, then responded obediently to Lisa's touch. It was only when they were once again stable, when the ground was no longer rushing up at them at a frightening rate, that she realized what had happened. Releasing the wheel as if it were on fire, she whirled in her seat to face Keith. He met her astonished stare with a look of grim satisfaction.

"That was quite a performance," he said, once again taking control of the craft. "It seems your friend taught you a hell of a lot more about planes than just how to read the tailpipe gauge! You really *do* continue to amaze me, Little Flower!"

Chapter Six

Neither of them spoke as Keith banked the Cessna and flew back to the airport, smoothly easing the craft onto the runway. As they taxied across the field the sun shone through the windshield to cast his lean, straight features into contrasting planes of shadow and light; the effect both dramatic and at the same time intimidating. But there was little illumination in those dark brown eyes, and Lisa could detect none of the little flecks of gold that had danced there this morning. As soon as the Cessna stopped, she fumbled to unfasten her seat belt. But before she could release the buckle, her wrists were imprisoned by an iron grip.

"Not so fast." Keith's low voice echoed in the small compartment, strangely silent now after the clamor of the engine. "You have some explaining to do."

"No more than you," she shot back. Lisa tried unsuccessfully to free the hands he held pinned in her lap. "That was a crazy, dangerous thing to do up there. We could both have been killed!"

"I thought you should have a chance to try your hand

at the controls," he countered quietly. "It seems my faith was justified. You did very well. *Unbelievably* well."

"You took me by surprise." Her eyes were accusing. "I told you I didn't want to handle the plane."

He smiled, but without humor; certainly the dark eyes remained scornfully cold. "That's what's so amazing, isn't it, Little Flower? Because when the time came you handled it pretty damn well."

Lisa bit her lip, searching for an explanation that he would accept. "Only because I was watching when you did those stunts." The excuse sounded pathetically thin, even to her, yet she went on, "If I hadn't paid attention I . . . I wouldn't have known what to do."

She was sure he hadn't missed the slight nesitation in her voice, any more than she could misinterpret the blatant skepticism in his.

"Come on, Lisa, you can do better than that. I don't know what kind of game you're playing, but I've had just about enough of it. How's about trying the truth for a change?"

"I don't know what you mean."

"You know very well what I mean, Lisa *Mason* Howard." His eyes glinted at her sudden intake of breath. "Care to tell me about it?"

Lisa's surprise quickly turned to fury as she realized the implications of his discovery. "Why you devious . . . underhanded . . . brute!" she sputtered. "You staged that whole scene up there just to trap me!"

"Don't forget I had a good teacher. How long did you think I'd buy that little-miss-innocence act you've been laying on me since our flight to Kyoto?"

Lisa's eyes blazed. "About as long as I was willing to fall for your down-home country boy routine." She fumed when she remembered the perfect yellow rose and the innocent face at her door this morning. "At least I didn't come bearing gifts."

Through her anger she was pleased to see him look embarrassed. "The rose had nothing to do with what happened up there," he shot back, momentarily on the defensive.

"Or what happened last night?" Lisa's cheeks burned with more than anger as she remembered his smooth performance in the Maserati. The knowledge of how she had been used cut through her like a knife. She grimaced in self-disgust as she considered her gullibility. How easily she had deluded herself into believing that Keith Brannon was interested in her, even if it was only for a one-night stand, when all he really wanted was revenge. She felt betrayed, and the pain was sharp in her chest. Keith Brannon was everything they said about him and infinitely more!

Lisa dug deep and came up with a last bitter vestige of pride. "I'd say that if we tallied the score, you'd be the winner hands down, Mr. Brannon. I hope you enjoy your victory."

"I never enjoy subterfuge, Lisa. And that seems to be the prime ingredient of our relationship. *So far.* But we're going to remedy that right now, aren't we?" Without releasing his hold on her hands, he shifted toward her on the seat. "The first thing I want to know is *why?* Your uncle's got one of the cleanest records in the business. Why did he suddenly stoop to something like this?"

"Uncle Leonard had nothing to do with it. He doesn't even know I flew with you on the Comet. Other than that I don't owe you any explanations."

His face grew taut. "Don't you?" Imperceptibly, the

pressure on her wrists increased. "I think you do . . . if you value your uncle's reputation."

Lisa wrenched her hands but couldn't pull free of his grip. "That's playing dirty."

"And industrial espionage isn't?" His eyes glinted hard in the sunlight. "Make no mistake. I'm not letting you out of this plane until you've explained."

She stared at him, realizing that he meant what he said, yet loath to give in to his demands. She realized that if it hadn't been for last night, she in all fairness would be eager to defend her uncle's honor. But the affair in the Maserati more than canceled her feelings of guilt. Preying on her emotions was unforgivable, no matter what the provocation. If she gave in now, his victory would be complete.

"I said I don't owe you any explanations," she repeated, her tone clipped and final. "Now let go of my hands!"

"And leave you free to bolt? No way. We stay right here until you explain." His eyes went to the tiny beads of perspiration that stood out clearly on her smooth brow. "Not that I don't enjoy your company, Little Flower, but I can think of more romantic places to hold your hands. In case you haven't noticed, it's getting damn hot in here."

Lisa heartily wished that she could blame the stuffy cockpit for the warmth invading her body, but she was too honest for that kind of self-deception. However she might despise the weakness, she was acutely aware of the tall, lean man sitting so close beside her, and she knew that the prickles shooting up from her wrists were caused by something far more dangerous than physical pain. Her refusal to speak was just prolonging a repugnant situation. Suddenly it was very important to be out of the plane and as far away from him as possible. To do this she had no choice but to explain.

"All right," she agreed through clenched teeth. "Though for the record, I consider it blackmail."

At her acquiescence he sat back watchfully on the seat, relaxing his hold on her hands somewhat. His face remained impassive, and she couldn't gauge his response to her story. Reluctantly, Lisa explained her uncle's unexpected trip back to the States and how surprised she'd been to find herself aboard the Comet.

"When I saw you at the airport I was every bit as surprised and *dismayed* as you were," she finished ungraciously. "But at least I was willing to make the best of a bad situation. I never dreamed I'd see you again."

"So you planned to get your information and run, huh?" he said caustically. "Well, you made too many slips for that. Did you really think I wouldn't wonder when you took over the Comet's controls, or question why you knew so much about the fire? Not too many people pick that up in one or two casual flights up with a friend." His look was mocking. "If you're going to succeed in the spy business, little lady, you'd better learn the ground rules."

Lisa had the infuriating impression that he was toying with her, and she refused to be drawn into his game of cat and mouse. "You've had your explanation," she told him tartly. "What you choose to believe is your business." She nodded pointedly at her lap. "I've lived up to my end of the bargain. Now let go of my wrists!"

Somewhat to her surprise he released her immediately, although she was unnerved when his hands remained resting lightly on her thighs.

"I said you could let me go now," she told him in a

voice not nearly as steady as she would have liked. "You got what you wanted. Accept your victory gracefully."

Still he made no effort to move. "How do you know what I want?" he asked her softly. She looked up at molten brown eyes much too close to her own. "Maybe I haven't gotten what I want at all." One of his hands tilted her chin up while the other folded her into the crook of his arm, holding her immobile. "But I will, Little Flower," he breathed. "I promise you, *I will*."

Even as she tried to jerk her head away, his mouth found hers, crushing it with devastating authority. Her mumbled objections were lost as his tongue forced its way through her teeth and into the warm recess beyond. It found hers, teasing it. At her involuntary moan, Keith pressed her closer until the metal zipper of his flight jacket rubbed abrasively into her chest. Then it was gone, replaced by the warm, rough touch of his hand as it undid the buttons of her blouse. Brushing aside the thin fabric, he moved to possess her breast.

"I plan to do all sorts of wild and wicked things to you," he murmured into her hair. "And you're going to love it, Little Flower. That's a promise, too."

"Keith, please . . ."

"Relax, Lisa, listen to your body. There's so much pent-up passion beneath that cool, businesslike facade. I want to put the match to it. I want to see it flame to life beneath my hands."

As if to illustrate his point, Keith's hand moved to the snap of her denim pants, unfastening it to slip beneath to the warm, silky skin below. Like a feather it roamed over her soft, firm stomach, then boldly moved even lower to push under the elastic edge of her lacy bikini briefs.

Lisa writhed in exquisite agony, breathless from the fiery sensations that burned uncontrollably beneath his hand. "Keith, stop. . . ." she moaned. "I don't . . . I don't want to do this."

"Of course you do," he breathed. "Your body is begging for it. Just like mine. Relax, darling. Don't fight me."

"But I . . ."

"I haven't begun to take what I want from you, Little Flower," he murmured into her throat. "My victory is just beginning."

"No!" The word ripped between them in the small cabin. Still imprisoned within his arms, Lisa looked up at him. "You're wrong," she told him, forcing calm into her ragged voice. "Your victory is finished. You're not going to make a fool of me again . . . not twice. Let me go!"

Keith pulled back but still retained his hold on her shoulder. "Whatever you say, Little Flower. Did your uncle give you orders not to fraternize with the enemy?" His eyes flickered with humor as they raked over her face. "You know I've always wondered what it would be like to make love to a beautiful spy." His lips traced one last time over her cheek. "And I think this one might prove to be much more amenable to the idea than she'd care to admit."

He was out of the plane before she could protest, and Lisa's mouth burned from the retort which died unspoken on her lips. My God! she thought. Hadn't he heard a single word she'd said? Or was he just amusing himself at her expense? No, she amended, at Uncle Leonard's expense.

The thought was sobering, and Lisa's mind was in a whirl as she followed him out of the plane, climbing down from the passenger seat unaided. She watched in silence as he secured the Cessna in its moorings. When the craft was anchored to his satisfaction, he unlocked the passenger door of the car and motioned her inside. She sat stiffly in her seat, counting the minutes until she would be back at the hotel where she could sort this out in private. Be it ever so humble, she thought derisively, at least it was away from Keith Brannon!

They had been on the road for several minutes before Lisa realized they were not headed toward the center of town.

"Where are we going?" she demanded. "This isn't the way to my hotel."

Keith kept his eyes on the road as he answered, but Lisa was surprised to hear him speak in a pleasant, almost friendly tone. It was as if their flight had been perfectly normal, as if there'd been no scene between them afterward. For the second time that day she wondered if he had the power to turn off unpleasant feelings at will.

"Why would I take you back there?" he asked, slipping the Maserati boldly through a break in the traffic. "I promised you my time today, and that's what you're going to get."

"But I'd much prefer to go back to my room," she protested. "I've had quite enough of your precious time today."

"Well, I haven't had enough of yours. Now sit back and relax."

"How can I relax when you think I'm some kind of industrial spy? I told you the truth. Why can't you accept it?"

He stole a sidelong look at her, and Lisa detected a trace of humor in his expression. "I don't think you've tried hard enough to convince me. I'm sure you can come up with something innovative and, ah, seductively *female* to prove I'm wrong. Aren't spies supposed to be resourceful?"

The amusement in his voice at once reassured and angered Lisa. At least he didn't seriously doubt Uncle Leonard, she thought with relief. On the other hand she resented being used as a plaything with which to act out his male fantasies.

"If you don't stop playing games, Keith Brannon, you may find out just how resourceful this spy *can* be!" she clipped.

"Umm," Keith agreed. "I'd like nothing better than to be in your power, Mata Hari." He grinned salaciously. "Take me, I'm yours!"

Lisa found it hard to resist his comically ribald expression. "Very funny," she said, forcing herself to remain serious. "Now please take me back to my hotel."

"All in good time, Little Flower. There are a few items on the agenda first." She flinched when he patted her knee condescendingly. "I'm afraid you're stuck with my company for the day, so you might just as well sit back and enjoy it."

When subsequent arguments proved futile, Lisa finally threw in the towel and did as he said. But she extracted one small ounce of revenge by refusing to be drawn into any further conversation. Stoically ignoring his occasional comments, she turned her back and stared out the window, holding her face carefully impassive.

As she watched, the character of the streets gradually changed as they moved out of the city proper. Lisa was enchanted when they passed a rice field and a charming old farmhouse settled comfortably to the side of the irrigated land. Further on they came upon a small bamboo grove perched incongruously between two factories.

"Where are we going?" she asked, curiosity winning the battle over stubbornness.

"You'll see," Keith answered, and she thought that he, too, looked relieved to leave the hectic city behind. "We're almost there."

A few minutes later they pulled into a small town, which Keith informed her was Kameoka. Turning the car off the main road, he parked by a cluster of buildings that bordered a broad, free-flowing river.

"No trip to Kyoto in the spring is complete without seeing the cherry blossoms," he said, opening Lisa's door. "And since Arashiyama has one of the best displays in the area, I thought you'd like to see it. Actually it's a little late in the season, but I think the blossoms will still be pretty spectacular."

"But you said this was Kameoka!"

Keith looked almost playful again, and Lisa decided this was when she was most vulnerable to his charms. Really, she thought in confusion, it was nerve-wracking trying to keep up with these mercurial mood changes. If he wanted to keep her off balance, he certainly knew how to go about it.

"It *is* Kameoka," he told her lightly. "But from here we can go to Arashiyama."

Lisa followed his eyes to a group of flatboats tied off the bank of the river. As she stared, a group of people, obviously tourists, were taking their places in one of the rubber rafts. "You mean . . . in one of those?"

She could see that her reaction amused him. "Yes," he said. "One of the most exciting ways to reach

Arashiyama is to ride the rapids down the Hozu River. It's six miles downriver from here and takes about an hour and a half to reach by raft." The smile he turned on her was infectious, and she made no resistance as he took her arm and led her quickly toward the water. "Come on, we'd better hurry or we'll have to wait an hour for the next group."

While Keith purchased their tickets, a nearly toothless man of undeterminable age took Lisa's handbag and sweater to place them in a waterproof locker attached to the inside of the raft, then handed her a bright orange life jacket. She saw that it was standard issue for river-rafting, with the flotation material placed in the front and around the neck to ensure a face-up position in the water. Grinning broadly, the old man quickly pantomimed how it should be worn, then turned back to help several of the other passengers with theirs.

Lisa easily donned the vest, climbed carefully into the eight-man boat, then moved toward the front to take one of the two vacant seats remaining. Behind her sat a young couple and opposite them a slightly older couple who held their paddles comfortably as if they had done this sort of thing before. Ahead of them, and directly across from Lisa, were two middle-aged women speaking rapidly to each other in what sounded like German. At the very back of the boat, between the two rows of passengers, was the seat the guide would take as he directed their progress down the river.

Settling into her place, Lisa thought of the occasional river-rafting she and Uncle Leonard had enjoyed over the years in the California Sierras. Although she did not consider herself expert at the sport, she was well able to negotiate a Class III, or intermediate, rapids

comfortably. Now as her eyes followed the course of
the easy-flowing water which stretched out like a curling gray-green ribbon, she decided that the Hozu did
not look more difficult than that. In fact, since it was
navigated by so many beginners, it was probably easier.
But she was pleased to see that it had sufficient
obstacles and a strong enough current to promise a
good ride, and she found herself eager to launch.

She didn't have long to wait. As soon as Keith
donned his own vest and took the seat behind her, the
little guide walked a few steps up the bank and called
out loudly in Japanese. Immediately, a young boy of
about fifteen ran from one of the buildings to stand by
the old man's side and Lisa was relieved to see that he
would act as interpreter. Both of the boatmen bowed
low to the passengers.

"Ichiro Matsudaira welcomes you to his humble
boat," the boy said in heavily accented but understandable English. "He says you listen good and learn how to
use paddle and everyone have very good time, *hai?*"

Ichiro held up a duplicate of the paddle they had all
been issued and, swinging it back and forth rapidly in
the air, did another remarkably lucid pantomine showing how it was to be handled. Motioning to the
passengers in the boat, he spoke to them in Japanese.
"Mizu kaki! Mizu kaki!"

"Ichiro says you do like him—use paddles—good
practice," the boy translated, and all eight members of
the newly formed white-water team obediently swung
their own paddles in silent imitation of their leader.

Then the old man changed directions and started
pushing his paddle backward in the air with quick,
hurried strokes. Loudly, he called out, *"Ushiro!
Ushiro!"*

"You paddle back now," the boy told them sweeping his hands back and forth. "Ichiro says to do this when you need to turn the boat."

The old man stopped paddling and pointed a bent and bony finger at the people on Lisa's side of the boat. Then once again he started his pantomime with the paddle as he cried out, *"Migi! Migi!"*

"Must turn boat to right now," the boy explained with a grin, clearly enjoying his important part in the demonstration. "Those on right must backpaddle fast. Those on left paddle forward. Understand, *hai?* If someone fall out, Ichiro say float with feet downstream so head not hit rocks."

"Hayaku! Hayaku!" the old man interrupted, bobbing up and down like a wizened old jumping bean, and Lisa heard Keith's soft chuckle behind her as the boy hastened to translate this last piece of information.

"Ichiro say sometime you must paddle very fast." He held his thin arms out in a wide circle until his fingertips touched. "Sometime big rock or long tree in way of boat. Must paddle fast to get out of way." He looked earnestly at the passengers. *"Wakaru?"* he asked them. "Everyone understand?"

Lisa nodded her head and noticed the other passengers doing the same. But it was obvious that they did not all share her enthusiasm. The two women directly across from her had become increasingly uneasy as the demonstration progressed, and now their expressions reflected open trepidation. It was not difficult to guess that they were both having second thoughts about their Hozu River adventure. Their expressions became fixed as they watched the old man take his seat at the rear of the boat, as if bracing themselves for the ordeal ahead. Lisa had to smile as the women determinedly clutched their paddles. No one could accuse them of not being game.

"*Mizu kaki!* Paddle!" their guide instructed, and the boat nosed out into the current to face, almost immediately, its first obstacle, the trunk of a large pine tree sheared off by last winter's floods. "*Migi!* To the right," the guide yelled, and Lisa's side of the boat instantly began backpaddling with short, choppy movements until the raft slid past the tree and into the middle of the river where they were soon gliding swiftly downstream.

Lisa felt a rush of exhilaration as she pulled her paddle through the water, enjoying the sensation even more when she realized that her strokes were in perfect synchronization with Keith's. Catching her eye, he winked, and Lisa's pulse skipped a beat, as if he had reached out to touch her. Anxious to disregard this response, she put her shoulder to the paddle and stroked with increased vigor. She started when her hair stirred and his mouth moved close to her ear.

"Take it easy," he chuckled softly. "Save your energy for later, when you'll need it!"

"*Mizu kaki!*" the guide repeated before Lisa could respond.

Suddenly there was no time to respond as the raft skittered through a churning, frothy stretch of the Hozu's white water. Lisa's attention was caught by a shock of cold spray breaking over the side and onto her face.

"*Hidari!* To the left!" the old man shouted. The little crew obediently increased their strokes and the boat neatly skimmed around several large boulders thrusting out from the shore. As one, the passengers cheered as they swept past the obstacles, instantly bound together by their success. Lisa felt a hand on her shoulder and, turning, found Keith's face bending toward hers. Their lips met for only an instant, but the effect couldn't have been more powerful. And as Lisa bent back to her paddle, she knew with bitter certainty that there would never be a river, nor an airplane, as thrilling and at the same time as dangerous to her as Keith Brannon!

For almost an hour they stroked, more or less in unison, as the little guide barked instructions, sometimes in a broken jumble of English, but more often in his native tongue. Lisa realized how difficult this must be for the German women, then noticed that they were taking their cue from the couple behind them who were stroking with practiced precision. Still, their movements were awkward and unsure, and several times the guide had to yell at them sharply when they became hopelessly out of pace with the others.

Unexpectedly, a more difficult stretch of rapids sprang out of nowhere. Fresh spray broke over the bow as the raft rushed around a maze of boulders and they were all quickly soaked. The speed of the boat as they bounced over the chop was thrilling, and Lisa nearly whooped with delight. The boat danced and bobbed on the frosted water like a fallen leaf, white water thundering all around as they sculled their way around several clusters of rocks. Tumbling around another turn, she watched as the front three-foot section of the rubber boat suddenly shot up vertically, then just as abruptly, bent nearly double from the force of the rapids.

Later, Lisa wondered at how quickly it happened. Had she not turned her head for one split second to her left, it might have been too late. One minute the

German woman opposite her was thrashing wildly with her paddle, ineffectively attempting to follow the guide's orders, and the next she rose high off her seat like a feather being tossed into the wind.

"Look out!" Lisa screamed, leaning over in an attempt to grab onto the woman's lifejacket. But another arm was faster than hers, and in one swift movement a familiar brown hand yanked the woman out of the water to lie wet and gasping in the center of the raft. Keith knelt by the frightened woman's side as she caught her breath, his arm comforting and strong around her shoulders.

"It's all right," he told her softly in German, rubbing her hands reassuringly. "We're in calm water now." Gently but firmly, Keith repositioned the woman until she was back in her place opposite Lisa at the front of the boat. "Stay low in your seat," he cautioned. "And try not to flail your paddle around so much. It puts you off balance."

The woman didn't speak—Lisa thought that she looked too petrified to talk—but the look she gave Keith was lavish with gratitude. She sat huddled in her seat for the remainder of the ride, her paddle lying useless in her lap, not even attempting to follow the guide's instructions. When they finally arrived at Arashiyama, she was the first one out of the boat, quickly helped ashore by her friend. Only then, with her feet firmly planted on the ground, did she reach for Keith's hand and pump it up and down.

"Danke, danke! Veilen dank!" she cried, and Lisa repressed a smile as Keith winced from the force of her gratitude. The woman shuddered as she looked back at the little craft, which was now bobbing harmlessly up and down by the shore.

"*Noch ein mal?*" Keith asked, smiling.

The woman shook her head so sharply that Lisa felt a spray of water from her hair.

"*Nein! Nein!*" she said with feeling, and Lisa needed no translator to know that the woman's rafting days were over!

Chapter Seven

"How does it feel to be a hero?" Lisa asked him as they walked up the path from the river. "And in German, yet!"

As soon as they'd collected their belongings and returned the lifejackets, the passengers had dispersed, all but the poor German women exhilarated, despite their soaked condition, by the experience.

Keith laughed. "I'm afraid my German is pretty much the classroom variety, but it comes in handy every now and then, especially when I travel. But you're the one who really saved her," he went on, and Lisa was very conscious of the arm which rested casually on her shoulder. "If you hadn't called out when you did, I doubt if I could have reached her in time. But she would have floated, at any rate."

"I'm not so sure she would have remembered to let her feet go first, though. She looked pretty terrified."

"Then she'd have a damn good headache by now." Keith grinned. He guided her toward a group of small cafes and shops which overlooked the river. "I don't know about you," he told her, "but all that work has given me a terrific appetite. How's about some food?"

Lisa looked at her watch and was startled to see that it was almost five o'clock. She nodded eagerly. "I'm so hungry I think I could eat a horse!"

Keith laughed and moved his hand to her arm, increasing their stride toward an unpretentious little cafe next to a boat shop. "I don't promise you anything as exotic as a horse," he said as they went inside, "but as I remember from my last trip here, they put together some pretty mean *tempura.*"

The blend of aromas that greeted them when they entered the cafe nearly did Lisa in, and she realized that she hadn't exaggerated her appetite. Fortunately there were few patrons in the little restaurant, and they were served at once.

They decided to make a picnic of it, Keith making the selections from a confusing array of dishes. First, he chose something called *norimaki*, which he explained was rice, egg and vegetables rolled into a cylindrical form before being wrapped in seaweed. Then, he selected the *tempura*—fresh fish and vegetables, dipped in batter and deep-fried in oil—which looked every bit as crisp and delicious as he'd promised. Next, he ordered a large dish of *soba*—long, cold buckwheat noodles, which she knew were extremely popular in Japan. For their last dish he chose *inarizushi*, or fried bean curd, folded into a triangular jacket, and filled with rice, mushrooms, bamboo sprouts and vegetables. For dessert, Keith included some sweet *mikan*, or mandarin oranges, and some delicious-looking golden persimmons, which he said grew abundantly around the Kyoto area. Finally, he picked out a large flask of *sake*.

"Won't the *sake* get cold on a picnic?" she asked. "I

thought it had to be served at just the right temperature."

"You can thank the guide books and James Bond for that misconception," Keith told her. "The truth is that *sake* can be drunk and appreciated either warm *or* cold." He gave a low chuckle. "I doubt if the old *samurai* had either the time or the opportunity to warm their *sake* before going out to fight. And their ability to consume *sake* is legendary."

Lisa was amazed when the small, wiry woman behind the counter deftly arranged their selections in a lovely red lacquerware box. At her surprised look, Keith explained, "There's a saying that the Japanese eat with their eyes. They believe, and I've come to agree, that the appearance of a meal is just as important as its taste. Even something as simple as a picnic is taken very seriously, and it's always served with as much artistry as possible." He looked down at her and winked. "That's what makes eating out in Japan so much fun."

Before leaving the cafe, they were given a length of bamboo padding, rolled tightly and fastened with yellow ribbons, which Keith said they would return before leaving Arashiyama.

"They're very trusting," Lisa marveled, impressed by the whole affair.

"They ought to be for the amount of the deposit I left them." He laughed. "Sorry to disillusion you, Lisa, but Japan isn't *that* different from the States."

After a brief scouting expedition, they found a small, private clearing that seemed ideal for their feast: a patch of green grass nestled serenely in a grove of large pines interspersed with maples and delicately blooming cherry trees. Stretched out between the trees was the gently flowing river, its banks decorated with a multicolored blanket of wild wisteria and azalea blossoms. Looking up through a lacy frame of fragile pink flowers, Lisa could see the clear azure sky, the few fluffy puffs of white clouds providing yet another contrast in nature's kaleidoscope. She was surprised and pleased to find so few tourists until Keith pointed out that they were picnicking rather late in the day.

"The crowds usually congregate earlier in the afternoon," he told her. "By this time they'll have gone back to Kyoto or flocked to the nearest bar for cocktails. And we're a bit off the beaten path here in this clearing. But you're right, Arashiyama can be pretty crowded during the season."

"I can understand why," Lisa said. She closed her eyes and inhaled the sweet scent of the cherry blossoms, content for the moment to put aside their differences. "This must be the most beautiful season of the year."

"Well, at least *one* of them." He laughed. "You'll find some dispute there. In the summer the mountains are a mass of vivid green, and in the fall the maple trees turn color, which can be as spectacular as the blooming of the cherry trees. And of course in the winter Arashiyama is a snow-covered paradise. Take your pick."

Lisa sighed and leaned back on the bamboo. "I think I'll take *now*," she decided, then wondered which had influenced her choice more, the setting or the company.

For a very brief moment, Keith's eyes rested on hers, and Lisa found them as unfathomable as ever. Then he was busy arranging the beautifully prepared dishes in the center of the bamboo mat. When the lacquerware box was empty, he poured out a small amount of *sake* and raised his cup to her.

"*Kampai!*" he said.

Lisa looked confused. "I beg your pardon?"

"It's a very old Japanese toast," he explained, "wishing the emperor long life—ten thousand years of it, as a matter of fact. It doesn't seem to daunt anyone that no emperor has lived up to it yet. It's still the most popular toast in Japan." Then his eyes warmed as he studied her across the mat. "But I can think of a better toast," he said softly. "To you." He made a sweeping gesture with the cup. "To you and the cherry blossoms and the *nagare kawa,* the running river."

Lisa smiled and inclined her head to acknowledge the toast; then sipped at the slightly sweet rice wine. *"Domo arigato gozaimasu,"* she said. "Thank you."

She raised her eyes to find Keith staring at something on her blouse, and for a moment she thought she might have spilled some of the *sake.* Following his gaze, she discovered something far more embarrassing than a stain. Pressing against the thin fabric of her still-damp shirt were the revealing contours of her breasts, the nipples beneath the sheer brassiere sharply outlined against the clinging material. Mortified, she reached for her sweater, throwing it around her shoulders and quickly fastening the top buttons.

"I was just going to mention that you must be cold," Keith said quietly, his eyes not missing the heightened color on her face. "I didn't mean to embarrass you."

"Well, I wish you'd said something sooner!" Lisa's flush intensified at the thought of how she must have looked in the cafe.

Sensing her agitation, he said, "If you're worried about the people in the restaurant, don't. Attitudes about nudity in Japan are much different than they are in the States, and so far they've been noticeably untouched by Puritan influences. To them the body is seen but not looked at." His smile betrayed that *he* had not been so unobservant. "You have a very lovely body, Little Flower," he added, his voice warming her far more effectively than the sweater. Keith's thick-lashed eyes darkened as he added, "You should never be ashamed to show it."

Lisa bent her head again to the *sake* as her body, with a will of its own, tingled in all the wrong places. She was furious that she had not been able to hide her reaction to his words, his knowing look—damn it—his presence! Now that she knew his motives it was doubly important that she not be taken in by a charming smile and empty flattery. Stubbornly, she brought her gaze level with his, matching him stare for stare, refusing to let him win this round. It was one thing to feel her emotions slipping out of control; it was quite another to let him revel in his victory. After several long minutes he turned away, and Lisa felt an exhilarating sense of satisfaction. Maybe she *could* get through the rest of the day without losing what little remained of her pride.

As they ate Lisa gradually relaxed, the exquisite setting combining with the delicious food and *sake* to ease away the tension.

"Obviously you've gone river-rafting before," he said when they were finished eating. He reached across the bamboo pad and refilled her *sake* cup, then sat back, his expression frankly curious. "I never know what to expect from you next."

Lisa swirled the amber liquid in her cup as she said, "There's no great mystery. My uncle and I raft up in the Sierras whenever we can. We're not all that good at it, actually, but it's a sport we really enjoy."

"What about the rest of your family?" he asked. "Do you have anyone besides your uncle?"

"No. My parents were killed in a plane crash when I was ten."

Keith's dark eyes reflected interest and sympathy, but, thankfully, not pity. "I'm sorry," he said simply, but Lisa knew instantly that the sentiment was sincere. "And so your uncle raised you," he prompted.

She nodded, remembering the time since her parents' death, the years that Uncle Leonard had lightened with his love and care, his seemingly endless patience in smoothing a lonely little girl's turbulent path to womanhood. She sighed. "I know it sounds trite, but he really was both mother and father to me. We're very close."

"And he taught you to fly." Keith's lazy gaze swept her face. "I gather he's your mysterious friend of tailpipe gauge and fire-light fame." It was an assessment, not a question.

"After my parents' death I was petrified of planes. I was quite prepared to live my entire life on good old terra firma." She smiled. "Poor Uncle Leonard. It took him months of cajoling and downright bribery before I finally worked up the courage to take that first flight with him."

"And . . . ?"

"That was all it took." She grinned impishly. "It was love at first flight, you might say."

Keith grimaced at the pun, then joined in her laughter. "And from there you went on to get your pilot's license."

Lisa nodded. "When I was sixteen. After that I couldn't wait until Uncle Leonard let me check out in one of his business jets." She looked wistful. "You know I'd forgotten until yesterday how good it feels to handle a plane like the Comet." Her voice dropped to a strained whisper. "Or perhaps I just didn't want to remember."

His eyes probed hers. "Jeff?"

Lisa was taken aback. "I didn't say that."

"No, but it wasn't too hard to deduce."

Lisa remembered her involuntary slip in the car the night before. "So you've known that all along, too."

Keith's smile was gentle. "There aren't too many people in the aviation business who don't know about your marriage, Lisa."

"But I feel like such a fool. Why didn't you say something?"

"When you mentioned his name last night in the car I was too upset to put two and two together. It wasn't until after I got home that I realized which Jeff you were talking about." He peered at her drawn face in the dimming light. "From the way you said his name I gather it wasn't a very happy marriage."

Lisa stared at the grove of trees that framed him from behind, but her eyes hardly noticed how the delicate pink blossoms were reflecting the bolder reds and oranges of the setting sun. She was only vaguely aware of Keith pouring *sake* into her cup and placing it in her hand.

"Here," he said simply.

She raised the tiny cup to her lips and sipped the sweet wine gratefully. When it was half gone she set it back down on the mat.

"Sometimes it helps to talk about it," he told her softly.

"I suppose," she admitted. "But I've gone so long . . . I've never even told Uncle Leonard."

Keith said nothing. He sprawled comfortably across from her on the mat, his long legs stretched out to one side, waiting, not coaxing, merely available. Lisa knew he wouldn't press her to speak and the knowledge was reassuring. Perhaps because of that, because he was willing to let her take the initiative, the feelings that she had held inside so long suddenly took substance in words.

"You're right, it wasn't a successful marriage," she started. "Actually, I'm not sure why Jeff married me in the first place. Certainly he had plenty of other women to choose from, both before and after our marriage." Her mouth hardened. "I should have known he'd never change his habits because of a piece of paper, but somehow I didn't see the danger signals until it was too late . . . *much* too late."

Haltingly, Lisa went on to relate her life with Jeff Howard. Her voice was so soft and toneless that Keith had to lean forward to catch the words as they floated away on the gentle evening breeze. It was only when she started to talk about the last few months that she faltered.

"There's more, isn't there?" he prompted.

Lisa nodded mutely and Keith seemed to sense her pain. Nimbly, he backtracked a bit in her narrative, giving her time to regain her composure.

"A few minutes ago you mentioned that you hadn't flown in nearly two years," he said. "Yet you're obviously a very competent pilot. Why did you quit?"

"I didn't exactly quit," she explained. "It was more like a tactical retreat." At his puzzled expression she went on. "Jeff had an enormous ego—perhaps justifiably so. At the time he was probably the best test pilot in the business, so maybe he had a right to strut a bit. Anyway, after a series of newspaper articles playing up his wife's flying ability, our family was suddenly too small to hold two pilots. Every time I went up we argued. When the fights got to be too much, it was simply easier for me to stay on the ground."

Keith's mouth was pinched, and Lisa knew he understood what this must have cost her. "So you let him win," he said tightly.

Lisa sighed. "I wanted my marriage to win. I was willing to do anything to keep it intact."

"Anything?" he repeated. "Including giving up a vital part of your life?"

"At that time my marriage seemed more vital. I kept deluding myself that we had a chance." She laughed shortly and her smooth brow furrowed in self-disgust. "When they said love is blind they must have had me in mind. It wasn't until the last few months of our marriage that I discovered that Jeff had never stopped seeing other women, my own friends included. Everyone knew about it but me."

Keith frowned but kept silent, waiting for her to finish on her own.

"I should have left him then—some part of me must have known it was hopeless. But I didn't. Maybe it was my pride that kept me there, I don't know. Perhaps I just couldn't admit defeat." Lisa shivered and pulled her sweater more tightly around her shoulders. "Whatever my motives, I soon found a much more important reason to stay. Our marriage had been good for something after all. I was going to have a baby." Her eyes misted, but she went on, groping for the right words. "Jeff was less than thrilled to find out he was going to be a father. And, of course, I got all the blame for being so careless. I even managed to look at *that* through rose-colored glasses, telling myself that he'd come around in time. He'd have to love his own baby."

Keith's eyes were unfathomable in the fading light. "What happened then, Lisa?" he urged. "Get it all out."

"It's . . . it's ironic in a way. That last day, the day Jeff was killed, I'd been so happy. I'd spent the afternoon shopping, buying little things for the baby, a few maternity clothes for me. That night Jeff came home late, and very drunk. He told me he was leaving me . . . for one of my best friends." Her face was white. "After all the signs, after all the warnings, I still couldn't believe what he was saying." She stared at Keith with glazed eyes, and he knew she was reliving the scene. "He called me a stupid little fool. He said he'd be well rid of me." She shook her head. "I guess I got hysterical then . . . it's hard to remember. I know I started screaming that he couldn't leave me, that I was his wife, that I was going to have his baby. But he wouldn't listen, he just kept going up the stairs."

Lisa stopped and took a quick gulp of air. "When I reached the bedroom he was packing. He was throwing clothes in his suitcase any which way. It's funny, I can still remember the sleeve of his favorite shirt hanging out the side of the bag. When I told him about it he swore and said it was just like me to care more about an old shirt than about him. He threw a few more things in and banged down the lid. I . . . I caught up with him at the top of the stairs." Lisa's voice was hoarse. "Afterward, I wished I hadn't."

The orange glow was gone from the sky, leaving the river tinged with faint gold. Lisa picked up her *sake* and drank down what remained in one gulp. She grimaced and returned the cup to the mat. Keith was still leaning back, his legs outstretched beside her. But he was no longer relaxed.

"Go on, Lisa," he said evenly.

Lisa spread her hands in a gesture of helplessness. "He pushed me. I . . . I don't think he meant to," she added softly. "He was much too drunk to know what he was doing. Jeff was like that when he drank—violent, I mean."

"And he just left you there?"

Lisa nodded; the pain had blessedly been blurred by the unconsciousness that had claimed her before she had reached the bottom of the stairs. She'd been taken to the hospital, suffering several cracked ribs and a concussion. The doctor told her that she was lucky to be alive. For a long time Lisa wasn't so sure. That morning, during treatment, she had lost her baby.

Keith stared at her, his drawn face shadowed in the fading light. "And that night he was killed?"

"His car hit a tree. According to witnesses, he was driving erratically, and much too fast. Judging from where the accident happened, he must have been on his way to get *her,* my . . . my friend, I mean."

"And you never told anyone the whole story? Not even your uncle?"

"No." Hot tears spilled over her lashes to rest on the graceful curve of her cheek. "It was all so humiliating. After everything that had happened between us I still . . . I still wanted the baby so much. . . ." She buried her face in her hands, appalled by her lack of control, wishing desperately that she had never opened the Pandora's box of her past.

She was aware that he had shifted on the mat, and strong arms reached out to cradle her trembling shoulders, pulling her into the warm, safe shelter of his embrace. "It's okay, honey," he told her gently. "Let it all come out. You shouldn't have held it in all this time. It's all right now."

His lips brushed her cheek, then caressed her hair as she sobbed unrestrainedly into his shoulder. Gradually the tears subsided, leaving in their wake a kind of peace she had not felt in years. It seemed so right having him hold her like this. She sighed contentedly and nestled closer into the protective arms. The crisp patch of hair that peeked out over the open V-neck of his shirt tickled her cheek, heightening her awareness of him. When his mouth made its way across her face she didn't turn away, allowing his lips to touch hers with tenderness. His kiss was warm and gentle, comforting rather than passionate, meant to console not arouse.

At what point it crossed over this line neither of them knew, but suddenly the sensations he was kindling in her were no longer innocent. Her awareness of him was overpowering, and she felt a sudden need to have more than he was giving. Her hands stole around his shoulders to probe and massage the corded muscles of his neck. Beneath his kiss her lips parted. Keith gave a little groan but held himself in check for a long moment before accepting her invitation. Then, as if losing the battle with himself, he pulled her more tightly into his arms, allowing his tongue to explore her mouth with such urgency that she was left breathless.

Suddenly, the sweater which was still draped across her shoulders was an obstacle preventing her from feeling as much of him as she craved. She reached up to undo the top button, but his hands were there first.

"You're right, you don't need this anymore," he murmured, dropping the unnecessary sweater to the mat. His eyes swept over her thin cheesecloth shirt, resting for a moment on the full, rounded swell of breasts beneath. "Your shirt's dry again," he said, smiling at her through the dusk. "But I think I liked it better when it was wet."

His look was hungry, and Lisa knew that she had deliberately fed the fire that burned now behind the dark eyes. The knowledge of her power was at once heady and frightening. When his hand reached out to cup her chin, she raised her face boldly to his, awaiting the confrontation that she no longer sought to avoid.

"What kind of a spell have you cast over me, Lisa Howard?" he asked. His eyes searched hers in the fading light. "I can't seem to get enough of you. I want to be as close to you as two human beings can get."

Then his mouth was feathering its way across her cheek to a point below her ear where it lingered for a moment, his tongue sending erotic messages to the rest of her body.

"I want to explore you. I want to know every inch of that marvelous body, Little Flower," he murmured.

Slowly the caress moved to the hollow of her neck, then lower to the opening of her shirt. Deft fingers quickly undid the buttons to allow access to the deep, warm cleavage below.

With the slightest of movements he lowered her to the bamboo, her lamb's wool sweater softly cushioning her head as she lay beneath him on the mat. There was no mistaking the raw passion in his eyes as he bent his head to continue the torturously sweet exploration of her body.

Lisa heard Keith moan softly as his mouth discovered the outline of a nipple pressed taut against the fragile lace of her brassiere. Instantly it was the warm captive of his mouth, and he gently probed and teased until it strained to pulsating life beneath the sheer material. Then his lips moved to the other nipple, lightly coaxing, tenderly massaging, until it, too, thrust achingly against the moist, thin restraint.

Suddenly frustrated by the lacy barrier, his fingers moved quickly to release the front-hooking clasp of her wispy bra. "You don't need this," he said, slowly separating the two flimsy pieces of lace.

She heard his sharp intake of breath as his eyes feasted on her nakedness. "My god, Lisa, you're beautiful," he groaned in wonder. His head bent as he brushed aside a last lingering scrap of shirt with his teeth. With a long sigh, his lips settled in the hollow between her breasts, where he left a trail of warm, fiery kisses.

"Oh, Keith," she moaned, "that feels so good."

No longer able to remain still under his practiced assault, Lisa writhed as shivers of pleasure shot through her veins. Moving closer into his arms, she held him so tightly that it seemed their bodies had fused together on the mat. Her hands moved to unbutton his shirt, brushing aside the flannel material to explore the hard, firm muscles of his broad chest. Her fingers moved down, tingling as they roamed feather-light over the soft, curly brown hair above his navel.

"God, Lisa, you're driving me crazy," Keith gasped and his arms tightened as he pulled her roughly into his bare chest.

"What do you think you're doing to me?" she whispered. "I shouldn't let you touch me like this. . . ."

His lips successfully silenced her objections. "I should and I must," he murmured huskily. His teeth nibbled delicately at her neck, then moved down to her bare shoulder. "Have I told you that you taste delicious?"

"I . . . I think so."

"Good. Then I'm telling you again."

When his lips were no longer satisfied with her shoulder they moved back to her mouth. "God, I want you," he breathed, and before she could answer, could tell him of her own, urgent longing, his lips crushed hers. This time their mouths came together with one insatiable craving, their eager tongues probing, penetrating, uniting. The soft, curly hairs of his chest tickled her bare breasts, and the sensation nearly drove her to distraction. She was in another world, a place where no one else existed except them. Nothing else mattered but this man.

His hands moved beneath her to find the line of her spine. Slowly, and with maddening care, they brushed up and down the full length of the column, sending thousands of erotic messages flying through the rest of her body. She felt the pressure of his fingers against her hips, and she trembled when he arched her back and pulled her tightly to his hard male need.

His voice was raspy with desire as he said against her lips, "I've wanted you from the first moment I saw you, Little Flower. I've wanted to touch you here . . . and here . . . and. . . ." He paused in his ardent voyage of discovery as her body was wracked by a long, lingering shudder. "And even here," he groaned. His hands moved beneath the waistband of her denim jeans to find the fragile underpants. She moaned softly as the fingers probed and explored, touching, stroking until she was nearly feverish with desire. Her hips rocked against him, arching in a desperate, aching quest for fulfillment.

The break came so suddenly that Lisa was left shaken and confused. In one jarring motion Keith's mouth was torn away from hers, and he had yanked them both to a sitting position.

"Shh!" he ordered as she started to speak, and through her shock Lisa noticed that his voice was raspy and still thick with desire. "Someone's coming."

Her pulse beating madly, Lisa fumbled with the clasp on her brassiere, then quickly buttoned her blouse. Behind her back she heard the sound of voices, but by the time the group reached the little clearing she and Keith were separated by a respectable distance.

"I should have known better," he said shortly after

the intruders had wandered further up river. "Arashi-yama in the spring is hardly private, even at this time of the evening."

Lisa stood and, with fingers still awkward, tucked the thin shirt back into her slacks. Moonlight bathed the river in a soft white glow and the fragile cherry blossoms rustled above them in the gentle evening breeze. "It's late," she told him, uncomfortably aware that her breath was still coming in short little gasps. She turned and picked up her sweater. "We should be starting back."

Keith pressed the little button that illuminated his digital watch. "You're right," he said, "it's after eight." "We were so, ah, preoccupied," he grinned, "that I lost track of the time. Don't worry, I'll call a taxi. Fortunately what takes almost two hours by raft is only minutes by car."

After returning the mat to the little restaurant, Keith stopped at a sidewalk phone booth, and in rapid Japanese summoned a cab. While he talked, Lisa sat down on a bench overlooking the river, suddenly exhausted by the day's activities and lack of sleep the night before. Stretching out tired legs, she slipped off her shoes and blissfully wiggled her toes, enjoying the sweet scent of cherry blossoms. Despite the rude interruption in the cherry orchard, Lisa still retained a warm glow from their lovemaking. Keith moved her like no other man she had ever known, including her own husband. Despite her reservations about seeing him again she had enjoyed the day enormously. *And especially the little scene just now?* she asked herself candidly. *Be honest, Lisa Howard, wasn't that the highlight of the day?*

Lisa shivered in the cool evening breeze. Even if she wanted to deny his power over her, her own body would have made the lie impossible; every square inch still quivered from his assault. The sensitive tips of her breasts tingled where his teeth and tongue had teased, and her mouth burned from the fiery intensity of his kiss. Her fingers remembered the hard muscles that had rippled beneath their touch, and his fresh, masculine scent still filled her nostrils. Once again she shivered, but this time she knew it had nothing to do with the wind.

Lisa pulled her sweater tightly around her shoulders. She had to make a decision. She had to make up her mind what she wanted from this relationship and, more important, what she was prepared to give in return. Would she live for the moment, wonderful as that moment might be, or would she be guided by the hard-learned lessons of the past? At the rate things were going she couldn't trust herself to keep matters on a platonic basis. Certainly Keith was open enough about what *he* had in mind. And what about her? Hadn't the last two days proved that her desire for him was every bit as explosive as his?

Lisa leaned her head back against the bench and sighed, a regretful sound that was immediately lost in the murmuring of the river. Inevitably, it came back to that. What was it to be—emotion or reason?—ecstasy or common sense?—Keith Brannon or emptiness?

Chapter Eight

The loud jangle of the phone pierced through Lisa's sleep, jarring her to a reluctant state of awareness. She groped for the receiver, one eye focusing on the clock to see that it was barely eight o'clock.

"Hello?" she mumbled.

"Morning, sleepy head," came the much too chipper voice on the other end of the line. "You sound like you're still in bed. I purposely brought you home with the birds last night so you could get going early this morning. Don't tell me my sacrifice was wasted."

His voice revived her like a splash of cold water. "Keith Brannon! I might have known it was you. You must get a perverse sort of pleasure from waking me up in the morning."

There was a low chuckle on the other end of the line. "It saves you the cost of an alarm clock, doesn't it? Although I should warn you, I do my best work in person." His voice became seductive. "If I were with you right now, I'd show you a *really* nice way to wake up in the morning."

Even over the phone his words stirred her, and she

had to clear her throat before answering. "Then it's a good thing you aren't here, isn't it or I'd never get an early start."

"Oh, I don't know about that." He chuckled softly. "We'd get an early start, all right, but it might not be the kind you had in mind." At her sharp intake of breath he hurried on, "Don't worry, Little Flower, unfortunately you're safe. I'm stuck here in the office all day. Which is why I called. You said you wanted to see the Kabuki troop tonight, so I thought I'd pick you up about six. The performance at the Minami-za actually starts in the morning and goes until late in the evening, but it's considered quite proper to drop in just for the evening portion of the program. I'm afraid we'll have to grab a bite to eat afterward, though."

"The Minami-za?" Her pulse was racing. She couldn't keep walking this emotional treadmill. Last night she had been too tired to come to a rational decision. Now, much too soon, he was forcing her hand. "But I was planning to see the Kabuki troop alone to . . ."

"Which is exactly what you *shouldn't* do," he broke in. "Unless your Japanese has improved miraculously since yesterday, you'll enjoy the performance a lot more with an interpreter along."

Her heart leapt at the opportunity to see him again, a clear reminder of how dangerous it could be. Still, he had a valid point. "Maybe . . ." she said hesitantly.

"Maybe nothing. How can you send home an intelligent report about the troop when you can't understand a word they're saying?"

"I'm sure Mr. Yakamoto will be happy to explain anything I don't understand."

Keith laughed. "If you think he has nothing better to do than translate for you, honey, you've got delusions of grandeur. Yakamoto will be far too busy behind the scenes to worry about how you're faring." His low voice was coaxing. "You're in for a rare treat tonight, Lisa. I want to share it with you."

She sensed his determination to win the argument even as she recognized her own willingness to let him. Even so, some small part of her—a more sensible side, she thought ruefully—held back.

"Thank you for offering, Keith, but . . ."

"Come on, Lisa. You'll have a great time. I promise." Lisa could hear muffled voices from the other end of the line as if Keith had pressed his palm over the receiver. After a few moments he was back on the line. "Sorry, honey. Like I say, it's a madhouse around here. Listen, I'll pick you up at six. Okay?" Without waiting for her to answer he rang off with a cheery, "See you then."

Lisa hung up the receiver, then sighed and pushed back the covers, lowering her long legs to the carpet to pad barefoot into the bathroom. She splashed cold water on her face, then shook her head ruefully at the tousled image that stared back at her from the mirror.

Just what did she expect from Keith Brannon tonight? Lisa asked the sleepy face. She paused as she considered this. Perhaps it was more to the point to ask what she expected from herself.

Lisa frowned and pulled out her toothbrush. In the end that was the most difficult question of all to answer, wasn't it? she asked the image. What *did* Lisa Howard want?

It was well past noon when Lisa left the crowded Kyoto Handicraft Center, her work binder bulging with notes. After enjoying a light lunch, she headed south for her next destination, the Kyoto National Museum. Normally she would have saved time by taking a cab, but the temptation to see as much of Kyoto as possible during her stay was too strong to resist. Hearing the faint lapping of water, Lisa sidetracked somewhat to follow the path of the Kamo River, a decision almost immediately rewarded by a scene which could have come right from antiquity.

Before her, a bridge protected by a parapet of timeworn pine-trunks spanned the river. There, to the obvious delight of the tourists who had collected on either side of the banks, a handful of dyers were steeping their gorgeous *yuzen* cloth in the clear running water. Lisa knew that the dying process used to make the decorated cloth was well over 300 years old, and that before completion of the process, the cloth was always washed in the Kamo River to preserve its remarkable color. She stopped for a moment as the women nimbly swished the multicolored silk around in the cool water, awed by this brief glimpse into the past. Again, as in the Katsura Villa, she had the feeling that she was suspended in time, a time when appreciation of and dedication to beauty were still of paramount importance. The scene filled her with a profound sense of peace as if, for a brief moment, she had become part of that world, and she marveled at a country that could provide such a harmonious blending of old and new. Where else in this troubled twentieth century could you find such supreme elegance in the guise of perfect simplicity? she wondered.

Then, as she watched the women lay long strips of cloth out to dry on the grassy banks, she suddenly wished Keith were here to enjoy the spectacle with her. Without him by her side the experience was somehow incomplete. She tried to tell herself that it was his little anecdotes she missed, the charming stories he told that seemed to bring Japanese history to life. But she knew that it was more than that.

The vague sense of unease stayed with Lisa as she roamed through Kyoto's National Museum. Finally, aware that she was giving the fine collection of art objects and ancient handcrafted treasures little more than cursory attention, she decided to call it a day.

Walking slowly back to the hotel, Lisa once again sidetracked, this time to wander through Kyoto's beautiful Maruyama Park. No sooner had she entered the charming nature area, however, than she knew the detour had been a mistake. The park's famous grove of cherry trees were a poignant reminder of the time she'd spent yesterday on the banks of the Hozu River. It seemed no matter where she went in this lovely old city, she was reminded of Keith. Why couldn't she get him out of her mind?

Lisa passed several restaurants and teahouses to find a quiet bench in a corner of the cherry orchard where she could sort things out in peace. Slipping out of her shoes, she wiggled her tired toes in the cool, lush grass, noticing as she did, a pair of lovers huddled on the lawn not far from her seat. Something deep inside Lisa ached when their heads came together in a long, intimate kiss, and the answer was suddenly clear. With a flash of insight she understood the feelings that had needled her all afternoon. For the first time in months she was lonely!

She missed Keith. It was as simple as that. Even as she realized this truth she couldn't help asking herself why. Her feelings toward him were conflicted to say the least. Even worse, they refused to stand still, but were forever shifting around. One minute she hated him, the next she was breathless from his touch. He was rude, condescending, brusque and outspoken. He was also sweet, understanding, patient, intelligent and downright fun to be with. And now, heaven help her, she missed him!

Lisa leaned back on the bench trying to make some sense of it all. Until her marriage to Jeff she had spent little time analyzing either her motives or her needs. Compared with the past few years, those early days with Uncle Leonard had been unbelievably simple. Since Leonard Mason tended to spoil his only niece, most of Lisa's needs had been met almost before she knew they existed. Of course that kind of indulgence carried its own price, and Lisa inevitably lived to regret her lack of independence. That was why the past two years had been so important to her. During that time she had learned to think for herself, to make her own decisions. She no longer depended upon someone else to rescue her from uncomfortable or awkward situations. She was finally self-sufficient.

So why was she having so damn much trouble extricating herself from this one? she wondered. For all her careful planning, why hadn't she foreseen the very real possibility of another love interest in her life? After all, she was still young; surely it was perfectly normal to expect that she might be attracted to a man again.

But not a man like Keith Brannon. That had never been part of the plan. Never in her wildest dreams had she expected to be attracted to a man so much like her late husband. The fact that Keith had shown that he could be warm and caring only added to Lisa's confusion. Especially when she remembered that she had felt the same trust and security with Jeff, too, when he was trying to maneuver her into his bed!

Lisa's head ached from trying to make sense of the situation. If she truly felt that sex was all that Keith was after, she had no business seeing him tonight. She ought to call him right now and cancel their date. But it was the other side of Keith, the gentle, understanding, charming side of him, that kept her from making the final break. For all her rationalizing, the simple fact remained that she wanted to see him again. Against all that was logical, she knew that she didn't want the relationship to end.

Lisa sighed and rose from the bench, aware that once again she had solved nothing. Well, at least this time she would be walking into the lion's den with her eyes open. "Discretion is the better part of valor," she quoted grimly as she started the short trek back to the hotel. And this evening Lisa intended to be very, very discreet indeed!

The Minami-za was large, capable of seating about 1500 patrons, and tonight the house was nearly full. The interior of the theater was dominated by the disproportionately wide, shallow stage, and by the *hanamichi,* a raised walkway from the rear of the theater through the audience to the stage. Although the Kabuki performance was continuous from mid-morning until late in the evening, there were periodic intermissions during the day when the audience was allowed to stretch or get food from the numerous vendors in the lobby. As they sat in their seats waiting for the next performance to begin, Keith added to Lisa's knowledge of Kabuki history.

"I'm sure you already know that Kabuki goes back to

the sixteenth century," he said. "But what a lot of people don't realize is that this all-male theater was originated by a woman."

"I'd heard that, of course," Lisa said, "but I still find it hard to believe. Kabuki today is so . . . so masculine."

"Anyway, back to my story. The lady's name was Okuni, and she was, by all reports, a very lovely dancing girl at the Shinto shrine at Izumo during the late sixteenth and early seventeenth centuries. Evidently, Okuni was not only beautiful but also a very clever opportunist. About the only stage performances available during that war-torn period were the austere Noh plays, and those were mainly reserved for the nobility. It didn't take Okuni long to recognize the general public's need for something more flamboyant, and so she started to perform some of her sacred dances publicly. She wore bright, colorful robes and used little bells and a chorus as accompaniment. With only this and Noh to choose from, the public went wild over her show; she was an overnight sensation. Naturally, it wasn't long before other young women got into the act."

"Yet today Kabuki uses no women at all," Lisa interjected.

Keith grinned. "Unfortunately, an ugly rumor soon circulated that the girls were giving private performances to special patrons after the theater was closed. Although no one suggested banning the parties, they did bar women from appearing on the stage. Ergo, the *onnagata,* which are the men who play all the female roles. The *onnagata* has become one of the most important elements of Kabuki. Actors spend their entire lives perfecting the art."

"It seems to me it would be a lot simpler if women were just allowed back on the stage," Lisa reasoned.

Keith nodded. "You're not the first one to come up with that idea. But so far no one has taken it seriously enough to change the rules." He smiled at her ruefully. "Besides, the most famous *onnagata* would argue that a woman is too secure in her own femininity to do justice to a female role." He laughed outright at her expression. "Take it easy, Little Flower, I didn't say I subscribed to the theory. Remember, it's a mistake to judge the Japanese by Western standards. Kabuki audiences never forget that they're in a theater to watch actors act. They half believe that the *onnagata* on the stage is a woman and half disbelieve it. That way they can enjoy the play *and* the skill of the man behind the costume."

Lisa looked unconvinced. "I suppose, but I still can't understand why—"

She was cut off by the staccato beating of wooden clappers which accompanied the opening of the next play. The curtain, brilliant in the Kabuki colors of black, russet and green vertical stripes, parted to reveal a set which nearly took away Lisa's breath. Before them, a full *nagauta* orchestra was seated at the rear of the stage. Even though she had been given a program with an English translation of the play, she was grateful for Keith's help in identifying the actors. From what he told her, Lisa recognized the huge figure in *suo* costume striding forward on the stage as one of the secondary characters in the plot. But to Lisa he was formidable in his boldly patterned blue and white costume and high black hat, and for several minutes he strutted imposingly across the stage as he delivered his monologue. When he was finished, there was a great fanfare from the orchestra, and Yoshitsune, one of the main characters, appeared on the *hanamichi* posing dramatically while his three followers and the other main character, Benkei, also appeared on the walkway. Lisa watched in fascination as the actors boldly emoted, using exaggerated facial expressions and extravagant posturing, the volume of their voices filling the theater.

The play, *Kanjincho,* which, Keith explained, was considered one of the masterpieces of the Kabuki theater, continued for more than an hour, then was followed almost immediately by another. At the start of the new play, Lisa was surprised to see the stage revolve smoothly to reveal an entirely different set. The process, Keith explained, was called *aka-ten.*

"In the past they used to rotate the revolving stage by hand," he explained. "Today, like everything else, it's mechanized. Not quite as Kabuki-like," he smiled, "but a good deal smoother."

After the third straight Kabuki drama Lisa found herself yawning. Although she attempted to hide her restlessness from Keith, he soon sensed it.

"This will go on for at least another two hours," he said, gathering their coats. "It's considered quite acceptable to leave before it's over. And I'm starved."

Lisa didn't argue as he led her up the aisle. She had enjoyed the Kabuki dramas enormously, but three straight hours of the noisy, highly stylized and largely incomprehensible plays were enough for one night.

They dined at a quaint restaurant tucked into a wooded hillside overlooking Arashiyama. Afterward, when Lisa expressed a desire to see Kyoto by night, he took her to the glittering entertainment area located between Kawaramachi and Kiyamachi streets. The area was crowded with bars and eating places, most of

them garishly decorated in plastic, glass, chrome and
neon. Crammed in with these were temples, shrines,
craft shops, clothing stores and other more sedate
businesses. Some of the smaller alleys and side streets
were more softly lit by paper lanterns, but it was the
main street that caught her attention, and she was
partly delighted and partly disappointed by the gaudi-
ness.

They entered one of the larger clubs and were shown
to a small table in the corner of the crowded room.
After they'd been served drinks, Lisa looked around
with interest, noticing several young, attractive women
approaching unattached male customers at the bar.

"Those must be the famous Japanese hostesses I've
heard so much about. Are they really as expensive as
I've been told?"

Keith nodded. "There's usually a flat hostess charge
based on an hour's company. Of course in addition to
this you're expected to buy her a drink or two and some
snacks. And at the end of the evening she'll expect
yet another tip. By the time the poor tourist goes
back to his hotel he may be poorer by quite a lot of
yen."

Lisa was revolted. "But surely you don't *have* to have
a hostess."

"You do if you want to stay in most of the bars. Some
of the bigger clubs have areas now where you can sit
and drink without having to pay for a hostess. But for
the most part the women come as part of the package."

"And afterward?" Lisa asked almost shyly. "Is it
true that they . . . ah . . . "

"Provide a more *private* sort of entertainment?"
Keith finished for her. He grinned. "Let's put it this
way, Little Flower, no single man in Japan has to go

without female companionship as long as he has enough money and a generous heart."

"Oh," Lisa said quietly. With a little chuckle Keith came to her rescue by changing the subject.

"What happens now?" he asked, taking a sip of his drink. "You've seen Yakamoto and the Kabuki troop's performance. Does that mean the exchange is all set?"

She shook her head. "No. We'll have to meet several more times to complete the arrangements." She smiled, more relaxed now that the conversation revolved around her work. "Before I left Evergreen my boss warned me that it's poor form to rush business affairs in Japan. So I'm taking things slowly."

Keith looked pleased. "Your boss is right. It's refreshing to meet someone who's willing to play the game by the rules, *Japanese* rules, that is. Too many Americans come to Japan and sit down at the negotiating table as if they were still in New York. Their behavior only makes the 'Ugly American' look even more repulsive."

His praise filled Lisa with a warm flush of pleasure. "That's the last thing we want to happen. We hope this will be the first of many successful exchanges with Kyoto. I'm meeting with Mr. Yakamoto again tomorrow to discuss the performance. I hope that we can wrap things up by the middle of the week."

"And then you'll fly back to Tokyo?"

Lisa's heart sank at the prospect. "Yes, to meet my uncle." The words clearly brought home the fleeting, hopeless nature of their relationship. She tried to sound casual. "By then Uncle Leonard's business should be finished, and we'll fly back to the States."

Keith's eyes twinkled at her in the candlelight. "And if he doesn't get the Fugi contract?"

Lisa lifted her chin, automatically ready to defend her uncle. "Then he'll go on to something else," she replied evenly. "But there's a very real possibility he *will* get the contract. After all he manages one of the top aeronautics corporations in the States." She studied him from across the table. "I could easily turn the question around. If he gets the contract, what will *you* do?"

She looked so serious that Keith laughed. "I think one of the first things I'll do is hire someone to defend me with the same kind of loyalty you feel for Leonard Mason. Are you always so touchy about your uncle?"

"I'm not touchy at all," she said defensively. "It's just that business is business and . . ."

"And you never mix business with pleasure."

"Keith, we're talking about a multimillion dollar contract. That's no laughing matter."

Keith's face grew mockingly serious. "Of course it's not," he agreed soberly, his brown eyes twinkling nonetheless. "Therefore I propose that we dispense with business and get right on with the pleasure." His hand closed over her fingers. "You're very beautiful tonight, Little Flower," he said softly. "And this place is much too public for the things I'd like to do to you right now."

The gleam in his eyes caused Lisa's pulse to race. "That effectively dispenses with business, all right," she said nervously, trying to keep her voice light. "Although I think I felt safer when the subject was aircraft."

"Ah, but sometimes it's much more interesting *not* to play safe. Why don't we leave now so I can show you what I mean?"

"But we just got here," she protested.

"And you've satisfied your curiosity to see Kyoto by night." His smile was inviting. "Now let me show you a much more quiet, intimate little place I know."

"Which wouldn't just happen to be your apartment?"

He shook his head sadly. "I was hoping you wouldn't figure that out until we got there."

Lisa stared at him, not knowing whether to laugh or be angry at the hangdog look on his face. "Keith, I can't go to your apartment."

"Why not?" he asked innocently. "I went to yours."

"You were uninvited, remember?"

"Ummm," he agreed lazily. "So invite me this time. I'm easy to get along with. I'll take your place *or* mine."

Lisa's body was filled with sexual tension, and under the circumstances the small table that separated them seemed hardly adequate. "Keith, be serious."

His eyes lowered to the tempting cleavage revealed in the low neck of her clingy chiffon dress. "Oh, but I'm very serious, Little Flower," he said softly. "I can't remember when I've been more serious." His eyes captured hers, and his voice was husky. "Come on, Lisa. You know you want this as much as I do."

Lisa's voice caught in her throat. "I . . . that is . . ." My god! What *did* she want to say? "Keith, I really need to powder my nose," she finished lamely. "Excuse me."

Lisa hurried from the table to seek refuge in the ladies' room. Since mirror space was limited, she stood stiffly to one side as a stream of Japanese women jostled her on their way in and out of the room.

This was most certainly *not* going as she had planned. How could she play it safe, keep their relationship on a casual basis, when he looked at her like that? Under that kind of pressure her will power was proving to be all but nonexistent!

Nervously she twirled the lovely pearl ring, daintily inlaid with diamond chips, that decorated the third finger of her right hand. The ring, a gift from Uncle Leonard on Lisa's eighteenth birthday, was very special to her.

"Enjoy this while you can," he'd told her, slipping the expensive band onto her slender finger. "It's the last ring you're apt to get without strings attached."

Lisa looked down at the delicate design; one large pearl in the center flanked on either side by two smaller ones and a sprinkling of diamonds. The queen of gems, she thought, admiring the perfect pearls, symbols of modesty and purity. Lisa had to smile at the irony of the situation. At the moment her thoughts were far from modest and pure. Keith was right when he said that she was as ready as he for the next logical step in their relationship. But was she *willing?* Could she knowingly walk the same path which had ended so disastrously with Jeff?

Lisa powdered her nose, then brushed her blond hair until it glittered with golden highlights. A dab of lipstick, and still she lingered, reluctant to leave the safety of the lounge.

"You're a coward, Lisa Howard," she mumbled under her breath as she stood before the mirror straightening the neckline of her dress. She sighed in frustration. Just a week ago she'd thought the dress so sophisticated when she'd picked it up in San Francisco in preparation for the trip. "So much for sophistication," she said aloud. "Tonight I'd be much better off dressed in sackcloth!"

Her words brought startled looks from several nearby women, causing Lisa to leave the lounge more quickly than she intended. She picked her way slowly through the crowd, conscious of the appraising glances of several men she passed on the way. A self-conscious smile died on her lips as she stopped several yards short of their corner table. Keith was no longer alone. Standing next to him was a beautiful Japanese girl, her arm draped casually over his shoulder as he sat in his chair. Lisa judged the woman to be about her own age, or perhaps a year or two younger, and she was struck by her loveliness. Slender and above average in height, the girl's long blue-black hair hung down her back, reaching nearly to her waist. Her Oriental sheath-style dress seemed to hug every curve of her body and was richly embroidered with intricately beautiful designs. The young woman's eyes sparkled with interest as she talked to Keith, and judging from their easy rapport, it seemed clear to Lisa that they must be very close friends. She composed her face into lines of polite indifference before continuing on to the table, then wondered why it should be necessary to put on a mask.

"There you are." Keith smiled, spotting Lisa through the crowd. "I thought you'd gone to the powder room by way of China." He rose and put his arm around the young woman. "Lisa, I want you to meet Yuki Matsu-ura. Yuki, this is a very good friend of mine from the States, Lisa Howard."

"I'm very glad to meet you, Miss Howard," the young woman said in nearly flawless English. "Is this your first trip to our country?"

"I'm pleased to meet you, too, Yuki," Lisa said, trying not quite successfully to match the other woman's friendly manner. "And, yes, this is the first time I've been to Japan."

"Ah," the young woman smiled, "then I hope you

will have a very pleasant stay. Kyoto is one of our most ancient cities. I'm sure you will find much that is beautiful to see while you are here."

As Yuki turned back to Keith, Lisa couldn't help thinking that she was probably gazing upon one of the loveliest sights right now. How could Keith, who had succumbed so completely to the charms of the East, resist this exquisite creature? Or, she thought with a sinking heart, perhaps he hadn't resisted at all. If what Clyde and Marion Gilbert said about his reputation was true, he had surrendered to quite a few local as well as not-so-local attractions.

The possibility loomed ever more probable as Yuki smiled up at him. "I must go now, Keith-san. But remember, we meet tomorrow at lunch." Her black eyes danced coquettishly. "You won't forget."

Keith pulled Yuki into his arms and kissed her lightly on the mouth. "I never forget a date with a beautiful woman," he told her with a grin. "Don't worry. I'll be there."

When Yuki was gone Keith picked up their previous conversation as if there'd been no interruption. "Ready to go?" He smiled.

Lisa was momentarily thrown off balance by this smooth performance. Then she remembered Clyde Gilbert's prophetic words at dinner the other night when he'd referred to Keith's reputation as a predator with the ladies. The love 'em and leave 'em type, he'd said and then laughed. Well, Lisa hardly felt like laughing now. A cold chill settled on her heart as she remembered how Clyde's comments about Keith had reminded her of Jeff. Thank God she'd had a glimpse of the real Keith Brannon in action before it was too late. She was damned if she'd make that kind of a fool of herself again!

"Yes," she told him coolly. "I'm more than ready to go back to my hotel."

"That's fine with me," he said, smiling amicably. "As I said, I'm agreeable to either place."

Lisa met his grin squarely, her gaze steady, although her stomach was churning. "I'll just bet it is," she told him icily. "Only I don't think you understand. When I get back to my room I intend to be quite alone."

His eyes narrowed. "That's some turnabout. Before your trip to the powder room you looked open enough to persuasion."

"Let's say I've had second thoughts," she said shortly. "Despite your obvious success with the opposite sex, it's about time you learned there are a few women left in this world who aren't dying to jump into bed with you. Now, can we please leave?"

Keith's mouth compressed into a grim line, and Lisa knew he was fighting to contain his temper. The realization that she had ruffled his pride brought a small measure of satisfaction. At least she had struck some blow in defense of all the women he had used in the past. She watched his eyes grow dark as they lost the golden highlights which had danced there just moments before. Still, his manner remained perfectly controlled.

"I see," he said quietly. He picked up her wrap and threw a large bill onto the table. "In that case, I'll be very happy to oblige."

Almost roughly he guided her toward the door, speaking clearly into her ear as they walked. "In fact, if I get you home early enough, maybe I'll have time to look up one of those women you were talking about— you know, the ones who are panting to fall into my bed."

Despite the coolness of his voice, Lisa was startled when she looked up to see his features darkened by an expression of grim anger. Mentally she cringed as he unceremoniously settled her in the car.

Inserting the key in the ignition, Keith studied her for a long moment, his expression cynical. "With that kind of a harem, I shouldn't have any trouble at all, should I, Lisa?"

Chapter Nine

"Are you sure you won't join us for lunch, dear?" The woman looked at Lisa with motherly concern as they left the Nishijin Orimonokan, the museum of Nishijin textile products.

"Thank you, Mrs. Nicholson, Mr. Nicholson"—with a smile Lisa included the woman's quiet, balding husband—"but I really have to get back to the hotel. Perhaps I'll see you there later."

"Of course, dear." The natural down-curve of Mrs. Nicholson's mouth was more pronounced than usual. "Although I'm sure you'd enjoy the *kaiseki* at the Hyotei," she persisted. "I hear it's absolutely delicious."

"I'm sure it is, Mrs. Nicholson." Lisa's tone was friendly but firm. Fond as she was of the couple, two days in their company left her eager for some time alone. Besides, in all honesty she had little appetite. "I'm a little tired," she told them, aware that the statement hardly described her true reason. "We've covered a lot of territory over the last couple of days."

"Don't blame you a bit," Mr. Nicholson put in, for once getting into the conversation before his wife. "Nice little nap at the hotel sounds mighty good to me, too. All this runnin' around is givin' me corns."

Lisa found it difficult not to smile. The Nicholsons were an odd match. Yet, in some peculiar way, they seemed to complement each other, with Henry Nicholson's natural reticence balancing his wife's gregariousness.

After saying her goodbyes, Lisa strolled slowly back to the hotel. The afternoon promised to be long and lonely; there was no need to hurry. How can I fill the hours? she thought listlessly. During the past five days such phrases had become a monotonous litany—how can I keep busy?—how can I forget? Of course she could take in Nijo Castle; it was one of the few Kyoto landmarks that she hadn't seen yet. Nijo was of interest not only because it was the seventeenth-century castle featured in the James Bond thriller, *You Only Live Twice*, but also because it housed some priceless paintings dating from the Tokugawa, or Edo, Period. Still, she could not bring herself to go through the motions.

In the last five days Lisa had visited the Golden Pavilion, the Nishi Honganji Temple, the Silver Pavilion, and dozens of lesser temples and shrines. In addition, she had taken in the Noh theater, which turned out to be every bit as staid and formal as she had expected it to be, the Takarazuka all-girl opera troop, a judo exhibition and even a Japanese baseball game.

Yet no matter where her body had wandered, her mind had been busy trying to forget, and then, perversely, struggling to understand. Her first reaction after seeing Keith and the beautiful Japanese girl in the Kyoto nightclub had been to deny her hurt. It was none of her business, she kept telling herself, if he had a dozen women like Yuki spread all over Japan. She was damn lucky to have been brought to her senses before she did something foolish.

But as she dragged through the next two days, meeting with Yakamoto to discuss the Kabuki troop's trip to Evergreen, then filling interminable hours with this or that tourist attraction, it became obvious that the ache was not going to fade away. If anything, her despondency deepened as the days passed and still there was no word from Keith. Without him, Kyoto had lost its charm.

On the third morning, Lisa fought the nearly irresistible urge to stay in her hotel room in case he called and forced herself downstairs to the coffee shop for some breakfast. It was there that she had met Catherine and Henry Nicholson.

The retired couple from the Midwest had been almost childishly delighted to meet a fellow American. Having decided not to see Japan with a regularly scheduled tour group, they were especially pleased to find Lisa's knowledge of the city broader than their own.

For her part, Lisa was grateful for the Nicholsons' company. With Catherine and Henry she was forced to pay attention to the sights, if only to answer Catherine's endless stream of questions, and it was difficult not to get swept away by their enthusiasm. They were a small, reassuring part of home, and it was not long before she felt a genuine affection for the couple.

This afternoon, however, Lisa was weary of the chatter. She longed for quiet, for release from the obligation to be cheerful, which she felt around the Nicholsons. But it was no use. The minutes dragged even more miserably in her room. She might run away from her friends, but she could not escape herself.

"Damn it, Lisa," she scolded aloud, restlessly pacing the dingy room. "What's the matter with you anyway? You knew from the beginning that Keith Brannon was nothing but a playboy. Yet here you are moping around as if you're in love with him!"

Lisa stopped short, the words as chilling as a bucket of ice water. It was impossible! How could she even think such a thought? There was no way she could be in love with Keith Brannon. Not another pilot; not another Jeff!

Still, the idea had been planted, and once there it grew like a wildflower. Yet how could it be? She'd hadn't known him long enough for love. All right, she conceded after several moments of self-examination, she'd admit to a strong sexual attraction to him. But how had that grown into this deeper need? How had desire turned so wildly, so hopelessly, into love?

Suddenly the room was too small, too stifling. Jumping up from the chair, she grabbed her purse and sweater. She'd see the Nijo Castle this afternoon after all, she decided impulsively. Anything to get out of this room. Anything to get away from the crushing, overwhelming truth.

She was actually in the hall when the phone rang. For several moments she let it ring, reluctant to answer. Right now she just couldn't cope with Catherine Nicholson's endless chatter. Yet what if it wasn't the Nicholsons? Her heart jumped. What if Keith had called her after all?

The notion propelled her back into the room and over to the bedside phone. It was several seconds before she realized that it was not Keith on the other end of the line.

"Etsu? Etsu Okura? How . . . how nice to hear from you." Lisa's mind was in a spin. Had Keith put his manager up to calling? Did he want to see her again after all?

Lisa knew her voice was unnaturally high as she forced herself to follow the amenities. "I've been meaning to thank you, and of course your lovely family, for having me to dinner the other night, Etsu. It meant a great deal to me to be a guest in your beautiful home."

Lisa could almost see the handsome Japanese bowing at the other end of the line. "It was our pleasure, Miss Howard. Our home was graced by your presence."

For several more minutes they followed the prescribed course for polite conversation in Japan. Only after he had courteously inquired about her health, her week in Kyoto and her family did Etsu finally get to the point of his call.

"I thought you might like to see an authentic *chanoyu,* a Japanese tea ceremony," he said politely. "I have spoken of you to a good friend of mine who is a *geisha* at the Gion-machi. She says she would be honored if you would accompany me there this afternoon as her guest."

Despite a momentary pang of disappointment that the call had nothing to do with Keith, Lisa was delighted, realizing that it was an honor to be asked to one of the finest geisha houses in Japan. Eagerly, she accepted the invitation, then had an idea.

"Etsu," she began, "would it be too much of an imposition if I asked some friends of mine to join us?—an American couple? I know it would mean a great deal to them to visit the Gion-machi."

"By all means ask your friends," Etsu replied without hesitation. "It is a small, private party. Your friends will be more than welcome."

As Lisa suspected, the Nicholsons were overjoyed to be included. Smoothly cutting off Mrs. Nicholson's effusive thanks, Lisa made plans to share a taxi with them to the Gion-machi.

Feeling somewhat better now that her afternoon had some real direction, Lisa quickly showered, then slipped on a light cotton skirt and blouse. She was putting the final touches to her makeup when the jangle of the phone once again cut through the room. Lisa jumped at the sound, then forced herself to wait a moment before rushing to the receiver. Still, her voice was breathless when she answered.

"Lisa? So you're finally home. I've been trying to reach you for the past two days. Where on earth have you been?"

Lisa smiled at the familiar voice, even as she again swallowed the sharp disappointment that it wasn't Keith. "I'm here on business, Uncle Leonard, remember?" she told him lightly. "I've had a lot to do."

"Well, all I can say is you certainly put your heart into your work. It's all but impossible to catch you." His voice became serious. "I thought you'd like to know I'm back in Tokyo—just in time to do some more work on the Fugi contract, as it turns out."

"What do you mean 'more work'? I thought it was just a matter of Fugi's board reaching a decision."

"That's what we all thought. But now they've decided they have insufficient information to award the contract. The competing companies have been asked to submit additional data by the end of the week." Lisa heard his low chuckle. "I've got my crew in California working around the clock. Still, there's a chance I'll have to fly back to the States and get the material myself if they don't get a move on."

Lisa was instantly on the alert. The doctors had warned Leonard Mason repeatedly to slow down. If anything, he had increased his workload since his illness the year before. How long could he keep up this pace without bringing on another attack?

"Do you think that's wise?" she asked him cautiously. "Is the Fugi contract really that crucial?"

She sensed rather than heard his hesitation. "Every contract is crucial right now, honey. With the economy the way it is we can use all the business we can get. I'd sure as hell hate to be forced into those layoffs."

Lisa knew that her uncle would go to any lengths to avoid giving a pink slip to even one of his employees. On the other hand, was anything as important as his health?

"Is there anything I can do to help?" she offered. "I'll be through here by early next week, couldn't I do the legwork for you?"

"Afraid not, hon. Fugi's set a deadline. They're not about to extend it for my convenience. Come on, Lisa," he teased. "You're turning into a regular worry-wart. I'm not taking any unnecessary chances. Trust me."

Lisa wished it was as simple as that. Long after she hung up she contemplated the alternatives. She was familiar enough with Mason Aircraft's financial situation to realize that if the company did lose the Fugi account, there would have to be cutbacks somewhere. She also knew how that would affect her uncle. Which would be more devastating? she wondered. The maddening pace her uncle was setting for himself now, or the inevitable consequences of a lost contract later?

Unfortunately, she could find no satisfactory answer. Either way, it seemed that Uncle Leonard had placed himself in a very dangerous no-win situation.

"The *chanoyu,* which literally means hot water for tea, has remained virtually unchanged since the fifteenth century," Etsu explained as they waited in a small anteroom for the call to the tea pavilion. "It was then that the first building was erected here in Kyoto exclusively for the 'teas' offered to the courtiers and distinguished guests of the Shogun Yoshimasa."

Catherine Nicholson looked awed, and for once her voice was hushed. "It's all so . . . so impressive," she whispered.

Etsu smiled. "The tea cult is sometimes called 'the religion of the art of life.' When practiced correctly, it enables one to better appreciate the finer things of life."

A gong sounded, and Etsu informed his guests that Miyume was ready to receive them. Having already washed their hands and rinsed their mouths, they left the anteroom to walk along a beautifully landscaped pathway toward the *cha-shitsu,* or tearoom proper. There, the Americans were surprised to find that they had to stoop low and almost crawl through the opening. Etsu whispered that the traditional reasons for this were to make it impossible for guests to conceal a sword beneath their robes, and to symbolize their leaving their pride outside.

The room was bare except for the graceful scroll hanging in the *tokonoma* alcove. Each of the guests was required to admire the scroll in turn. This ritual complete, they lined up on their knees to await the arrival of their hostess.

Miyume entered the tea pavilion like a ray of sunshine, lighting the simple room with the sheer splendor of her beauty. Lisa thought the *geisha* was the loveliest creature she had ever seen, easily capturing every eye in the room as she bowed low to her guests and sank with modest, yet fluid grace, to her knees in front of them. Her brown, almond-shaped eyes were warm and friendly; her oval face, as smooth and fair as the most delicate alabaster. Miyume's hair, lustrously thick and black, was piled high on her head in the classic and beautifully complicated *geisha* style, gracefully fastened with colorful combs and jewels. Her robes were lovely, delicately designed in the most costly brocades, causing Lisa to compare her to the exquisite dolls that she had admired so much that last afternoon in Tokyo.

Lisa knew by the sudden hush that settled over the room at Miyume's entrance that everyone else was as thoroughly captivated as she. Especially Etsu. She hardly needed his audible intake of breath to guess the young Japanese's utter devotion to the lovely *geisha*. His eyes never left her; they followed her every move as if she were the sun, the moon and the stars wrapped up into one magnificent package.

The silence in the pavilion was nearly complete as the *geisha*'s shy smile acknowledged her guests. Then, with time-honored solemnity, she bent her head to the brazier before her and slowly began the ceremony. Lisa looked with interest at the array of implements arranged artistically next to the fire, aware from Etsu's earlier explanation that most of them were very old and extremely valuable. There was the jar of fresh water, a bamboo ladle, the bowl-washer, and finally the delicately painted bowl itself, complete with bamboo whisk, spatula and tea caddy.

Miyume was reaching for the spatula when Lisa sensed an imperceptible change in the room. Turning her head slightly, she saw a tall form slipping quietly into the pavilion. Her heart leapt wildly as the latecomer sank softly to his knees beside her. It was Keith Brannon!

Keith glanced at her briefly, his expression unreadable, then shifted his attention to the beautiful *geisha* and the ancient ceremony she was performing. Dazed, Lisa did the same, trying to ignore the scent and feel of him as he knelt so close beside her in the small room. As if from a great distance, she watched Miyume's graceful hands slowly put the green tea powder in the bottom of the bowl, then carefully pour hot water onto the mixture. With a minimum of perfectly controlled motions, the *geisha* gently beat the preparation with the whisk made of bamboo switches until it was entirely covered with green froth. Still on her knees, she bowed formally and offered the bowl ceremoniously to Etsu. The young man flushed, then solemnly raised the bowl to his lips before passing it to his employer as the second guest of honor. After sipping his share, Keith turned and handed the bowl to Lisa.

For a long moment their eyes met over the tea. Lisa knelt motionless, her heart beating madly in her breast, the tea forgotten in her hands. For a few seconds outside of time no one else existed in the room. It was only when Etsu gently cleared his throat that Lisa reluctantly came back to the present, raising the bowl awkwardly to her lips. Even then she was only vaguely aware of the bitter taste of the brew or of handing the bowl on to Catherine Nicholson.

After that the ceremony seemed endless. Miyume's every movement was performed very slowly. Lisa had the feeling that the ritual was being enacted in slow motion, that she was watching it in a dream. Only the man next to her was real.

Finally, Miyume solemnly handed the utensils to the guests to be admired. Lisa knew that Etsu was explaining the ancient associations attached to the costly implements, but his words droned on meaninglessly, hardly piercing her consciousness.

Then, at last, it was over, and Lisa was aware of a tingling sensation followed by profound relaxation, as if her tired body were sinking into a steaming bath. When she stood, her knees were so stiff that she could hardly straighten, and she noticed that it took both Etsu and Keith to help Mrs. Nicholson to her feet. Even Henry Nicholson was limping slightly as they walked out of the pavilion.

They walked about the grounds surrounding the Gion-machi until sunset as Miyume shyly explained the meanings of each of the many features of the traditional tea garden. Fascinating as it was, Lisa had a difficult time concentrating. Miyume's patient answers to Catherine Nicholson's excited questions seemed endless, the small group a huge crowd of intruders. Were they never to be alone?

Finding the others looking at her strangely, Lisa realized that Etsu was speaking directly to her and Keith. She had completely lost the drift of the conversation.

"The festival is called *Aoi Matsuri*," he was saying, "because part of the ritual consists of offering leaves of the *aoi* tree to the gods. It is very ancient and very colorful. I'm sure you would enjoy it, Hana-san. Please say you will join us."

As if sensing Lisa's confusion, Keith came to her

rescue by answering for them both. "We'd be honored, Etsu," he said with a slight bow. "Of course we'll join you."

Lisa turned to him in surprise, but he was busy putting the Nicholsons into a taxi. Unsure whether she should accompany them or not, Lisa started to follow only to be stopped by a strong hand on her arm.

"No, I want to talk to you," Keith told her under his breath.

She nodded mutely, smiling vaguely at her American friends as they continued to offer lavish thanks for being invited to the ancient ceremony. After promising to see them the next day, the couple drove away, well pleased with the afternoon.

Keith and Lisa left Etsu to say his own private goodbyes to Miyume. It was obvious that the young couple were eager to snatch what few moments they had left together before she was called inside. The depth of their devotion to each other was obvious, however they tried to conceal it beneath layers of convention and propriety.

Keith took Lisa to dinner at a small, intimate restaurant off Higashioji-Dori. Lisa was aware that the food was excellent, but, as at the *geisha* house, she could hardly taste a thing. After dinner they strolled up the Higashiyama hillside toward the Kiyomizu Temple, which was perched regally above.

As they walked Lisa was unnervingly aware of his closeness, of the warm, strong hand at her waist.

"I made a surprising discovery during the past five days," he told her softly. "I missed you."

Lisa's pulse was racing, yet she said nothing, afraid that he might stop speaking.

"At first I told Etsu I couldn't come to the Gion-machi today," he went on. "But it kept eating at me

that you'd be there. I couldn't think of anything else."
He turned and took her hands. "What have you done
to me, Little Flower?"

Lisa paused, searching for the right response. She
wanted desperately to believe him, yet some small part
of her mind argued caution.

"So in the end you came," she said, realizing that the
words were slightly inane.

They had stopped walking and were standing on the
temple's wooden platform, famous for its spectacular
view of the gorge below, the hills around and the city
beyond. Keith's profile was etched clearly in the moonlight as they stood before the protective railing. It was
all Lisa could do to stop herself from reaching out to
touch the dimple in his tanned cheek.

His hands reached around her waist, pulling her
closer. "And so I came," he answered simply.

She looked up into his eyes, but what little she could
read there only heightened her need to know more.
Nothing was worse than the wondering and the doubts.

"What do you want from me, Keith?" She met his
eyes boldly, marveling at her control, the steady throb
of her pulse testifying to the importance of his reply.

His hand tightened fractionally on her back. When
he spoke his voice was soft and he was, she sensed, a bit
confused, as if he were dealing with unfamiliar feelings.
"Most of all I guess I want to be your friend," he
started slowly. "The way you looked at me the other
night—it just about tore me apart. You made me feel
like some sort of a monster."

When she answered she was surprised that her voice
sounded almost normal. She was relieved that it would
not betray the emotions that had prompted the episode
at the nightclub. "I don't know what got into me," she
lied glibly. "I guess I was just frightened that things

were moving too fast between us. Chalk it off to nerves if you like."

"I thought matters were moving along at a very nice rate myself," he said, his breath lightly brushing her hair.

His lips grazed her forehead, and she felt a shock, as if she'd been touched by a small volt of electricity. "I've never felt like this, Lisa," he whispered. "You do something crazy to me."

His lips touched hers, warm and inviting, then moved to nibble seductively at the sensitive lobe of her ear. Tightening his arms around her, he pressed her to his chest, his voice nearly lost in her hair. "I feel as if I've been drugged. What's this spell you've cast over me?"

Lisa shuddered as his mouth returned to hers, hot and urgent now. She made no resistance as he coaxed her lips apart, searching between them with an insistence beyond her power or her desire to resist. For if a spell had been cast, surely she was equally a victim. Whatever sense, whatever sanity she had fought to maintain earlier in their relationship seemed no longer important. All that mattered was being back in his arms with his mouth hungrily feasting on hers.

She moaned lightly, suddenly aware that here, on this faraway hillside in Kyoto, she had found a happiness greater than any she had ever known. The love she felt for this man transcended distance, bridged differences. Only in his arms was she truly whole.

His hands gently massaged her back, then slid down to her hips, pressing them firmly into his muscled length. Lisa felt weak with longing. Warm pleasure swept through her like a wave, and she luxuriated in it. No man's kiss had ever affected her like this. She could hardly get her fill of him, of his hard, lean body, of his deliciously clean male scent. Her arms crept around his neck, and her hands fastened themselves in the crisp, dark hair which curled about his collar. Gently, instinctively, she rotated her hips as he ground them into his loins.

At her movement, his kisses seemed to explode. Eagerly his tongue sought hers. With a peculiar noise deep in his throat, Keith pressed her even closer, molding her to his body until Lisa was acutely aware of his male need for her.

With a louder groan, his lips left hers to bury themselves in the warm, gentle curve of her neck. Tantalizingly, he trailed kisses down to the opening of her blouse while his hand moved up under the thin material to cup her breast.

"Why do you have to be so damn beautiful?" he rasped, tracing a rough thumb around a nipple until it grew hard. "You're driving me crazy!"

"And just what do you think you're doing to me?" she gasped, vaguely aware that other tourists had stepped out onto the terrace. Reluctantly she pulled out of Keith's grasp and tried to calm her breathing. "It isn't exactly private here," she murmured, trying to hide how much he had aroused her.

Keith moved his hand lightly over her chin and throat, then let his index finger trace a path to the V-neckline of her blouse. "But I know a place that is," he told her seriously. For a poignant moment their eyes met in the moonlight, and a message as old as time passed between them. Then, as if in silent affirmation, they turned and moved arm in arm toward the stairs.

Without questioning, without caring about the consequences, Lisa mutely followed Keith's lead. Suddenly, it was terribly important to preserve the fragile thread which bound her to this man. Whatever came tomorrow would have to be faced on its own terms. Tonight was for them. Tonight was for the making of dreams.

Keith's apartment was located in a large building near the downtown area. In fact, Lisa thought ruefully, remembering the five days of misery during his absence, she could probably have looked out from her hotel and seen his windows.

When he opened the door and switched on the light, Lisa saw a large, comfortable room. The low, uncluttered lines of the furniture blended well with the dark brown carpet and glass-topped coffee table. It was a masculine room, and it bore the mark of its owner. On a sideboard, next to several framed pictures featuring what Lisa assumed to be Keith's family, were half a dozen small, detailed models of Brannon Aeronautics' planes, including their latest, the Comet. Hanging on the opposite wall were a collection of color photographs depicting a series of jet planes in flight, some shot at dramatically unusual angles. Over the fireplace was a beautifully executed oil painting of Mount Fugi, its familiar symmetrical cone rising majestically over a handful of mountain lakes at its base. The fourth wall, opposite the fireplace, was composed almost entirely of windows which revealed a sweeping vista of the city below. It was a pleasant room, a comfortable refuge, and Lisa felt relaxed here, as if she had just come home from a long journey.

Without thinking, she walked toward the view and was conscious that Keith had followed her only when she felt the short jacket she wore slipping off her shoulders. Turning, she found him looking down at her, his expression blatantly hungry. He tossed her jacket onto a nearby chair and took her gently into his arms.

"I've been waiting for this since the first day I met you," he murmured. His eyes drifted to the low opening of her blouse. Lisa flushed beneath his look as a tingling sort of excitement coursed through her body. She wanted him. Her body had known the truth long before her mind and emotions finally reached the inevitable conclusion. No matter what the cost, she wanted to give herself to this man completely, irrevocably. If this was what it felt like to be in love, then her feelings for Jeff had been no more than wispy shadows of the real thing.

He stooped to kiss her forehead, then let his lips graze her mouth in a feathery kiss. "I want you, Little Flower," he whispered into her cheek.

"I know," she said softly, searching for his mouth. "I want you, too. I've never wanted anyone so much in my life."

With a little groan he brought his mouth back to hers. His tongue boldly slipped through the opening she had provided, eager to explore the sweet warmth beyond. "Why do you have to taste so damn good . . . ?" he murmured. His hands moved to her hips, pressing the softness of her flesh against the growing hardness of his own. ". . . and feel so soft and pliable? It's as if we were made to fit together."

Her mouth yielded to the increased intensity of his assault, meeting his tongue with eager assent, joining it in an urgent mating which left her weak and breathless. Keith's fingers massaged and kneaded her hips, moving her body in a steady sensuous rhythm against his own.

"I want it to be as perfect for you as it's going to be for me," he whispered, not quite relinquishing the corner of her mouth. His hands slid over her body, leaving a trail of fire and excitement wherever they passed. "I'm going to enjoy every inch of your fantastic body," he breathed. "Just as you're going to enjoy mine."

He couldn't miss her response, their bodies were too close for her reaction to pass unnoticed. At her shudder he smiled, then moved one hand up to release the top button of her blouse. Gradually, the thin material gave way to reveal her breasts, only partially hidden beneath the flimsy wisp of a brassiere.

Brushing the blouse onto the floor, Keith's hands went around her back and unfastened the hook of her bra. Slowly, taking all the time in the world, he eased the scrap of material forward until he had completely exposed the pink-tipped globes. She heard his sharp intake of breath as he gazed down at her, then gasped herself as he cupped a full breast in each hand, and then bent his head to cover each pulsating nipple with his mouth, letting his tongue and teeth coax the rosy points into sharp tautness. When she was tingling with ill-concealed anticipation, Keith again lowered his hands and deftly released the side button of her skirt. Never taking his eyes off her, he lowered her cotton skirt slowly to the floor.

She stood before him clothed only in her stockings and flimsy lace bikini panties. With infinite care, Keith gently rolled the pantyhose down from her waist, painstakingly smoothing them over the graceful swell of her hips, then down the length of her long, slim legs. As if mesmerized, her eyes never leaving his, Lisa stepped out of her hose, then stood looking up at him, lips slightly parted, ready, eager for whatever might come next.

He moved his hands almost reverently along her satin-soft body, and she felt her skin burn as if she had been branded by the touch. With a shock, Lisa felt his fingers move under the elastic edge of her lacy briefs, running feather soft back and forth across the flat surface of her abdomen until her breath was little more than a gasp. Her hips moved sensuously against him as his slightly roughened hands eased down the last flimsy restraint until it, too, drifted onto the carpet.

With one smooth movement, Keith swept her into his arms and walked toward the bedroom. Lisa barely had time to glance at the huge, king-size bed before he was gently settling her within the folds of the caramel-colored spread. The material felt cool and unbelievably erotic against her bare skin. Lisa's long lashes dusted her cheek as she lowered her eyes, suddenly modest, suddenly frightened by the intensity of her emotions.

He was looking down at her, wonder etched on his handsome face. "You're beautiful," he said huskily, his voice the barest whisper in the darkened room. Keith moved to the side of the bed and flicked the light to its lowest beam. "I want to watch you, Little Flower," he said, undoing the buttons on his shirt. "I want to see your face when you come to life beneath me."

As he quickly stripped off his clothes, Lisa frankly admired the clean lines of his body, the broad shoulders, the flat stomach, the firm, muscled legs, and, finally, the hard evidence of his desire. Then he was lying beside her on the bed, his hands lightly moving over her, caressing, arousing her to a fevered pitch of longing. The passion in his eyes only fed the flame in her own, and she responded eagerly, her hands making their own voyage of discovery. Wantonly, she moved them over the muscles of his arms, the firm hardness of his chest, the taut male nipples, and down to the curling hair beneath his navel.

The movement of her hands seemed to set him on fire, and his mouth closed on hers with frantic hunger, only breaking away to rain a flurry of kisses onto her face and neck. Her body tickled from the crisp hairs of his chest as he shifted lower to continue the onslaught, her breasts his next target. Gently he tugged at her nipples with his teeth, causing them to form hard, aching peaks as his hand moved even lower to find the warm, moist place between her legs. Slowly, inch by inch, her eager body came to life beneath his adventuring hands and mouth. Her own hands and mouth were causing Keith to tremble, and he groaned hoarsely, "Oh, God, Lisa, you're driving me insane!"

The hand between her legs became more insistent, his lips more demanding. When she could no longer stand the fire burning in her loins, she raked her nails down his back.

"Keith . . . please," she cried. "My God! I want you!"

"Yes, darling," came the gasping reply. "I want you, too. Now."

In one quick shifting motion he fused their bodies, binding them together so completely, so perfectly that it was as if they had been made from matching molds. With a little cry Lisa felt herself swept to another time, another plane, as she surrendered totally to the rhythm of his body. Through the haze of their passion each knew the miraculous harmony of their union. It was right, the giving was total.

Gradually the rhythm increased until Lisa thought she would explode. And then she did. Only as she sank to the heavenly, blissful other side of pleasure did Lisa realize that it was her own voice she had heard, her own cries at the violent surrender of her body. She shuddered one last time as she felt Keith's final, driving response, then they were still.

Completely spent, they lay together, cradled in each other's arms. Together they had reached the pinnacle. They had had their glorious moment of fulfillment.

Chapter Ten

*K*eith was already dressed when she awoke. He had been quiet, but the unfamiliar noises coming from the bathroom and then the kitchen finally broke through Lisa's consciousness. It had been more than two years since she'd heard the sound of an electric razor or the low, murmured curse of a male voice accompanied by the smell of burnt toast. The combination was enough to bring Lisa to life in a hurry.

Throwing on Keith's blue terrycloth robe from the foot of the bed, Lisa wound the long belt several times around her slim waist, then padded to the bathroom. Quickly she splashed her face with cold water and ran a comb through her hair before hurrying to the kitchen. There she found Keith, dressed in gray slacks and a pale blue dress shirt with the sleeves rolled up, fighting unsuccessfully to turn an omelette. The familiar shock of dark brown hair had fallen over his forehead from the effort. He grinned as she walked into the room.

"You just spoiled the surprise. I was going to serve you breakfast in bed."

Lisa's eyes went to the counter and the stack of

blackened toast resting on a small plate, then back to the stove where the omelette he'd been wrestling with sat in the pan looking rather the worse for wear. Catching her expression, he grinned.

"Okay, so I'm no Julia Child. Remember, it's the thought that counts."

Lisa's heart melted at the woebegone look on his face. How could a man as successful, and notorious, as Keith Brannon still appear like such a lost little boy at times? With a rueful smile, Lisa wrapped a towel around the robe and nudged Keith out of the way.

"You man the coffee," she directed. "I'll see to the eggs."

Despite its somewhat ragged appearance, the omelette was delicious. Freshly cooked toast and several strips of crisp bacon, which Keith produced with a proud flourish from the oven, provided a hearty breakfast. After they had eaten, they lingered over coffee in the sunny nook off the kitchen, enjoying the early morning stirrings of the city below.

"What's on your agenda for today?" Keith asked, pushing his empty plate to one side.

"Nothing very spectacular," Lisa admitted. "Although I've arranged meetings with several groups that may be exchange possibilities, nothing's on for today." She looked at him speculatively. "Why? What do you have in mind?" .

Keith's look turned boyish again as he winked at her over his coffee. "Oh, I just thought it might be fun to mix a little business with a lot of pleasure this afternoon. Have you been to Kobe yet?"

Lisa shook her head. She knew that the major port city of Kobe was spread out along the shores of Osaka Bay about forty miles southwest of Kyoto. It was on her list of possible places to visit if time permitted. "Actually, I was thinking of making a trip there with the Nicholsons," she told him. "But we haven't worked out the details yet."

"How about going with me instead? Fugi's asking for more data before they award the Tokyo contract, so I have to run some stuff over to Kobe Aerospace Test Lab this morning. I thought you might like to go along for the ride." He grinned. "There's something special I'd like to show you afterward."

Lisa's smile of acceptance was automatic, and she hoped that it hid the slight constriction she was feeling around her heart. For the first time it came home to her that she had just made love to her uncle's major competitor. When she was in Keith's arms it was easy to forget this other, and to Lisa, more threatening, side of his life. Or perhaps she had just willed herself not to think about it. Matters between them had seemed complicated enough without letting business considerations enter the picture.

But now, with the mention of the Fugi contract, she could no longer ignore her concern. Just how much of a chance did Keith have of snagging the Fugi business away from her uncle? She remembered her conversation with Uncle Leonard the afternoon before, his insistence that every contract right now was crucial to the company, the worried tone he'd been unable to disguise. What if Brannon Aeronautics *did* land the Fugi contract? What would it do to Uncle Leonard? And, heaven help her, how would she feel then about the man who had caused her uncle's pain?

These thoughts continued to run through Lisa's mind long after Keith had returned her to her hotel room, promising to pick her up at about eleven. She continued to mull the matter over as she showered and, later, as she slipped into a pair of blue cotton trousers and a short-sleeved off-white sweater. She wished now that he had never mentioned Fugi International, or suggested the drive to Kobe on business which she now knew was directly tied to the contract. Somehow going with him made her feel as if she were being disloyal to Uncle Leonard.

None too gently, Lisa fastened a simple gold chain above the scoop-neck of her sweater, put on a matching pair of gold chain earrings, then brushed her hair fiercely and yanked it into a practical knot at the back of her neck. Looking at her reflection in the mirror she hesitated, remembering Keith's earlier criticism of the severe style. Then, almost perversely, she turned away from the mirror, determined to leave her hair exactly the way it was. If Keith didn't like the way she looked that was his problem. What he was doing to Uncle Leonard didn't earn him any special considerations!

All of which was totally irrational, she realized, taking the elevator down to the lobby just before eleven o'clock. Keith was a businessman, and the whole idea behind running a company was to make a profit. Winning the Fugi contract was simply good business.

Still, she couldn't shake a small pang of guilt as they began the drive to Kobe, especially since Keith continued to discuss the reason for the trip.

"Having Kobe Aerospace use models of the Comet in their wind tunnel will save us weeks of our own testing," he told her. "And since Fugi expects the results by the end of the week, that's time we simply don't have right now."

Despite herself, Lisa was interested. "Are the wind tunnel tests really as valid as tests done on actual planes under real life conditions?" she asked.

"They're remarkably accurate. All the tests are

computer controlled, so it's possible to get some pretty exact results. And it's a whole lot faster, and cheaper, than doing the tests ourselves with the real thing."

"When will you get the results?"

"They're rushing the job, so we should have them back in a day or two. Then we'll have to reduce the data, of course. That'll take Etsu at least one more full day."

Lisa tried to keep her voice casual as she asked, "Will you make the deadline?"

"There's no denying it'll be close," he replied seriously. "But we're going to give it a damn good try."

And who would she be rooting for? Lisa asked herself as Keith became momentarily absorbed in traffic. If his data didn't get to Tokyo on time, Uncle Leonard might have a chance. And if it did—who would win then? Who did she *want* to win?

Lisa leaned her head back against the seat and closed her eyes. Why did life have to be so damned complicated? It seemed impossible that a little over a week ago her most serious problem had been completing negotiations with the Kabuki troop and scouting for other groups to follow their tour to Evergreen. Now look where she was—in love with a pilot, and not just any pilot at that but a *test* pilot, and one who also happened to be her uncle's major rival. Good lord! If she had set out to make a mess of things, she couldn't have done a better job.

She yawned. The steady motion of the car was soothing her despite her problems. Yes, it was all very complicated, she decided drowsily. If only she'd never met Keith . . . if only he'd never taken her into his arms . . . or touched her . . . or made love to her. . . .

"Hey, sleepy head. Wake up."

She felt the pressure of Keith's hand on her arm and opened her eyes to find that the car had stopped. Looking around, she saw that the Maserati was parked in front of a modern, well-landscaped plant much like the ones she was used to seeing back home in California.

"This is only going to take a minute," he went on. "You can stay here or come inside with me if you'd rather."

"No, I'll wait here," she said quickly. It was one thing to come along for the ride and quite another to help hand over the enemy's chief weapon. She would wait right where she was.

Twenty minutes later he was back in the car and they were off, this time heading south toward Osaka Bay.

"Now you're really going to see something special," he said a few miles later, pulling the car to a stop next to a long pier. "I couldn't take enough time off for the full day's tour, but there are plenty of smaller ships that make the shorter trip in the afternoon." His smile was infectious. "How's about it, Little Flower? Are you ready to cruise the Inland Sea?"

As they steamed along they munched sandwiches and sipped tea bought from one of the vendors operating aboard the ship. They sat forward on the small steamer, and because the ship was not one of the regularly scheduled liners, they had a portion of the deck to themselves. The day was clear, and the blue water of Osaka Bay seemed to beckon them as they sped outward toward the nearly 3000 islands that dotted the Inland Sea.

While they ate Keith told his usual intriguing tales from ancient Japanese history. "The story goes," he told her, "that several million years ago this area was rocked by volcanic activity of such gigantic proportions that it split the islands of Shikoku and Kyushu away from Honshu, creating the Inland Sea. Some of its islands are large enough to support human life, while others are little more than rocks jutting out of the water."

"And it stretches for over 300 miles," Lisa said, remembering a few isolated facts about the famous Japanese landmark.

"That's right. Actually, the Inland Sea is a chain consisting of five separate bodies of water, like Osaka Bay, linked together by narrow channels. We'll pass through Naruto Straits in a little while before we come to Shikoku Island."

The small steamship glided over the water like a swan, passing other steamers, small freighters and numerous junks with billowing esparto sails. Lisa was astounded to see one island appear after another, most of them verdant with trees, hedges and other vegetation. They seemed to go on forever, as far as the eye could see. Every so often one of the larger islands afforded a peek at farmers working their rice paddies, and she was stirred by the peace and harmony that were so much a part of the pastoral scenes.

"It's so tranquil," she sighed. "It's hard to believe that all this exists in the same time-frame as the rest of the world."

Keith nodded, seeming to share her wonder. "I know. I've never lost my awe of it either. Traveling through the Inland Sea, you get a glimpse of old Japan. Sometimes I look over my shoulder expecting to see a pirate ship moving up on us from the rear. In the past, when the sea was of much greater economic importance than it is now, buccaneers plagued these waters.

I've often thought that must have been an exciting time to live in this part of the world."

Lisa grimaced. "And dangerous." She looked up at him, head cocked thoughtfully to one side. "Somehow I can imagine you more easily as one of the pirates than as a peaceful farmer."

The message she read on his face caused a shiver to run down her spine. "I don't think I'd mind that," he told her softly. "When I pillaged your ship I could claim you as part of the booty." His dark eyes gleamed. "And then, fair maiden," he leered, "you'd have to do my bidding."

"Or walk the plank?"

He pulled her into his arms. "Never. I'd never let you go that easily. There are better ways than that of making the booty obey."

"Oh?" She glanced coyly up at him, enjoying the game. "Such as?"

"Such as this. . . ." Hungrily, his lips fastened on her mouth as if he would devour it. Without waiting for an invitation, his tongue pressed between her lips, eager to explore the softness which awaited within. She felt his raw need as his hands moved over her back, pressing her breasts against his chest.

"Keith . . ." She tried to protest, embarrassingly aware of the other passengers around them on the deck.

Again and again he kissed her, heedless of their awkward position, not seeming to care if the whole world were watching. He showered her with kisses, as if he couldn't get enough of her mouth, her skin, her hair. With a groan of defeat, Lisa's arms went around his back, aching to feel as much of him as she could through the confining layers of their clothes.

"You're not putting up much of a fight," Keith

whispered into her cheek. "I like my booty to present more of a challenge."

With an explosion of laughter, Lisa pulled out of his arms. "You *are* a rogue, Keith Brannon. I'm just glad the days of the pirates are over. I don't think I'd like being your booty."

"Of course you would," he said, planting a light kiss on her nose. "You'd love every minute of it." He looked around at the other passengers in annoyance. "For two cents I'd prove it to you right now."

Lisa inched away from him on the wooden seat. "Oh, no you won't, Mr. Buccaneer. Fortunately I've got plenty of protection out here, so you'll just have to forget your dastardly plans." She looked out at the chain of islands they were passing. "How far are we going, anyway?"

Keith pointed to the southwest. "This ship only goes as far as Takamatsu before it circles back to Kobe. That's the principal port-of-call on Shikoku Island. Most of the regular tour cruises go from Osaka to Kobe and then out as far as Kyushu, a trip that takes about fourteen hours. We're going considerably less than half that distance." He looked as if he regretted that fact. "I wish we had some time to go ashore at Takamatsu, but . . ."

"I know," Lisa interrupted, annoyed that he had once again reminded her of the Fugi account, "business prohibits."

He grinned. "'Fraid so."

As the hours passed, Lisa found it impossible to dwell on her problems. The scenery was simply too unique, too glorious to be wasted. Although they couldn't go ashore, they spent satisfying moments admiring the relatively unspoiled shoreline as they passed Takamatsu before drifting north for the return trip to Kobe. As the sun settled lower in the orange-tinged sky, they sat on the deck and sipped warm *sake* from the small flask Keith purchased inside. When the *sake* was gone, Lisa nestled comfortably into the crook of Keith's arm, and together they watched the flaming ball that had been the sun as it disappeared behind the shadowy crest of a faraway mountain. Then they were back in Kobe, slowly docking in the dusk which had stealthfully settled over the bay.

"Where to now, Captain Kidd?" Lisa asked as the Maserati sprang to life.

"Dinner, fair maiden. First I'm going to wine you, then dine you, and then further your education in Japanese culture."

Lisa raised a well-shaped brow. "Oh? And just how do you plan to do that?"

The passing lights revealed all too clearly the gleam in Keith's eyes. "It's time you were introduced to a very ancient and very sacred Japanese custom," he told her with mock gravity. "After dinner, Hana-san, I plan to show you the exotic wonders of the hotsy-bath."

Lisa hadn't noticed the door leading off the main bathroom the night before. Now, Keith slipped off her jacket and led her into a room which contained a large, oblong wooden tub more closely resembling a small swimming pool than a Western-style bathtub. Alongside the tub, several tiny wooden buckets and a low benchlike seat sat over a slanted, tile floor. Behind the buckets was a single faucet set low in the wall. When Lisa asked why Keith had an additional room for bathing when his bathroom already contained a very adequate shower, he explained.

"The Japanese love bathing. They consider it a sensuous and social experience as well as a means of getting clean. In the years I've been here I've come to appreciate this wisdom. There's nothing like a nice hot soak at the end of the day. It does a lot more to help me unwind than a shower."

Lisa was slowly circling the large tub. "It's huge," she said, peeking over the rim. The water in the tub looked at least four feet deep, and the tub itself was about five feet wide by six feet long. Curious, she examined the wooden buckets stacked neatly on the side. "What are these?"

Keith's eyes were twinkling. "They're to rinse off with. It would be very bad manners to get into the family tub dirty or to have even a bubble of soap on your body." At her startled expression he went on with a smile, "In the old days, whole families would line up to use the tub every night. And since very few homes could afford to change the water more than once a day, if that often, it became a common courtesy to scrub and rinse thoroughly before you got in."

"I've heard of the practice, of course," Lisa told him. "I guess I just didn't expect to find it here, in a Western-style apartment."

Keith gave Lisa a teasing grin. "There's real value in knowing which customs to adopt and which to let be, Hana-san. This is one I wouldn't do without." His eyes grew serious as they swept over her slender body, taking in every deliciously rounded curve. She saw the flicker of desire within their dark depths as he walked toward her, stopping so close that his sleeve brushed against her bare arm. Deftly, he moved his hands to her hair and quickly removed the pins and combs which held it confined at the nape of her neck. With an easy flick of his wrists he set it free, allowing it to cascade in a soft, golden mass around her shoulders.

"There," he sighed, "that's better." Lisa's heart fluttered as his hands moved from her hair to the hem of her sweater. "You've had a long day," he said thickly. "Let me help you to relax—Japanese style."

Effortlessly, he pulled the soft, off-white sweater over her head and tossed it without a glance to the side of the room. His eyes grew hungry as they took in her full breasts, the sheer lace of her bra revealing far more than it concealed. Firm, rosy nipples pressed against the taut material, teasing him, daring him to touch.

Slowly he exhaled, then moved his hands around her back. A second later the lacy constraint was flying across the room to land beside the sweater.

He feasted on her partially naked body, reveling in the smooth, satin sheen of her skin. Very slowly he reached out and ran his hands over her shoulders, letting them come to rest just above her elbows. Keeping his hands on her arms, his thumbs reached out and gently stroked the sides of her breasts, softly massaging until the rosy nipples strained upward.

Bending his head, he kissed each hard tip, coaxing it to life before allowing his hands to roam downward until they reached the front fly opening of her blue cotton trousers. In a moment the clasp was released, the zipper eased down. Lisa caught her breath when she felt one of his hands slip smoothly inside the opening.

"Oh," she cried, as his fingers moved in soft, caressing circles on her sensitive skin.

"I know," he answered, his breathing uneven. "You feel wonderful."

He eased the trousers down over the soft swell of her

hips and let them fall in a careless heap around her feet. Without taking her gaze from his face, she quickly stepped out of them and stood facing him, clad only in her lacy briefs.

"God, you're beautiful," he said hoarsely. "I want to see all of you." With one impatient movement he removed the last flimsy barrier, and she stood naked beneath his hungry gaze.

He paused long enough to strip off his own clothes, then led her over to one of the wooden buckets. Reaching for a bar of soap, he turned on the low faucet and quickly worked up a good lather between his hands.

"Is this the way the Japanese do it?" she asked shakily, as his hands slowly began to soap her back. Although the lather was only comfortably warm, her flesh felt hot wherever he touched.

"If the Japanese aren't doing it this way," he said softly, his breath ragged with desire, "then they don't know what they're missing."

Carefully, he turned her around and began the same, tantalizing assault on her front. He worked carefully and systematically, as if holding himself in close control. Starting with her shoulders, he sudsed downward in short, agonizing circles. When he reached her breasts he seemed to take particular care, running his hands slowly over the silky flesh. When Lisa thought she could no longer stand the searing pleasure, he moved lower, covering her hips and abdomen with the soft suds.

"My God, Keith . . ." she gasped as he found the warm, pulsating center of her womanhood. Gently he kneaded and stroked, his fingers sliding smoothly with the lather until she thought she'd surely explode. Her body moved against his hand, aching, searching for release.

Her own hands went to his bare chest and lost themselves in the mat of dark brown hair which covered the tan skin. He sucked in his breath as she traced a path to his hips where her fingers gripped at the firmly layered muscles. Aflame with desire, she dug her fingers into his flesh, kneading and massaging until she heard his anguished groan in her ear.

"God, Lisa, what are you doing to me?"

He grew reckless in his exploration of her, touching, stroking, setting her body ablaze. Hungrily their mouths came together, their tongues mating with an urgency as uncontrolled as their embrace.

"Keith, I need you," Lisa moaned, unable to stand the delicious torture any longer.

Keith pulled away long enough to spread a thick bathmat on the tiled floor. Carefully, he lowered Lisa to the rug, then stretched out beside her, his hands running over the slippery length of her wet body. When they reached her breasts they moved with an excited tension, as if there were a fire raging uncontrolled within him.

Her fingers dug deeper into his back as he nudged apart her legs, once again claiming that most vulnerable area of her womanhood. With ever more frantic strokes he coaxed her to pulsating life, until she arched into him in an aching quest for fulfillment.

"Keith . . ." she moaned, writhing beneath him.

"I know," he gasped, "I can't remember ever feeling like this before. I want you so badly!"

She could hear the near-desperate passion in his strangled voice, and could feel his hard, throbbing response to her as he pulled her against his body.

Eagerly she reached out for his rigid manhood, stroking and massaging, fanning the already flaming inferno of his desire.

"My God! I can't hold off any longer." With a loud groan he rose above her. Slipping his body between her legs, he inhaled raggedly and sank down, thrusting boldly into her exquisite softness. Again and again he plunged, catapulting them both to the dizzying, wondrous edge of the precipice. With a gasp, Lisa felt herself hurtling toward the pinnacle, racing out of control until she cried out with one incredible burst of pleasure. Then Keith moaned, his whole body shuddering as he followed her over the brink and into the peaceful valley beyond.

Lisa rested her head on his shoulder as their breathing gradually returned to normal, both of them too exhausted to move. Never before could she remember feeling so relaxed, so completely fulfilled. For a few short moments everything in the world had been right; there had been no tomorrow.

"A penny," Keith said, running a finger lightly down between her breasts.

Lisa jerked involuntarily from his touch, then laughed. "I was just thinking that this is an unlikely spot to get romantic . . . the floor of your bathroom."

He raised up on one elbow and eyed her mischievously. "And what's wrong with the floor of my bathroom? Can you think of a cleaner place to make love?" He grinned. "Besides, I didn't notice you complaining a few minutes ago."

She made a face at him. "I was tricked. You lured me in here under false pretenses. May I remind you that I was promised a genuine Japanese hot bath?"

Keith looked at her in mock seriousness. "Good heavens woman, you're right!" He scraped a fingerful of lather off her shoulder. "Did you know you're full of soap?"

Lisa sat up with a giggle, scraping some lather off Keith's chest. "So are you."

"See what you do to me?" He laughed. "You looked so darn delectable I completely lost track of what I was doing. Come on, let's rinse off."

He stood up and pulled her easily to her feet, then scooped up the bathmat and threw it over a hook on the wall. Filling one of the wooden buckets from the low faucet, he poured the water over her shoulders.

"Wait," she cried before he could stoop to fill another. "It's my turn."

For the next ten minutes they splashed and poured buckets of water over each other like a couple of children. Over Lisa's squealed objections, Keith insisted on washing her hair and then delighted in dumping pail after pail of water over her head to rinse it.

"You did that just so you could drench me," she sputtered, trying to duck the last deluge.

"You're already drenched," he pointed out, moving aside as she flung the contents of her own pail back in revenge. He reached out and grabbed her naked body, parting her wet hair with his fingers so he could see into her face. "You know you make a beautiful wet person," he said softly. "The water glistens on you in all the right places. In fact you look so damn delicious I may just have to soap you down all over again."

Lisa tried to pull away in alarm. "You'll do no such . . ."

Her protests were effectively cut off by Keith's mouth pressing against hers, moving seductively over her lips until all objections were forgotten. "Hush," he murmured against her cheek. "You're interfering with your education again. Besides," he added, his eyes gleaming, "the Japanese are very clean. We have a hard example to follow."

Leisurely, he soaped her again, taking his time, smoothing the suds over every hill and vale of her satiny skin. When he was finished, she lathered him, enjoying the excuse to feel the lean, muscled expanse of his chest, and the powerful bulge of his arms. When they were through, they rinsed thoroughly, this time with slow, deliberate movements, glorying in each other's bodies, knowing that they had all the time in the world. Then at last they soaked, gradually inching their way into the nearly scalding water to sit on comfortable built-in seats with only their heads above the water.

Lisa thought the tub was similar to an American Jacuzzi, except that the water was much hotter and of course it didn't swirl around. But the experience was quite different. She was more relaxed, more in tune with herself as she sat in the sweltering water. Although Keith told her he kept his bath temperature some degrees lower than the average Japanese would, Lisa felt waves of heat envelop her, making her feel light-headed and extraordinarily free. Or perhaps she was just feeling a reaction from their passionate lovemaking on the floor. She'd never made love like that before. Everything was so new, so wonderful—the ocean voyage this afternoon, the warm *sake,* Keith's embraces— all so fantastic. She closed her eyes to clear her head. Strange that the *sake* should still have such an effect on her after all this time. . . .

His voice was low and reassuring, but the touch of his hands below the level of the water was sending conflicting messages to her muddled brain. "Come on, Little Flower," he coaxed, "it's time to get out. You've had quite enough of this for the first time out."

She felt the pressure of his hands under her shoulders as he tried to raise her out of the water. "What's wrong?" she asked him, groggily. "Did I fall asleep?"

"You sure tried to," he said, helping her the rest of the way out of the tub. Quickly he wrapped her in an oversized towel. She smiled like a pleased cat and indeed almost purred as he proceeded to rub her down from head to toe.

". . . feels good," she sighed, yawning deeply. "Can't remember . . . can't remember when I've been so tired, though."

Keith grabbed his own towel, then scooted her through the door to the bedroom. "Perfectly natural, sweetheart. It zaps you every time, especially when you're not used to it." With one hand he supported her weight while with the other he tried awkwardly to turn down the covers. "Here, lie down now," he told her, slipping off her towel.

Lisa snuggled down between the cool, smooth sheets. She looked up at him sleepily through long lashes. "Keith . . . ?"

He sat on the edge of the bed and took one of her hands, gently rubbing the fingers and palm. "Yes?"

"Keith . . . ?" Her blue eyes looked puzzled for a minute, then very heavy, as if she were having great difficulty keeping them open. "Never mind . . . can't remember. . . ."

"Then sleep, darling," he soothed, tucking the blankets under her chin. "For a beautiful little flower you've had a very busy day. Just sleep now."

And she did, barely hearing the last words he spoke as she drifted off into a delightful, sheltered world of soft lights and shimmering water. In the distance she saw a beach, and a line of trees, and farmers toiling beneath a benevolent sun. She stretched out in the sand, feeling more relaxed, more wonderful than she had ever felt in her life.

Sometime during the night she felt the warmth of another body next to her own, and the weight of an arm stretched across her breast.

She sighed in her sleep, content that he was near. The man she loved was beside her; all was well. Just for tonight the world was secure. It would be all right.

Chapter Eleven

*T*he next few days were wonderful. As long as Lisa refused to examine her situation too closely, they were very nearly perfect. With each passing day Keith seemed more at ease with her, almost as if they had entered a new, higher plateau in their relationship. When they weren't working, they spent virtually every moment together. Sometimes Keith took her to little-known nooks and hiding places far off Kyoto's tourist trails; sometimes they simply relaxed together in his apartment.

If the days were exciting, the nights were idyllic! In Keith's arms it was easy to forget all the tomorrows which were yet to come. Never had Lisa imagined she could find such fulfillment, such happiness with any man.

She spent most of her time in Keith's apartment now, returning to her hotel room merely to collect messages and exchange clothing. In the mornings she cooked breakfast for them in his modern kitchen, and in the evenings that they didn't go out they worked together to prepare dinner. Later, they would come together with a passion as fresh and explosive as if they were experiencing it for the first time. If anything, their hunger for each other seemed to grow; it was as if they had developed an insatiable craving that refused to be satisfied no matter how often it was fed. And if Lisa experienced occasional anxiety that it must soon end, that their love could only end in disaster, she quickly buried it. She learned to live for the day, sometimes for the hour. Thinking of tomorrow was too painful. Surely, she told herself, it was all right to exist for the moment, to be content in the knowledge that she was happier than she had ever been in her life.

Four days before she was scheduled to complete her business and return to Tokyo, Keith took her on an overnight trip to Nara, a nearby city even older and more steeped in legend than Kyoto.

"In 710, Nara became Japan's first permanent, settled capital," Keith told her as they sipped tea in a lightly wooded area of Nara's famous Deer Park. "The seventy-four years it remained here saw the beginnings of Japan's written history as well as its formal culture."

Keith looked so serious as he spoke that Lisa laughed. "You know you're really remarkable, Keith Brannon. Touring with you is like walking around with my own private encyclopedia. Is there anything about this country you don't know?"

"Lots." He grinned. "But I'm trying to make up for it by studying up on a place like crazy before I take you there."

"Keith, you don't!"

He winked disarmingly. "I'll never tell. Besides, I'd rather you kept the impression that I'm brilliant."

"You *are* brilliant." She laughed. "And you love this

land. It's obvious in every word you speak and in the way you look around with a kind of awe in your eyes. That's why you settled here, isn't it?"

"Yup. I came, I saw and I just couldn't leave."

Lisa sat thoughtfully for a minute, quietly sipping her tea. Although she tried to avoid discussing flying with him, she couldn't deny her natural curiosity to know everything she could about him. "I guess what I still wonder about," she said at last, "is why you decided to become a pilot instead of a farmer like your parents. It's quite a switch, you know."

It was Keith's turn to look thoughtful. "Yeah, I guess it is." He looked out at the grove of huge Japanese cedars, oaks and cypress trees which surrounded them. Other visitors were taking advantage of the many paths that wound through the trees and open meadows and alongside the still ponds that dotted the area. She and Keith had already met some of the tame deer, the "divine messengers," as the natives called them, which roamed the park freely. In the distance she heard the sharp trill of a bird, and almost immediately the answering call of its mate. Lisa waited patiently for Keith to go on. She knew intuitively that he was about to share something very special with her.

"As far back as I can remember I loved the farm," he told her. "Even though there was always plenty of hard work to be done, we made sure we had our fair share of fun." He looked wistful. "You know I think I might have been very content to stay a farmer if my dad hadn't taken my two brothers and me to the county fair when I was about eight. There was an air show that day, and I remember I finally pestered my dad into letting me go up in an old Beechcraft Twin-engine Bonanza that was taking people up for five dollars a head. As far as I was concerned, that was it." He looked at her with a sheepish grin. "Like someone else I know I fell in love at first flight."

"Touché." Lisa laughed. But she knew exactly how he must have felt. It was the same wild, wonderful feeling that she had experienced when Uncle Leonard took her for her first flight when she was ten. "So you took flying lessons?"

"No, we couldn't afford it." There was no bitterness in his tone that he'd had to wait while she'd been handed the opportunity on a silver platter. It was a simple statement of fact. "I consoled myself by learning everything I could about flying—reading whole sections out of the library, taking what few classes were offered in aerodynamics at school, even doing odd jobs around the airport. When it came time for college I guess I was a pretty big disappointment to my family. Instead of following my older brother to our local agricultural college, I managed to land a scholarship to Northwestern."

"And from there it was the Marines?"

Keith nodded. "I was planning to join even if 'Nam hadn't come along. It was obvious that the military provided the finest aeronautics education available. The war simply gave me some practical experience a little sooner than I'd planned."

"And introduced you to Japan."

"Yup. I guess I owe the Marines that one, too."

"And from being a 'leatherneck' you went on to start your own company."

Keith smiled. "I'm afraid it wasn't quite as simple as that. Before I started Brannon Aeronautics I worked for several other aircraft companies, learning the ropes, and trying to decide where I fit into the scheme of things." He drained his teacup, then reached for the pot to pour more tea for them both. "Building your own company is not a decision you make overnight."

Lisa remembered Uncle Leonard's stories of his own struggles. "I know," she said softly, thinking how very much alike the two men were. But the thought only brought home anew who she was with and how he might affect the man to whom she owed so much. She felt as if she were being tugged in opposite directions. She loved them both. Why must her loyalties constantly be divided?

"Where are we going after Nara Park?" she asked with false brightness, regretting now that she had ever broached the subject of Keith's past.

Keith looked at her over his tea, and she was sure that he had caught the subtle change in her mood. Yet he answered in kind, evidently deciding not to pry.

"After we see Nara Museum here in the park I thought we'd go to Tidaiju Temple to see the *Daibutsu,* or Great Buddha. The *Daibutsu* is the largest bronze statue in the world." He smiled. "What it may lack in reverence it more than makes up for in size."

They saw the museum, then the Great Buddha. While Lisa was duly impressed with the huge, 452-ton statue, the real highlight of the afternoon came when they visited the Shinto shrine of Kasuga, set in a peaceful grove of trees on the eastern edge of Nara Park. Keith carefully planned their entrance to the shrine, walking from Sanjo-dori through the park's two vermilion *torii* gates, so that they approached the shrine along the avenue of stone lanterns.

"People have been donating lanterns to the shrine for years," Keith explained. "By now the collection's reached more than three thousand. Twice a year the lanterns are lit, and believe me it makes a spectacle even Hollywood would be proud of."

As soon as they entered the shrine Lisa was struck by an intense feeling of sanctity and tranquility. But it was the peace she sensed in Keith that made the visit special. He seemed to relax here, as if the simplicity and cleanliness of the Shinto shrine had carried over to him, influencing his mood.

For a long time after they had explored the sanctuary they sat quietly on a bench overlooking one of the strangest trees Lisa had ever seen. Keith explained that it was a graft of wisteria, *nanten,* camellia, maple, cherry, *niwatoko* and *iso-no-ki.* Altogether a peculiar mixture which had somehow managed to blend into a unique whole. It was a peaceful place to be. And as Keith draped his arm intimately across her shoulders, Lisa leaned her head against him and sighed, content to enjoy these few precious moments without thought for what must follow.

"Happy?" Keith tipped his head to see into her face.

"Yes," she sighed. "Very happy." She looked at him. His half-smile clearly revealed the dimple in his left cheek, and Lisa gave in to the urge to trace it with her finger. Playfully, he caught her finger with his teeth.

"Mmm, I like that." He laughed, moving one hand to tilt up her chin. "And you know something else?" he went on. "I like *you,* too."

Then his lips were on hers, the touch light and caressing. With infinite tenderness, he stroked her hair, then let his mouth trail to the corner of each eye. "Did you know that your eyes are almost the same color as the sky? And I could just as easily get lost in their depths." His tone grew more mischievous. "In fact, I think I will. Later."

And he did. That night they made love on great soft *futons,* or quiltlike blankets, which were placed directly on the *tatami* floor-covering of their room. The peace and serenity of the Japanese *ryokan* inn where they were staying only seemed to add to the excitement and urgency of their lovemaking. Stifling their voices because of the thin, sliding walls of the *shoji*, Keith undressed her, then cupped her full, flawless breasts in his powerful hands. Taking one nipple into his mouth, he gently sucked and probed until it grew hard, then he did the same with the other one, teasing it until it, too, throbbed. Her skin tingled and burned as his fingers moved softly down her stomach, caressing and stroking a path of fire to her navel.

Lisa felt every inch of her body quiver beneath his marauding hands. The touch of his warm skin on hers, coupled with the faint smell of spice in this strangely erotic room, added to the frenzy of her desire. Eagerly she reached out for him, running her hands through the thick coils of his hair, her body moving against him in wild little circles as she became more and more aroused.

Gently he eased apart her legs, searching for the soft center of her femininity. Finding his goal, his fingers massaged and cajoled, probing the warm, moist depths until she writhed beneath him in a kind of painful ecstasy.

"Oh, my God! Keith!"

Lisa felt an electric current course through her loins as she realized that his fingers had been replaced by his mouth. Straining her hips upward, she groaned as the movements of his nimble tongue brought her to unknown heights of pleasure.

"Oh, Keith. I've never felt like this," she gasped.

Keith's voice was low and husky. "Relax, darling. Relax and enjoy."

She had to bite her lip to stop herself from crying out to him in her bliss. The entire lower part of her body seemed to come alive under the agile movements of his mouth. When it seemed that she could stand no more, when the smoldering fire between her legs threatened to explode, he deftly shifted positions, pulling her on top of him.

"It's your turn," he said hoarsely. "Make love to me, Lisa. Please."

Sensuously, she rose above him and his eyes were drawn to her firm, swollen breasts, peaking with the desire he had kindled. She looked down on him, entranced by his perfect physique, the broad expanse of his shoulders, his muscular chest and the iron-hard arms. Instinctively, she lowered herself to move against him, reveling in his sharp intake of breath as she slid along his body. She deliberately allowed the hard, rosy tips of her breasts to brush lightly against his naked chest as she moved downward. With the same tantalizing care he had used with her, she explored his navel, running her tongue around the crisp hairs and firm, hard skin of his stomach. When he twisted in frantic ecstasy beneath her, she moved even lower, using her tongue and teeth to nibble a string of tiny bites to the very edge of his swollen manhood.

"My God, Lisa," he groaned, twisting his hands in the long, luxurious flow of her thick hair. "Where did you learn to do that?"

Lisa's soft lips curled in a teasing smile, but she didn't answer. Instead, she continued her journey, letting her hands smooth and caress the sensitive skin of his lower abdomen and thighs until she felt his breath coming in excited little gasps. Her fingers lightly teased him, bringing his body to a fever pitch of excitement that only heightened her desire.

"Lisa, please," he moaned, the muscles of his lean

body knotting tautly. "I can't take any more of this. Come here."

Keith reached for Lisa's hips and skillfully lowered her onto him, exclaiming aloud as her soft flesh closed around the hard, pulsing spear of his desire. For a moment Lisa felt uncertain in this new position, then, as the rhythm of their bodies was established, the doubt was lost in a torment of rocketing sensations. Her body responded wildly, and she rode him with abandon. Keith's hands came up to stroke the full ripeness of her breasts, kneading them until she arched back in delicious agony. Gradually the rhythm of their bodies increased, building rapidly to a crescendo until Keith groaned and shifted positions so that he once again towered over her on the *futons*.

"My god, Hana-san," he breathed, his eyes ablaze with desire. "You make my blood boil like no woman I've ever known. How have I managed to go on so long without you?"

Lisa could not answer; she could hardly breathe. Her fingers dug into his back, pulling him down to her, desperate to have him inside her again.

Once more he entered her, and she arched to meet his urgent thrusts, eager to be swept with him to the quaking, incredible summit of their love. Spasms of fulfillment shook them both, and they shuddered in the violent, sweet explosion which seemed to rock the very foundation of their souls.

Then they lay limp in each other's arms, exhausted and sated. Tenderly, Keith cradled her, his lips brushing the soft line of her hair.

"Good night, Little Flower," he mumbled, his words already thick with sleep.

"Good night," Lisa answered. She cuddled closer,

her head burrowed into the crook of his arm. Only when the slow, even rise of his chest told her he was deeply asleep did she turn her head to whisper, "I love you."

Lisa smiled and closed her eyes, more content than she had ever been in her life. Slowly she drifted off to sleep, already reliving within the exquisite fabric of her dreams, the sweet experience of their lovemaking.

They returned to Kyoto the following afternoon. That evening Lisa was scheduled to dine with Onoe Fukai, manager of the city's Noh theater group, and Keith laughingly complained that he'd better get back to the office before his desk was buried beneath a ton of paperwork.

"What will you do with yourself tonight?" Lisa asked as he dropped her off at her hotel.

"Oh, I'll keep busy, don't worry," he replied lightly. "When you set up the date with Fukai I decided to take care of some unfinished business of my own tonight." He stopped the car in front of the hotel and brushed her lips with a kiss. "Just don't be too late getting back. I've got some very interesting after-hours entertainment planned for tonight."

Keith's promise stayed with Lisa throughout the afternoon, and she found herself humming happily as she showered and changed for her appointment with Fukai. She had already met the group's manager on two previous occasions, but tonight would be the first time that they would seriously discuss the Noh troop's possible visit to Evergreen.

"The Japanese are never to be rushed," Lisa told herself with a smile as she remembered her polite maneuvering with Fukai over the past few days. She pulled on a lightweight wool dress, cut simply and attractively in the palest shade of mint green, then brushed her hair back into the no-nonsense chignon so disparaged by Keith. Lisa had to laugh as she recalled Onoe Fukai's open admiration on the first two occasions they'd met. Given the handsome manager's obvious interest in her, she thought this might be one time Keith would approve of the severe style.

The small but handsome young Japanese picked her up promptly at seven, and after much bowing escorted her to one of Kyoto's more popular restaurants. Lisa knew the attractive restaurant well, having eaten there with Keith several times during her visit. She felt relaxed in the familiar surroundings and pleased that she was finally knowledgeable enough to order competently from the menu.

When the last of the dishes had been removed, they sat comfortably over their tea and discussed business, finally arriving at some definitive plans for pursuing future negotiations once Lisa returned to the States. It was well after nine before they rose to leave.

Lisa was feeling very satisfied as they left the restaurant. There remained only one or two minor details to be worked out with Hiruka Yakamoto, the Kabuki director, before the troop's trip was set, and already she had made splendid progress lining up possible groups to follow.

But the main reason for her tingle of expectation was Keith. In just a little while she would be with him. She remembered the "plans" he'd hinted at for the evening and flushed. For no apparent reason she beamed at a passing waiter and almost laughed at his startled expression. Good heavens, she thought as Fukai guided her smoothly around the tables. She felt like a school girl eagerly waiting for her first date!

They were making their way past a small corner room

off the main body of the restaurant when she saw them.
Her eye had been caught by an extremely handsome
couple closeted together toward the rear of the tiny
room. The woman was Japanese and beautiful, her
long, shiny black hair framing a vivaciously lovely face
and long, slender arms. Lisa's world reeled as she
recognized her. It was Yuki Matsuura, the striking
young woman whom she had met at the nightclub the
week before. With a terrible lurch of her heart she
recognized the man as well. He was sitting attentively
close, his dark, handsome head bent intimately toward
hers as they seemed to share a private joke. She caught
the glitter in his dark eyes as he raised his cup to the
young woman in a kind of salute. There was no
mistake. It was Keith!

She had seen all she could take. Turning her back on
the pair, Lisa hurried from the restaurant, then pleaded
a sudden headache and asked Onoe Fukai to take her
directly back to the hotel. Once there, she bid the Noh
manager a pleasant but firm good-night and finally
escaped into the impersonal refuge of her room.

Without caring where they landed, she threw her
purse and wrap onto the chair, then went to stand
dry-eyed and shocked in front of the window. Somewhere down there Keith was with another woman,
smiling at her, perhaps even embracing her with the
same warmth he had shown Lisa only that morning.
Her world had turned suddenly topsy-turvy; rational
thought was impossible. The only thing Lisa knew for
sure was that once again she had let a man make a fool
of her!

Lisa awoke early the next morning. From the faint
light peeking through the faded drapes she realized it
couldn't be long after dawn. She turned over sleepily,

vaguely aware that something was missing. Then, with a sinking heart she knew what it was. She was alone. Gone was the familiar warmth next to her, the strong, eager arms ready to close around her and waken her to the new day.

The previous night came back with a sickening jolt. About an hour after Fukai had brought her back to the hotel she'd heard the knock, and Lisa had braced herself for the moment she'd been dreading. It had been Keith, of course, coming to bring her back to his apartment for the night. What had he done with his Japanese girlfriend? she wondered, and found that the thought helped her resist his continued entreaties to open the door. What excuse had he given the girl when he left her to come here? Had he promised Yuki that in a few days she'd be his principal interest again? Did she love him enough to be patient?

Lisa had known that the DO NOT DISTURB message she'd left at the desk earlier would not be enough to stop him. He might not be able to get through to her on the phone, but if he were really determined, there was no way she could keep him from her door. So she had lain perfectly still in the dark room, hardly daring to breathe, trying to block out the voice she loved so dearly, even now, despite what he had done.

After what seemed an eternity he'd left, but for a long time Lisa had not been able to sleep. At last she allowed herself the luxury of tears, and the night seemed to stretch interminably as she examined the mistakes that had led her to this state.

Finally she admitted that no matter how badly she had handled things in the past it was the future that must be faced. And right now that loomed dark and exceedingly empty. In two days she would leave Kyoto; it would soon be over. But she would only be kidding herself if she thought the pain would stay behind when she left this "Land of the Gods." She knew that there could be no easy release from a man like Keith Brannon!

Lisa was out of her room by seven, anxious to be away from the hotel in case Keith should come back. She forced herself to eat toast and eggs at a nearby restaurant, then lingered over coffee trying to plan a course of action for the day. The most important thing was to keep busy. Her final appointment to see the Kabuki director was set for eleven o'clock the following morning. And last night marked the completion of her search for possible groups to follow the troop. So how could she fill the day? she wondered in desperation. Inaction would only give her more time to think. She had to do something, *anything*, to keep her mind occupied.

Of course she could always shop, she thought suddenly. It would be a shame to leave Kyoto without at least a few reminders of her stay. That was it, she decided abruptly. She'd go shopping. Darned if she'd sit around all day mooning over Keith Brannon. This was her last full day in Kyoto. She'd make the most of it!

Paying her bill, she set out purposefully for the crowded stores on Shijo-dori, one of Kyoto's main shopping centers. She bought several delicately hand-painted lacquerware bowls to bring home as gifts, then tried on a number of silk brocade dresses for herself. But as Lisa pulled on one dress after another she found that she was judging them on one factor alone—would Keith find them attractive? Angry with herself for permitting him to influence her choice, Lisa defiantly chose a beautifully cut royal blue brocade and tried it on. It fit her rounded curves like a glove, emphasizing the sensuous swell of her breasts and hips and the slender indentation of her waist. Leaving it on, Lisa gathered up her parcel and marched to the cash register, eager to pay for the dress before she changed her mind.

When she left the store she felt somewhat better. But after another half-hour of aimlessly wandering the streets, she had to admit that, as therapy, the morning was a failure. Try as she might she could not purge Keith from her thoughts. Everywhere she walked, each park and tree and temple reminded her of the wonderful days she had spent here with Keith. One moment she ached from missing him and the next she was consumed with anger and hurt that he had been so successful in deceiving her.

Inevitably, her fury turned back to herself. She had known about him from the beginning, she told herself ruthlessly; it had been a hopeless situation from the start. More than that, she'd had reason to know the terrible risk she was taking. There was only one person to blame for her incredible gullibility, for the empty, throbbing loneliness she felt now—herself! Damn it, she thought, blinking back a surge of fresh tears. Why couldn't this knowledge help heal the wound? Why did the prospect of spending the rest of her life without him seem so totally shattering?

The morning was well advanced when she realized that the streets had become unusually crowded and that there was an increased level of expectation in the air. In the distance she could hear the loud bang of firecrackers, and several nearby children were happily waving Japanese sparklers. Looking around, Lisa realized that she had strayed close to the grounds of the Imperial Palace and that the bustle of activity seemed to have its center there. She noticed that people were lining up on either side of the main street leading out from the palace. It was almost as if they were expecting a parade. Curious, she moved forward, joining the fringe of a group standing directly opposite the Imperial Park entrance.

Almost immediately she saw an ox-drawn chariot being pulled out of the park, accompanied by much noise and hundreds of gaily costumed attendants. The sight of all the men and women dressed in the costumes of Japan's old Imperial Court brought home what was happening. It was the celebration Etsu had been talking about several days ago at Miyume's Gion-machi tea ceremony. She was witnessing the start of Kyoto's ancient *Aoi Matsuri,* or Hollyhock Festival. Lisa remembered Etsu's polite request that she and Keith join him. Keith had accepted Etsu's invitation on behalf of them both. She shouldn't be here alone, she thought dismally. She and Keith should be watching the spectacle together!

The realization brought with it a fresh wave of pain, and Lisa followed the elaborate procession in a kind of daze. She knew from what Keith had told her that the festival dated back to the sixth century, a time when Kyoto was still the capital of Japan. Once each year the emperor and empress of Japan would leave the Imperial Palace to pay homage at two shrines in the city. The procession she was following now was a faithful recreation of their journey, and up ahead she could see men on horseback who represented the police of ancient Kyoto, and others on foot carrying the emperor's standards. The women in the parade, beautifully outfitted in authentic court costumes, either walked or rode along behind the chariot.

After what seemed miles of walking, but was actually

less than a dozen city blocks, the procession arrived at the first shrine, the Shimogamo Jinja. As the chariot pulled up before the shrine, Lisa moved closer for a better look at the sacred ceremony that would be performed there by the Shinto priest. She was so engrossed in the ritual that she started violently when a hand suddenly closed on her shoulder. She whirled around, and her heart jumped at the angry face that glared down at her.

"Well, well, look who we have here," said the low, mocking voice. "So you decided to come out of your lair after all." Keith's other hand reached out and cupped her chin, inching up her face until she had no choice but to look into those dark, menacing eyes.

His voice was little more than a whisper as he spoke to her over the crowd, but she had no difficulty hearing every curt, clipped word. "Now would you be kind enough to tell me what in hell is going on?"

Chapter Twelve

*L*isa winced at the pain in her arms. His hands had tightened until she felt as if she were being held in a vise.

"Keith, you're hurting me," she gasped.

Immediately his grip loosened, but not enough to allow her to escape. "I should throttle you for what you've put me through since last night," he spat. "What in the world's come over you, Lisa? You were in your room last night. Why didn't you open the door when I knocked?"

"I . . . I was asleep," she stammered, unwilling to tell him the truth. Never had she seen him look so furious, so out of control.

"Like hell you were!" His eyes blazed into hers, and she could see a small nerve pulsating in his temple. She felt herself tremble beneath his scrutiny. But this was not the time to discuss their differences, and certainly not the place. Glancing behind Keith, Lisa was surprised to see Miyume, the lovely *geisha's* face revealing her embarrassment at their confrontation. With typical

Japanese respect for privacy, the young woman seemed to be looking right through them as she watched the *Aoi* ritual, which was being enacted on the steps of the shrine.

"Well?" His impatience showed as he once again increased the pressure on her arms.

"Not here," she whispered, nodding her head toward Miyume. "We can talk later."

He hesitated for a long moment, searching her face. "All right," he said at last. "But no games, Lisa. Understand? I want to know what's going on."

"Yes," she agreed. "I understand." Her initial shock at seeing him had given way to anger at his brazen attitude. "I understand only too well."

His eyes swept her suspiciously. "What's that supposed to mean?"

"Only that I'm through playing games, too, Keith. I'm as anxious as you are to settle matters between us."

The ceremony at the Shimogamo Jinga went on for another two hours. During that time Miyume patiently explained the significance of this or that rite, although it must have been painfully clear that neither of her companions was paying more than perfunctory attention. At two o'clock, the procession recommenced, this time heading in the direction of the Kamigamo Jinja where the second ritual would be performed.

Although Lisa would have preferred to return to her hotel, she was drawn along by the ironlike hand on the small of her back. Keith was not letting her out of his sight. And without creating a scene there was little she could do to get away.

The service at the Kamigamo Jinja was much like the first, although possibly more enthusiastic. The sound of fireworks was louder now, and Lisa realized that, at least on the outskirts of the crowd, the celebration was growing more raucous.

It was late afternoon before the cortege finally started back for the Imperial Palace. The throng seemed to move more slowly now, as if they were determined to draw out the festivities for as long as possible. It was only as they started to follow the plodding progress of the chariot that Lisa thought to question Etsu's absence.

"He had to spend the day reducing the data from the Comet's wind tunnel tests," Keith explained shortly. "We got the test results from Kobe Aerospace yesterday, and since they're due in Tokyo tomorrow, the work had to be done today. He's supposed to meet us back at the palace."

But there was no sign of Etsu when they returned to the Imperial Park. As soon as Keith discovered that his manager was not waiting at their prearranged meeting place, the three combed the thinning crowd in a futile effort to find him.

"Perhaps he is still working at the plant," Miyume ventured shyly, obviously concerned over Etsu's absence.

Keith nodded, seeming to find no better explanation. "He must be. Although the job shouldn't have taken this long. That is, unless he ran into some problems."

Miyume bowed low to the others. "You will excuse me, please," she said softly. "But I must go to the plant now. If Etsu-san is there, I will find him."

Keith answered by taking both women by the arm. "We'll all go, Miyume," he said. "If Etsu's still poring over those test results, we'll rout him out."

Keith's car was parked several blocks from the palace. Settling Miyume in the back, he helped Lisa into the seat next to him. The ride was slow, for people continued to mill about the town, still consumed by the holiday spirit. As they drove, Lisa saw fireworks displays burst brilliantly into the air before they fell, lifeless and spent, back to the earth. They passed several groups of children, primarily boys, shooting off firecrackers or small rocket displays of their own.

Not knowing where Brannon Aeronautics was located, Lisa watched as they passed slowly through the main part of town and into an unfamiliar outlying area.

"It's just a few blocks now," Keith told them, turning a corner. He stiffened as a low, dark column of smoke curled into view a short distance ahead. She heard Miyume's surprised gasp and knew that the *geisha* had spotted the black cloud as well.

"It is very close to the plant." The young woman was leaning forward in her seat, her face directly over Lisa's right shoulder.

"Too close," Keith replied tersely. Lisa looked at him sharply. His lean face was tense.

Fear clutched Lisa's heart. "Keith! You don't think it's Brannon Aeronautics, do you?"

Keith didn't turn his head. She could see that his whole attention was focused on the gathering crowd ahead. "I don't know. But wherever it is, it means trouble. Once a fire gets started around here it can level an entire block in a matter of minutes!"

The shrill oscillating sound of a Japanese siren pierced the car. Lisa held her breath for a moment listening to the high then low *pee-po, pee-po* sound. The trucks were coming closer.

"Damn!" Keith brought the Maserati to an abrupt halt at the curb. "There's no sense trying to drive any further," he told them brusquely. "You two wait here.

I'll be back as soon as I know what's going on up there."

Then he was gone. Lisa lost sight of him as he jogged quickly around the next corner to the left. The sound of several more sirens had joined the first, forming a frightening din that chilled Lisa's blood.

She turned to Miyume. "How far ahead is the plant?"

The look of alarm on the *geisha's* artificially whitened face was clear even in the fading light. "It is only three, perhaps four blocks from here." She pointed a perfectly manicured finger to the left. "It is around that corner—where Keith-san ran."

Lisa followed Miyume's finger and saw several more people dashing in the direction Keith had taken. Over her shoulder she could see that a much greater number had been attracted by the sirens and were rushing toward the scene from the rear. Sounds of the firetrucks were much louder now, as if they were converging only a few blocks away.

"The fire can't be very far from here," Lisa said, more to herself than to the woman with her. "And I don't like the idea of waiting helplessly in the car."

"No, it is very bad that we do not know what is happening." The young *geisha's* worry transmitted itself to Lisa. If the fire were at Keith's plant and Etsu were still inside . . . She would not let her thoughts go any farther. It was time for action, not speculation!

"Come on, Miyume," she said abruptly. "Nothing's worse than just sitting here worrying!"

The *geisha* needed no further persuasion. She allowed Lisa to help her out of the back seat, and the two women conscientiously locked both doors of the car then hurried toward the corner, moving as quickly as the narrow hem on Miyume's brightly printed kimono would allow. As soon as they turned to the left they could see the fire. Two blocks ahead, on the right-hand side of the street, a large office building was ablaze. Several fire engines were parked in a half-circle in front of the burning building, while firemen rushed about pointing gushing hoses at the flames. The size of the crowd watching the blaze grew even as they hurried closer, and a small group of policemen was working hard to hold the gawkers behind a cordoned-off area.

Lisa felt a terrible lump in her throat as she watched the men battle the spreading blaze. She reached out and took the *geisha's* arm, raising her voice to be heard above all the noise.

"Miyume, is that . . ."

The *geisha* nodded her lovely head miserably. *"Hai,* Hana-san. It is Keith-san's plant." Lisa watched as the young woman's almond-shaped eyes filled with tears. "What if Etsu . . . ?" The sentence remained unfinished. Placing a small, dainty hand over her mouth, she looked at Lisa with mute appeal, her dark eyes horror-struck at the possibility she dared not verbalize. Instinctively, Lisa reached out to comfort her.

"I'm sure he's safe, Miyume," she said, praying desperately that she was right. "They must have gotten everyone out."

But privately Lisa admitted her darkest fears. Searching the crowd anxiously, she could see no sign of Keith's tall, powerful body towering over the much shorter Japanese. What if Etsu *had* still been inside when the fire started? If Keith went in there to find him . . . She looked back at the building, mesmerized by the flames shooting out of a good number of the windows. My God! she thought with a fresh rush of terror. What if both men were still inside that inferno? What if Keith and Etsu were trapped?

Lisa was suddenly driven by one impelling need. She had to find Keith. Telling the *geisha* to wait, she made her way through the crowd, elbowing when necessary, not caring in her anxiety whom she pushed out of the way. At last she reached the front of the barrier, face ashen, heart thumping wildly as she tried to get someone's attention. Calling out loudly to one of the policemen, Lisa tried desperately to communicate to him that two men might still be in the blazing building. In vain she exhausted her meager knowledge of Japanese only to watch him shake his head in confusion.

"Wakari-masen. Wakari-masen," he repeated impatiently. Then, as he was bumped from behind by a fireman repositioning a hose, he dismissed her with an abrupt wave of his hand. *"Atchi ni itte kudasai! Watakushi waima isogashii desu ka!"*

Lisa almost cried as he moved away to try to control the crowd, her panic mounting. *Please God let him be safe,* she prayed with all her heart. *Let them both be safe!*

Looking around, Lisa saw that the policeman was occupied now with an unruly bunch of youngsters trying to push closer to the firetrucks. Jumping at the chance, she stooped and slipped under the rope used to keep back the crowd. She ran to the closest fireman.

"There may be two men in there," she shouted, pointing toward the burning building. "You've got to send someone in to look for them. Please!"

The fireman's face was flushed from the heat and smudged with soot. *"Do nasai mashita ka?"* He spread his hands in a gesture of helplessness and added haltingly, "No talk English."

Lisa was almost in tears. "Then please find someone who does!" She jumped as a large section of the upstairs wall fell to the ground with a crash. *"Please!"* she screamed. "Two men may be trapped in there! You've got to find them!"

"Wakari-masen." The man shook his head and started to move away. *"Watakushi waima isogashii desu."* He pointed toward the building. *"Kaji."*

Through her frustration and tears, Lisa recognized the man's last word. "Yes," she yelled at him, reaching out to hold onto the sleeve of his coat so he couldn't move away. "I know there's a fire. That's just it. There may be two men trapped in the fire." Lisa fought to be calm, to rein in her panic. She had to keep her head; Keith's life might depend upon it. Desperately she held up two fingers. "Two men," she enunciated slowly. "Two men in there, in *kaji*. You have to do something before it's too late!"

The fireman shook his head and pulled out of Lisa's grasp. *"Watakushi waima isogashii desu,"* he repeated motioning to the building. *"Kaji!"*

"Oh, God! *Please!*" she cried. "Please make someone understand me!"

In her panic, Lisa searched the crowd for someone who might speak English. For the first time since her arrival in Japan she felt terribly alone and helpless. During most of her stay in Kyoto, Keith had provided the key to all the strange doors she would have had to face on her own. And now she could do nothing to help him. Why had she told Miyume to wait so far back in the crowd? Right now she would give anything to see a friendly *English-speaking* face!

Lisa was so distraught that it took a moment before she realized that several members of the press had

managed to sneak under the heavy rope which cor-
doned off the fire area. Unobtrusively, they were
attempting to interview some of the police and firemen.
Her eyes were drawn to the solitary woman in the
group, a young, slim girl with long flowing black hair
reaching nearly to her waist. Even though the girl's
back was toward her, she seemed vaguely familiar. Lisa
watched the way the young woman moved—her ges-
tures quick and sure, yet graceful—she was sure she
had seen her before. Then the woman turned, and Lisa
felt a shock of recognition. It was Yuki Matsuura,
Keith's friend from the nightclub, the girl who had
chilled Lisa's heart at the restaurant the night before.
What was she doing here? Why had she come in with
the reporters?

A few seconds later Lisa realized that the young
woman was a legitimate member of the press team.
Yuki had pulled out a note pad and pencil and was
questioning one of the policemen guarding the crowd.
With none of Lisa's language difficulties, she was
obviously getting the story she was after. Lisa seized
the opportunity. Running over to the woman she cried,

"Yuki, it's me, Lisa Howard. You've got to help me.
Keith and another man may be trapped in the fire.
We've got to get someone to go in and look for them
before it's too late!"

Startled, the girl looked at her for a moment before
her face lit with recognition. "You are Keith's friend!"
With the realization came a flash of alarm. "And you
think he may be inside?"

At Lisa's frantic nod the girl sprang into action.
Ignoring the policeman she had been questioning, Yuki
hurried over to a man who seemed to be directing the
fire-fighting operation. She spoke to him in rapid

Japanese, gesturing toward Lisa, then pointing at the burning building. The fireman glanced briefly at the American, as if trying to make up his mind, then turned to two of his men and issued crisp orders. Immediately, the firemen started for the building and disappeared inside. In Lisa's near hysterical state it seemed the men were gone forever, although a more rational voice told her it had been mere minutes since they'd entered the burning building. When she thought she could stand no more of the agonizing suspense, she caught a faint movement inside the doorway. Eyes stinging from smoke and tears, she strained to catch a better look. Yes, something was moving. Her heart nearly stopped beating as she watched a lone figure emerge through the dense curtain of smoke and flames.

For a moment Lisa thought she was seeing an illusion. Then the figure moved again, struggling slowly out into the open beneath the limp burden it carried slung over one broad shoulder. Behind the man she could see the two firemen now, guiding the tall figure as he made his way through the maze of firefighters and their paraphernalia. Lisa's heart leapt with joy, and tears of relief flowed unchecked down her cheeks. It *was* Keith! And now she could see that the smaller form he carried, arms and head dangling to the rear, was Etsu. Somehow Keith had found the other man. Even more miraculously, he had made his way through the fire and smoke to bring him out. Thank God! Thank God, they were safe!

It was almost midnight when they finally left for Keith's apartment. It had not taken the hospital's emergency room staff long to dress Keith's few superficial burns, but he and Lisa had remained with Miyume until there was definite word on Etsu's condition. The general manager had sustained both first and second degree burns on parts of his hands and arms, but it was the severe smoke inhalation that he had suffered which had the doctors worried. An hour ago they had finally pronounced the young Japanese out of danger, although he would be kept in the hospital overnight so that he could be observed for possible complications, including pneumonia. Reluctantly, Miyume had been persuaded to leave for the night, and Keith had taken the *geisha* back to the Gion-machi before turning the Maserati toward home.

"For heaven's sake, why didn't Etsu get out of the building sooner?" Lisa asked, free, now that Miyume was gone, to voice the questions which had bothered her all evening. "Did he tell you anything when you spoke to him?"

Before leaving the hospital, Keith had asked to be alone with his manager. He had come out of the room smiling, but highly secretive.

"When the fire started—which, incidentally, they now know was caused by some careless fireworks in the neighborhood—Etsu's first thoughts were to put it out. Of course that's how he got all those burns on his hands and arms. When he finally realized he was getting nowhere, he called the fire department and then tried to save as many company files as possible before leaving. In a matter of minutes he was overcome by smoke and so disoriented that he couldn't find his way out."

"My God, Keith," Lisa exclaimed. "You mean Etsu risked his life to save a few documents?"

"That's just what he did." He grinned at her in the darkness. "Don't worry, I've already given him a piece of my mind on that score. Of course it was pretty hard to stay angry with him when one of the files he managed to salvage was the reduced data on the Comet's wind tunnel results. Without those we wouldn't have had a prayer of getting the Fugi business." His face lit with mischief. "I think a pretty healthy reward is called for in a case like this, don't you, Little Flower? Say one substantial enough to buy off a certain young lady's contract?"

"Keith! Do you mean it? But that's wonderful. Have you told him yet?"

"I did." Even in the dim light Lisa could see that Keith's eyes were sparkling. "Of course I'll have to admit to an ulterior motive. I can't have my general manager lallygagging around in a hospital when there's important work to be done. Knowing that he and Miyume have a future to be planned should get him out of there in pretty short order."

"I couldn't be happier for them, Keith," she said with sincerity. "Etsu and Miyume deserve to be together, and I think it's wonderful that you're making it possible for them. But what you did, what *both* of you did, was so dangerous!" She felt a sudden chill run the length of her spine. "If you hadn't gone in for him, Etsu might not have gotten out at all!"

Keith's hand moved to her thigh, giving it a reassuring squeeze. "And if you hadn't sent in the rescue squad, I doubt that I'd be sitting here right now talking to you. There was so damn much smoke in there I couldn't see two inches in front of my face. I'll tell you those two firemen were a mighty welcome sight!"

"Thank God they found you in time! I've never been so worried in all my life."

"I'm glad to hear that." He laughed irreverently.

Over Lisa's sputter of protest he continued, "After last night I wasn't sure what was wrong with you. Looks like a little worry turned out to be a good thing."

"Why you . . . you self-centered, conceited . . ."

"Male?" Keith filled in for her. "Guilty as charged. I'll admit you've delivered a pretty mean blow to my male ego during the past twenty-four hours." His voice grew serious. "Maybe I was taking us for granted, but I thought we had progressed to the stage where we could be honest about our feelings . . . work out our differences together. What happened, Hana-san? What went wrong?"

His attitude was not what she expected. Still wary, she knew that she had to set matters straight. "Wait, Keith. Before we get into that there's something I have to know." She searched for the right words. "That friend of yours, the woman I met in the nightclub last week . . ."

"Yuki?" Keith sounded surprised. "What does she have to do with this?"

"Keith, please, let me finish." Lisa was finding it difficult to put her thoughts into words. "Yuki was at the fire tonight. Evidently she was covering it for her newspaper. I guess you didn't see her because they hustled you and Etsu off in the ambulance so fast. Before Miyume and I left to follow in your car, Yuki gave me a message for you. She sends her love and says she's not surprised you turned out to be a hero."

Lisa watched him closely as he drove through the quiet Kyoto streets, waiting for his reaction. She heard him chuckle softly. "So she thinks I'm a hero, huh? I'm sorry I didn't see her. She's one neat lady. Not only that, she's one hell of a reporter. That young woman has a real future in journalism."

Lisa waited for him to continue. When he didn't, she pressed. "Is that all? I mean, you never told me she was a reporter."

"Hey, come on, you make it sound as if I were deliberately misleading you. Frankly, I just didn't think to mention Yuki's job when I introduced you two the other night." He grinned meaningfully, rubbing his hand lightly along her leg. "As I recall, I had other things on my mind at the time."

Lisa couldn't stand the suspense any longer. Without any preamble she blurted out, "Keith, just how much does Yuki Matsuura mean to you?"

Taken aback by the question, Keith withdrew his hand from Lisa's lap. "That's a damn funny thing to ask. But if you really want to know, Yuki is a very good friend of mine. In the past two years she's been the only member of the so-called objective press who has written a halfway honest story about me. I don't think it's an exaggeration to say that since Brannon Aeronautics has come into its own, I've been maligned, misrepresented, misquoted and generally mistreated by nearly every reporter who considers a wealthy, eligible bachelor fair game. I realize that success brings a certain amount of notoriety, but I still hold to the notion that at least *some* of the stories written about me should be true. Fortunately, Yuki subscribes to the same notion. So now when I want the world to see my side of a story, I give Yuki an exclusive interview."

"And that's what you were doing last night in the restaurant—giving Yuki an interview?"

Keith looked surprised. "How did *you* know I had dinner with Yuki last night?"

Lisa dropped her head, grateful that the night was too dark for Keith to see her flush of embarrassment.

"Onoe Fukai and I had dinner at the same restaurant," she admitted softly. "I saw you."

"And immediately leapt to the conclusion that she and I had some sort of secret assignation. No wonder you wouldn't answer your door last night. Lisa, do you have so little faith in me? Did you really think I'd run straight from our bed into another woman's arms? Don't tell me you're going to be the kind of wife who turns green every time her husband so much as looks at another woman."

"Wife?" It took a moment for the word to register. "Keith, are you saying what I think you are?"

"If you mean do I want to marry you, yes. Actually, it's the only sane solution. When you're not around I can't work, I can't sleep, damn it, Lisa, I can't even think straight! I thought I'd lose my mind last night when you wouldn't open that door for me. I guess it's a matter of getting married or living the rest of my life as a zombie. Frankly, I prefer getting married."

Keith pulled the Maserati into the garage beneath his apartment complex. Turning off the ignition, he slipped an arm around her shoulder and pulled her into his arms.

"Lisa Howard, you have ruthlessly and shamelessly cast a spell over me. As of this moment I'm officially acknowledging my surrender." Tenderly, he kissed the tip of her nose, then went on softly, "I'm totally, madly and deliciously in love with you, Little Flower. Now, what are we going to do about it?"

Their lovemaking that night possessed a new, almost magical quality, a sublimity that had not been present before. Sensitive to Keith's burns, Lisa took the initiative, first pulling off his jacket, then unfastening the buttons of his shirt. She didn't hurry, her movements were slow and deliberate, calculated to arouse him. Gently she eased the shirt off his shoulders, then let it fall lightly onto the floor.

When he stood before her naked from the waist up, Lisa paused for a moment, running her fingers over the solid, compact expanse of his bare chest and down the long, corded length of his arms. She could feel his firm muscles tense as she leaned forward to run her tongue lightly around his nipples, delighting in the crisp, curling hair that tickled her upper lip. Teasing him now as he had tormented her so many times before, she took one of his nipples gently between her teeth and tugged on it lightly until it grew hard and taut in her mouth. She heard the deep groan in his chest as she moved to the other nipple, rolling it between her lips until it grew firm and eager like the first.

"Lisa." The word was a soft whisper in her hair and she hurried to assuage the need which she could feel growing even through the barrier of his remaining clothes.

Working more quickly now, Lisa removed Keith's shoes, then released the snap on his trousers and pulled down the zipper. She lowered his pants until he stood clad only in the tight-fitting cotton of his white bikini briefs. Then those, too, disappeared, and she stood very still, frankly admiring the clean lines of his perfectly formed torso.

"Did you know you're quite a hunk, Keith Brannon?" Lisa teased, her hands roaming slowly over his lean, hard body.

"And did you know you're driving me crazy, Lisa Howard?" Lisa looked up to find his forehead damp with perspiration. His dark eyes were fastened on her with a kind of mute appeal, and she felt a heady sense of power.

"I certainly hope so," she murmured. "It's only fair after what you've put me through over the past two weeks. Now hold still, I'm not through with you yet."

Obediently, Keith allowed her to finish her journey of discovery, her hands moving seductively over every inch of his body. Only when her own desires threatened to get out of control, did she stop, lowering him gently to the bed so that he could watch her own, deliberately erotic striptease.

She slowly unfastened the buttons of her shirt, then casually threw it across the room. Next she undid the zipper of her skirt and slowly slithered out of it to stand before him clad only in lacy bra and panties. Keith moved convulsively on the bed, and Lisa could see the muscles of his arms contracting and she knew he ached to reach out for her. She smiled sensuously, the knowledge of her effect on him acting as a stimulus as she continued to undress. She raised her arms gracefully, and slowly lowered the thin straps of her brassiere. Hugging herself tightly, she peered at him seductively through thick lashes before reaching behind her back to undo the hook of her bra. She allowed the scrap of black lace to fall slowly forward, letting him glimpse only one tantalizing inch of creamy breast at a time until Keith's breath was coming in short, ragged gasps.

"Lisa . . ." Only his lips formed her name. There was no sound as he stared at the perfect curves that were completely revealed now to his eager eyes.

Her hands dropped to run lightly inside the elastic band of her tiny bikini briefs. Keith gaped at the swell of her hips as she slowly lowered the panties and let them trail easily to the carpet. Totally naked now, Lisa smiled like a contented kitten, then raised her arms high above her head, full breasts thrust forward, hips slowly revolving as she stretched sensuously before him.

Gradually, she lowered herself to the bed, eyes never leaving his face as she spread her long legs to straddle his body. With endless forebearance she claimed his lips, teasing them in a long, lingering kiss which left both of them trembling and breathless. Before he could recapture the embrace, Lisa slid further down his body, allowing the firm tips of her breasts to skim his chest as she moved. He swallowed hard as she ran a string of kisses down to his navel, and she could feel his body tremble as she ran her warm tongue ever closer to his hard thighs.

"God, Lisa, have pity. I can't stand much more of this!"

Still she didn't stop. Weaving her fingers with a feather-light touch over his abdomen, she showered him with tiny kisses until, with a loud groan, he buried his hands in the thick silk of her hair.

"Enough! Good God, that's enough!"

Grabbing Lisa's waist, he pulled her roughly down beside him, then twisted until he towered above her, his face damp and flushed with desire.

"You ignite my body like no woman I've ever known," he gasped. "Now help me put out the flames!"

He entered her swiftly, and then their bodies were moving together in unison, in a beautifully choreographed dance of two perfectly tuned beings.

Higher and higher they soared, Lisa's hands kneading, pressing, scratching deliriously as Keith carried them to the zenith. For one long moment they hung suspended, then they found the ultimate release, and, shuddering together, they subsided into the final, wonderful throes of fulfillment. At last they were still, too spent to move, too much in awe of what had passed between them to speak. Lisa lay content in Keith's arms, his lips buried in her golden hair.

"I meant what I said, you know," he told her at last, stroking her hair away from her smooth, damp forehead. "No woman has ever affected me the way you do. Just the sight of you is enough to start my heart pounding." He touched her cheek gently with his lips and whispered, "I love you very much, Little Flower."

Lisa's heart melted, his words the perfect music she had thought never to hear. "And I love you, darling." She brushed away tears which had surprised her.

Keith sat up in concern. "Hey, why the tears?"

"Because I'm so happy," she told him, choking up again at the distressed look on his handsome face. "It's all right, darling, really. I guess I just didn't know it was possible to love another human being like this. It takes some getting used to."

Keith's teeth nipped at her sensitive earlobes. "Good. I hope it takes a whole lifetime of getting used to, because that's how long we'll be giving it."

Lisa settled into his arms and sighed, content to feel his hard body next to hers, happy to let the gentle cloak of sleep enfold her weary body. Keith loved her and she returned that love with all her heart. At last she had found happiness beyond her wildest dreams.

Why then, did a heavy hand seem to close over her heart as she drifted into sleep? Shivering slightly, Lisa moved closer to Keith's warmth and wearily tried to analyze the vague sense of unease. But she was too tired to think.

And then it was too late. Safe in Keith's arms, Lisa was soon asleep. And if some of her dreams that night were troubled, she would not remember in the morning.

Chapter Thirteen

"But Keith, it's too dangerous to fly to Tokyo this morning! You admitted yourself that the ceiling is 300 feet and coming down."

Keith continued to dress, calmly ignoring Lisa's comments from the bed. "Which simply makes it more of a challenge." He tucked in his shirt and walked over to where she lay with the edge of the sheet pulled modestly up over her naked breasts. "Did anyone ever tell you that you look particularly delectable first thing in the morning?"

"No, and don't think you can change the subject with flattery. In case you've forgotten, Keith Brannon, I happen to be a pilot too. I know how dangerous it is to fly when you can barely see half a mile ahead of you."

"How can I possibly forget when you keep reminding me of it every two minutes?" He sat down beside her on the bed and took her hand, running the side of his thumb gently over the palm. "Listen, darling, I know you're worried, but there's no need to be, honest. I really can't afford to wait around in the hope that the ceiling might lift. On this island that could take hours, even longer. Etsu risked his life to save those test results; I can't blow it now. If that data doesn't reach Fugi International before noon today, we're out of the running."

Lisa felt hot tears stinging the corners of her eyes. Resolutely she blinked, determined not to let him see her cry. "And are those papers more important than your life?"

"No, but they could be very important to our future. We need this contract, honey. I don't intend to lose it because of a low fog bank." He kissed her lightly on the cheek, then let his lips drift to her mouth where they lingered in a long, tender caress. For a moment Lisa held back, then with a little moan she answered his kiss with all the love and fear that was in her heart. Her arms reached out to clutch him, holding him as if this might keep him with her forever. With a deep chuckle, Keith pulled away.

"Keep your lustful hands off me, woman," he said, grinning, "or I'll never get out of here."

"Would that be so bad?"

"Hmmm. I don't know." Keith's eyes seemed to strip her body of the clinging sheet. "No, damn it, woman, I will not be led astray. Business before pleasure is the order of the day. But tonight . . ."

He leaned over and gave her one more quick kiss. "You're scheduled to finish up your business with Yakamoto today, aren't you?"

Lisa nodded mutely.

"Good. You wrap things up and when I get back from Tokyo later this afternoon we can celebrate." He gave her a cheerful wink. "Okay?"

Numbly, Lisa fought back her tears. "Keith. Don't

go." The words came out as a whisper, but the intensity behind them struck Keith like a physical blow.

"Honey, I have to. I'll be all right, I promise. Now you go ahead with your day and leave mine to me."

"There's nothing I can say to change your mind?"

"Not a thing. Come on, Lisa, you're just tired." He grinned. "It must be all that exercise we got last night. You'll feel better after you have some breakfast." He blew her a kiss from the doorway. "See you this afternoon, honey."

But Lisa didn't feel better after breakfast. Even a vigorous shower couldn't shake her apprehension that Keith was placing himself in a very dangerous situation. He was risking his life and everything the future might hold for them for the sake of a single business deal. Why was he being so stubborn? And why couldn't she shake this cold, clammy fear which was worse than anything she had ever experienced in her years with Jeff?

Lisa kept her ten o'clock appointment with Hiruka Yakamoto, but the knot in her stomach persisted as he signed the final papers and approved the itinerary the Kabuki troop would follow during their tour. They completed their business well before noon and parted amicably, both assuring the other how much they looked forward to the exchange.

On the way home she discovered that the gnawing in her stomach had become painful and regretted that she had ignored Keith's advice and eaten so little breakfast. Stopping at a little coffee shop near Yakamoto's office, Lisa tried to remedy the situation by ordering a substantial lunch, then ended up picking at it. She pushed aside the unfinished meal and sipped her tea, watching the clearing skies outside the window.

Was it going to be like this every time Keith took off on a flight she disapproved of? Would he continue to put business before his own safety even after they were married? And if his flight to Tokyo this morning frightened her, what in heaven's name would she do when he went out on an even riskier flight to test an unproven plane?

Last night they had been swept away by passion. It had been easy not to reason, to live only for the moment. Today she could no longer ignore the harsher realities of their situation. Keith was a test pilot, like Jeff; his job put him in constant danger. Could she live with that again? Did she even want to try?

Lisa knew that she had to do some thinking. Quickly she paid her bill and hailed a taxi for the hotel. Even in her confusion she knew that she could never work out her problems logically as long as she was with Keith. In his presence all resistance melted; she was willing to stay with him at any price. She had to get away from Kyoto and all the bittersweet memories it held for her; she had to be where she could work matters out in her mind without interference from her heart.

Two hours later Lisa was on a flight from Itami Airport to Tokyo. Having phoned ahead, she looked eagerly for Uncle Leonard's face when she landed. Then she saw him, smiling at her as she walked down the long enclosed ramp and into the airport building. Her initial joy at seeing him, though, turned quickly to alarm when she noticed how pale and drawn he had become.

"You've been working too hard again, haven't you?" she accused, searching his thin face. "You promised you'd slow down."

Leonard Mason smiled wanly. "Unfortunately, some

promises are more difficult to keep than others. I hope that after this Fugi business I'll be able to take things a little easier."

Lisa was not surprised that her uncle had taken a taxi to the airport; she knew he studiously avoided driving in Tokyo whenever possible. And, climbing into the waiting cab, she thought that this suited her purposes much better anyway. If Uncle Leonard were not preoccupied with driving, she could carry on a quiet conversation with him on their way into town.

"You finished your business okay?" Mason asked as they left the airport complex.

"Yes. It went very well as a matter of fact. And I take it you got the new test data to Fugi on time this morning?"

"I hand-delivered it yesterday afternoon," he said proudly. "I wasn't taking any chances on being late. This contract's too important."

Again, Lisa felt caught between the two men. Just this morning Keith had told her how much the Fugi business meant to Brannon Aeronautics. But only one of them could win the contract. And either way part of her would lose.

"Uncle Leonard . . ." Lisa straightened her skirt, suddenly nervous about what she had to say. "Uncle Leonard, I've met someone."

"Keith Brannon," her uncle said without hesitation. Startled, Lisa turned to find him smiling at her. "No, I haven't become a mind reader. Brannon came to see me this morning about the Fugi affair. He mentioned that you and he had become good friends. *Very* good friends. It seems the young man has marriage in mind."

"Yes," Lisa murmured uncomfortably. "That's what he told me last night."

"Well, I must say you don't look too excited about it.

Does that mean you don't return the young man's affection?"

"Oh, I return it, all right. That's part of the problem. I return it too well."

Leonard Mason chuckled softly. "I hope you don't mind putting that in terms an old man can understand. I know I'm from a different generation, but I didn't think things had changed *that* much over the years."

"Oh, Uncle Leonard, it's Jeff all over again. There are some things . . . some things about my marriage to Jeff that I never told you. We weren't, at least *I* wasn't, very happy."

Mason's voice was gentle; his kindly eyes rested on Lisa with compassion. "I know that, honey. Long before Jeff's death I knew something was wrong between you two."

"But why didn't you say something?"

"I didn't want to interfere. I was always there, honey. Any time you needed me you had only to ask."

Lisa gave him a quick kiss. "I know, Uncle Leonard. You've always been there. I . . . I just didn't want to involve you in my problems. I had to work them out for myself."

"And you did. Very capably, too."

"But, you see, that's part of it, part of the reason I'm here, I mean. I love Keith. I never thought it possible to love anyone that much. But I'm terrified of making the same mistake all over again."

"You mean because Keith is a pilot, don't you? Honey, are you afraid that Keith Brannon will treat you as shabbily as Jeff did?"

"No, of course not." Lisa hurried to explain. "Keith could never be like Jeff. It's the constant worry that goes with the job I'm afraid of: the sleepless nights, the terror whenever the phone rings unexpectedly and he's out on a flight. I don't know if I could take the fear of wondering if this will be the day he doesn't come home." Lisa's eyes brimmed with tears. "Uncle Leonard, I love him too much for that. If it was bad with Jeff, it would be a nightmare with Keith!"

Mason put his arms around her, patting her head as he had when she was a child. "It's okay, honey. Your fears are perfectly natural. What you have to do is put the problem in a little different perspective, that's all."

"I . . . I don't know what you mean."

"Of course you don't. You're too close to the trees to see the forest. But it's all there. You have only to rearrange things a bit."

Lisa smiled at him through her tears. "You always make things seem so simple."

He patted her hand. "Isn't that what uncles are for? Come on now, let's think about this problem of yours for a minute. First of all, you're assuming that Keith is going to take the same reckless chances that Jeff took. Yet you just finished telling me that they're two very different people. Not all test pilots have a neurotic need to prove themselves, honey. Believe me, a really top-notch pilot puts the safety of his passengers, his machine and himself above heroics. And we all know that Keith Brannon is one of the best."

"I know that, Uncle Leonard, but it's such a risk. I'm so afraid to lose him."

"*Life* is a risk, Lisa. The first step in any commitment is to be willing to take a risk. I did it when I started my company—even when this craggy old bachelor took in a lonely, confused little girl. You'll have to do it too if you hope to form any kind of meaningful relationship. It would be a very dull world if we didn't take a risk now and then."

"But it can hurt."

"Sure it can hurt! And it can hurt *not* to love, too. To love means to take a chance, Lisa, but without love life is meaningless." He put his arm around her. "Keith has a natural gift, honey. Trying to squelch that gift would be as cruel as Jeff's attempts to keep you on the ground during your marriage. When two people join their lives there has to be trust, and enough love to allow each person to follow their own path." He tilted her chin up with his finger. "Isn't that what you expect from your husband, Lisa? Can you offer any less to him?"

They rode quietly for several minutes, Lisa's head resting lightly on her uncle's shoulder, his right arm cradling her gently. Lisa felt at peace; she was safe here. It would be so easy to escape the harsh realities of the world by crawling back into this warm, sheltered refuge of her childhood. But it would solve nothing. The world would still be out there; she couldn't run away forever.

At last Lisa lifted her head and kissed Mason on the cheek. "Thanks, Uncle Leonard, I needed to hear those things. But now what I need more than anything is some time to think. I have to sort it all out. And I guess you're right, I have to put a few things in perspective."

Lisa asked to be dropped off a few blocks from the hotel, preferring to walk for a while alone with her thoughts. Uncle Leonard understood, as she knew he would. They both realized that there was only one person who could make this decision, only one person who would have to live with the consequences.

She wandered aimlessly, hardly caring where her feet carried her. Uncle Leonard's words revolved in her

mind, making sense one minute, demanding too much
the next. Yes, life was a risk. But did she have to risk
everything to have love?

The sun had begun its nightly plunge into the western
sky when Lisa found that she had strayed onto the
grounds of the Imperial Palace. Behind her, sounds of
traffic swirling around the perimeter of the palace were
already receding, replaced by the tranquility of the
peaceful retreat. This late in the afternoon few people
congregated on lawns which were filled every noon
with office workers from the nearby Marunouchi district. She was surrounded by wonderful old gnarled
pines and the soft gurgling of the palace moat. Finding
a bench that afforded a clear view of the Nijubashi, or
the Double Bridge, Lisa sat down, stretching out her
tired feet.

She looked out at the two bridges which arched
across the moat in front of the palace. Graceful swans
glided noiselessly in the still waters, seemingly at peace
with themselves and with their environment. Lisa en-
vied them, and at the same time she felt sorry that their
lives were forever restricted to this one body of water,
however lovely it might be.

Yet isn't that what you're trying to do to Keith? a little
voice asked. Wasn't she trying to lock him just as tightly
within the confines of a nice, safe, nine-to-five job? No
matter how idyllic their marriage, was it fair to impris-
on him within boundaries drawn by her without regard
for what might be right for him?

The notion of herself as a jailer was jolting. Lisa sat
for a long while absorbing the idea that some of her
fears might be motivated by selfishness. Yet it was true,
she decided at last. Jeff had tried to mold her to suit his
own needs and she'd been miserable. By asking Keith

to change such a vital part of his life wouldn't she be demanding more of him than she was willing to give herself? Wasn't the real question whether she loved Keith enough to share the rest of her life with him, not as the person she might prefer him to be, but as the person he actually was?

Lisa sat very quietly and watched a flock of birds peck about the lawn in search of crumbs left by this afternoon's luncheon crowd. A sudden blast of horns from nearby Sakurada-Dori interrupted their meal, causing them to soar suddenly into the sky in a flight as graceful and free as the Comet's. As she watched them climb as high as the trees and beyond, Lisa remembered the thrill she had experienced that first day in Keith's jet when she'd taken over the controls. She had felt set free, as if she'd finally been released from Jeff's bondage. And Keith had made it possible. He had returned a precious gift. He had helped to make her whole again.

Lisa watched the birds until they disappeared. She had made her decision. She could no more ask Keith to give up his test flying than she could clip the wings of these wild birds. It hadn't worked for Jeff; it wouldn't work for her. Uncle Leonard was right, to love did not mean to stifle but to support and encourage. That was what she wanted from Keith; that was what she must give to him in return.

Lisa didn't wait until she got upstairs to Uncle Leonard's room; she had to talk to Keith immediately, to tell him why she had left and how she felt about things now. Hurrying to a little alcove in the hotel lobby, she placed a call directly to his apartment in Kyoto. When she received no answer she had the operator try his office at Itami Airport. Her blood chilled when she was informed that Mr. Brannon had not yet returned from Tokyo. His flight was three hours overdue!

Declining to leave a message, Lisa replaced the receiver. A rational section of her brain told her it was foolish to worry. Keith could have been detained for any number of reasons, perhaps he had even chosen to land at a neighboring airport instead of Itami. But that didn't make sense either. He knew how worried she'd been. He'd be all the more anxious to get back on schedule.

Lisa ignored the elaborate line of elevators and headed for the wide carpeted staircase. Using the exercise as a kind of emotional release, she resolutely climbed the seemingly endless stairs to Leonard Mason's ninth floor room. Before she reached the seventh level, she had herself under control. How far would she get in this marriage if she let herself think the worst every time Keith was a few hours late? She had to put his safety in the hands of a power greater than her own. She had to live each and every hour with him to the fullest, letting go of the past and allowing the future to take care of itself.

Leonard Mason's door flew open only seconds after she knocked. But it was not her uncle who stood glaring at her from the threshold.

"Keith!" She stared at him in shock. He seemed to fill the doorway, his broad, muscular shoulders straight and rigid as he returned her gaze.

"It's about time you got back! You've been gone for hours."

"I . . . I needed time to think," she stammered, finally collecting herself enough to enter the room. She walked through to the gracious sitting room of Leonard Mason's suite. "I didn't expect to find you here."

"I might say the same thing about you. The last I heard, you and I were going out to celebrate tonight, remember?"

"I tried to call. But your office said you weren't back yet. My God, Keith! They told me you were three hours late." Lisa could not stop tears of relief from flooding her eyes. "I thought you might have . . ."

"Crashed? I didn't even leave. You looked so damn miserable when I left this morning that I called your hotel early this afternoon. All they'd tell me was that you'd checked out without leaving a forwarding address. That really threw me until I figured you'd probably come here. So I stayed in Tokyo." Lisa was surprised to see real anguish in his eyes. "Lisa, you really had me going there for a while. What made you leave?"

In her anxiety to work out her own problems, it had not occurred to Lisa to consider how her abrupt departure from Kyoto might affect Keith. The pain she saw in his eyes now made it even more difficult to explain. "I guess I panicked," she began, trying to put her confused feelings into words. "I was looking for the safe, comfortable life you didn't seem willing to give me. But all I found was emptiness. I discovered that without you, safety and comfort don't mean very much."

Keith reached out and touched her hair with unsteady fingers. "What are you trying to say, Lisa?"

"I'm trying to tell you that if you're still looking for a wife, I'd like to apply for the job. I can't promise never to be concerned when you fly—I love you too much not to worry just a little—but I give you my word I'll do my best to keep my mouth shut. And from now on I'll always be there when you get back."

"But you don't have to worry anymore, honey. I did

some thinking today, too. I decided that if my flying really bothers you that much, maybe it was time I retired and became a full-time desk jockey."

"You'll do no such thing!" Lisa was vehement. "Listen Keith Brannon, I fell in love with you exactly the way you are, *because* of what you are. I don't want you to change one single hair on your head for me. Flying is your life. I could never take that away from you."

"No, you've got that wrong, Little Flower," he said softly. *"You're* my life now. Now and forever."

In two huge strides he bridged the distance between them and enclosed her in his arms. Finding her lips, he caressed them softly with his own.

"Have I told you lately how much I love you, Hana-san?"

"Hmmm," Lisa grinned. "Not for at least five . . ."

But Keith didn't wait for her answer. He'd found a much better use for her lips and crushed them in a long, satisfying kiss.

They heard a low cough at the door. "It seems you two have worked matters out after all. And quite satisfactorily from the looks of it."

Keith raised his head but kept Lisa firmly locked in his arms. "Very satisfactorily, thank you. I'd say our merger is off to a very good start."

Lisa looked up at him in surprise. "Merger? What are you talking about?"

"I guess Keith's been too busy with, er—other things to mention our little business transaction. You do recall my telling you that your young man visited me this morning."

"Yes, but . . ."

"Well, Keith came up with a business proposition I couldn't refuse. As you never tire of pointing out to me, I'm getting to an age where I can't keep up the pace I used to. When your young man here suggested that we merge our businesses, I must admit it sounded very tempting." His light blue eyes twinkled. "What do you think, Lisa? Shall we throw our fortunes in with this brash young pilot?"

Lisa ran to throw her arms around her uncle's neck. "Oh, Uncle Leonard, I'm so relieved. Of course, we should merge. It's like an answer to a prayer. Now you can take life a little easier and enjoy yourself for a change. And I don't have to feel as though I'm being sliced in two every time you both bid on the same contract."

Mason kissed his niece lightly on the forehead. "Somehow I thought you'd approve." He moved toward the door. "Now if you'll excuse me, I think it's time for dinner. Would you care to join me, or would three be a crowd tonight?"

"Give us a few minutes and we'd be delighted to join you, Mason," Keith replied. "This has been a pretty big day for me . . . for us. I think a first-class celebration is in order."

As soon as the door closed behind her uncle, Lisa was once again in Keith's arms.

"You knew I was worried about him, didn't you?" Lisa thought she had never loved him as much as she did at that moment.

His arms tightened around her as he said, *"I* was worried about him, honey. When I came here this morning and saw how tired and ill your uncle looked, I realized that the strain of running the company was getting to be too much for him. I also sensed how torn you felt worrying about which of us would get the Fugi contract. The merger just seemed like a very sensible solution for all concerned."

"It's a wonderful solution. And I love you for suggesting it." She hesitated, hardly knowing how to broach the one last problem which was bothering her. "Keith," she began slowly.

"Oh, oh, now what? When you get that look in your eye I know something's about to hit me. Come on, out with it."

"Well, it's my job. I've worked very hard to get where I am, and I'm proud of my accomplishments."

"I'm not disputing that. I'm proud of you, too. So what's the problem?"

"It's just that I don't know what I'll do now. Not only will I be starting all over, but I'll be doing it in a strange country. Keith, I can hardly put together a dozen words of Japanese. You'll have to admit it's rather intimidating."

"Yeah, it could be, if we let it. But I think we can work it out. Your degree is in speech and drama with a minor in fine arts, right?"

Lisa nodded.

"Japan has some of the finest museums and art centers in the world. Your kind of talent is valuable anywhere, honey, and your credentials as well as your understanding of Western culture would be terrific assets in landing a good job. Once we get started on your Japanese lessons I think you've got a brilliant future ahead of you." He gave her his irresistible little boy look. "Although I kind of hope you'll want to take *some* time off to increase the American population in Japan. Say two, or three, or four or even . . ."

"Stop!" Lisa laughed, "before you overpopulate the island. Good heavens, Keith, I didn't know you wanted to raise an entire baseball team!"

He kissed a stray lock of golden hair from her brow. "I do if they all look like you." His lips moved to her cheek, then down to her mouth. "There you go with that magic of yours again. Good lord, Lisa, you make me feel like an oversexed teenager. Whenever I'm with you I can't keep my hands to myself."

"So I see." Lisa shuddered as his hand came up to fondle a breast already aroused by his kiss. "And I only have one thing to say, Mr. Brannon."

"Oh? And what's that?"

"Don't ever grow up."

Keith laughed and swept her up into his arms. "Know something, Hana-san? I think we're going to be late for dinner tonight."

Lisa curled her arms around his neck as he carried her into the spare bedroom. She sighed and buried her lips in his hard, masculine shoulder.

"Mmmm. I think we're going to be very, *very* late." She chuckled softly.

MORE ROMANCE FOR
A SPECIAL WAY TO RELAX
$1.95 each

2 ☐ Hastings	21 ☐ Hastings	41 ☐ Halston	60 ☐ Thorne
3 ☐ Dixon	22 ☐ Howard	42 ☐ Drummond	61 ☐ Beckman
4 ☐ Vitek	23 ☐ Charles	43 ☐ Shaw	62 ☐ Bright
5 ☐ Converse	24 ☐ Dixon	44 ☐ Eden	63 ☐ Wallace
6 ☐ Douglass	25 ☐ Hardy	45 ☐ Charles	64 ☐ Converse
7 ☐ Stanford	26 ☐ Scott	46 ☐ Howard	65 ☐ Cates
8 ☐ Halston	27 ☐ Wisdom	47 ☐ Stephens	66 ☐ Mikels
9 ☐ Baxter	28 ☐ Ripy	48 ☐ Ferrell	67 ☐ Shaw
10 ☐ Thiels	29 ☐ Bergen	49 ☐ Hastings	68 ☐ Sinclair
11 ☐ Thornton	30 ☐ Stephens	50 ☐ Browning	69 ☐ Dalton
12 ☐ Sinclair	31 ☐ Baxter	51 ☐ Trent	70 ☐ Clare
13 ☐ Beckman	32 ☐ Douglass	52 ☐ Sinclair	71 ☐ Skillern
14 ☐ Keene	33 ☐ Palmer	53 ☐ Thomas	72 ☐ Belmont
15 ☐ James	35 ☐ James	54 ☐ Hohl	73 ☐ Taylor
16 ☐ Carr	36 ☐ Dailey	55 ☐ Stanford	74 ☐ Wisdom
17 ☐ John	37 ☐ Stanford	56 ☐ Wallace	75 ☐ John
18 ☐ Hamilton	38 ☐ John	57 ☐ Thornton	76 ☐ Ripy
19 ☐ Shaw	39 ☐ Milan	58 ☐ Douglass	77 ☐ Bergen
20 ☐ Musgrave	40 ☐ Converse	59 ☐ Roberts	78 ☐ Gladstone

MORE ROMANCE FOR
A SPECIAL WAY TO RELAX

$2.25 each

79 ☐ Hastings	87 ☐ Dixon	95 ☐ Doyle	103 ☐ Taylor
80 ☐ Douglass	88 ☐ Saxon	96 ☐ Baxter	104 ☐ Wallace
81 ☐ Thornton	89 ☐ Meriwether	97 ☐ Shaw	105 ☐ Sinclair
82 ☐ McKenna	90 ☐ Justin	98 ☐ Hurley	106 ☐ John
83 ☐ Major	91 ☐ Stanford	99 ☐ Dixon	107 ☐ Ross
84 ☐ Stephens	92 ☐ Hamilton	100 ☐ Roberts	108 ☐ Stephens
85 ☐ Beckman	93 ☐ Lacey	101 ☐ Bergen	
86 ☐ Halston	94 ☐ Barrie	102 ☐ Wallace	

*LOOK FOR SUMMER COURSE IN LOVE
BY CAROLE HALSTON AVAILABLE IN SEPTEMBER*

*AND A THISTLE IN THE SPRING BY LINDA SHAW
IN OCTOBER.*